BURN THE WATER

A NOVEL
BY BILLY RAY

SCHOLASTIC PRESS
NEW YORK

Copyright © 2026 by Billy Ray

All rights reserved. Published by Scholastic Press, an imprint of Scholastic Inc., *Publishers since 1920.* SCHOLASTIC, SCHOLASTIC PRESS, and associated logos are trademarks and/or registered trademarks of Scholastic Inc.

The publisher does not have any control over and does not assume any responsibility for author or third-party websites or their content.

No part of this publication may be reproduced, stored in a retrieval system, or transmitted in any form or by any means, electronic, mechanical, photocopying, recording, or otherwise, or used to train any artificial intelligence technologies, without written permission of the publisher. For information regarding permission, write to Scholastic Inc., Attention: Permissions Department, 557 Broadway, New York, NY 10012.

This book is a work of fiction. Names, characters, places, and incidents are either the product of the author's imagination or are used fictitiously, and any resemblance to actual persons, living or dead, business establishments, events, or locales is entirely coincidental.

Library of Congress Cataloging-in-Publication Data available

ISBN 979-8-225-00674-7

10 9 8 7 6 5 4 3 2 1   26 27 28 29 30

Printed in India   197
First edition, March 2026

Book design by Maeve Norton

FOR JULE

She was bigger than the water...

ONE

The young woman sighed.

London had drowned, peril had won, and there was so much she didn't yet know.

She didn't know if she'd survive this day, or the next one. Didn't know that a pax—peace—was possible. Didn't know that one day Love and Water would finally clash, and that one of those two giants would win. Uncertainty was her lot.

But she had courage, and courage matters. It wins wars and builds nations and inspires the doubtful and crosses rivers. And she had so *many* rivers to cross.

So she continued. Bravely.

Autumn had come and the air was cold and insects flitted above Shooter's Hill, darting and humming and feeding and flying. Their sounds were rebirth; the river couldn't touch them. Shooter's Hill was elevated, rising above the swollen Thames, part of London's "Dry Ten," the 10 percent of the city that *wasn't* underwater, off the A205 road. Once—when pavement had meant promise and progress, and vehicles were a necessity—this hill had been a charming suburb. Little shops, humble homes, a quiet park.

Now, in the twenty-fifth year of the twenty-fifth century, it was lush jungle, trees and grasses wildly overgrowing, smothering what had formerly been black asphalt with verdant green, oxygenating the air for all those winged miracles flittering above—while on land, dreams continued to drown.

Rain had fallen that morning, and all that foliage—along with a thin layer of mud—felt slick underfoot. She hobbled over it, grimacing in pain, an empty sack slung over her shoulder.

Jule. Her ankle was broken, but her hands were strong and her face was kind, unmarked save for a single small but permanent scar on her chin, its origin known only to her.

Like everyone else in England, she wore clothing that had survived centuries of weather, abandonment, theft, and reuse: a leather jacket, denim jeans patched over dozens of times with needle and thread. Her shirt was made from a version of cotton grown in greenhouses. Her sweater was woolen. Her boots were old and reshod.

It was hard for her to walk down this village road without imagining what it had once been, before the Great Soak and that sadly historic British day in the 2100s when the Thames first climbed over its banks and stubbornly refused to retreat. Jule now passed what were once shops and small eateries, long since gutted, mere shells suffocated by the swarming embrace of branches and leaves. Each business had been someone's livelihood and someone else's refuge. People had congregated on this very lane to make commerce and to talk about the news or a football match or the tabloids or a relative's wedding.

Jule envied them all, nostalgic for a time she'd never actually lived.

She felt it every time the sky went pink, or trees whispered, or grass glistened, or a parent held a child, or the world felt clean. But she kept her longing buried inside like a hidden wound and hobbled on, each step labored. There were no vehicles here. *Anything* made of metal had been seized long ago to be repurposed into sluggers, mini-balls for guns, by two rival armies, the Rogues and the Crowns, in their centuries-long war. Every mailbox from every building, every door handle and lock, they'd all been forged, Crowns and Rogues surrendering individual privacy in order to make it easier to kill one another. Both Houses had rules forbidding *any* personal use of metals. The only jewelry one saw was made of twine. Jule didn't wear any.

With that slick grass underfoot, she hobbled toward a street corner where two male soldiers stood at ease, lazily guarding a beech tree.

Beech trees mattered in London. People killed for them.

The two soldiers wore armbands, black ones, which told the world, *Here stands a soldier of the Rogue Army.*

When they saw Jule approaching—slowly—the two men broke into drunken grins. She was injured, helpless. Not even a crutch to protect her. And she wore no armband—black *or* gold—which meant she was a *Hab*, and therefore belonged to neither of the two warring Houses. That made her unsponsored, unimportant.

The taller of the two Rogues called out to Jule, his tongue a bit thick. "What's your business?"

Yes, drunk.

Jule, still twenty feet away, answered: "Just a Hab. May I pass?"

The tall soldier smiled at his mate, then: "Well, that depends. This is a toll road."

Jule sighed. "A toll road."

"Yup. And a girl like you might have to pay *twice*." He laughed. So did his fellow soldier. Jule knew what was coming. It had happened before. She approached slowly. "Sirs, may I pass?"

"That hobble of yours looks pretty bad, missy. Maybe you should just lie down for a bit."

She was close enough to speak quietly now, almost an exhale. "Must it always come to this?"

The tall one nodded. "Yes. It must." He felt a stir in his groin and he obeyed it, grabbing her.

That fast, Jule produced a dagger from the back of her belt and slashed his throat with it—one short, sharp thrust. Before the other could react, Jule gutted him. Their bodies fell.

Just eighteen, Jule cleaned her blade on their clothes, then used it to saw some bark off the beech tree, gathering it in the sack, which had been her aim all along.

Two dead Rogues. Two fewer enemies to kill in battle, two fewer threats to the army she'd spent her life serving.

She marched down the A205 road, her ankle healthy and well.

And while it didn't help them much, those two sloppy soldiers would enter the afterlife knowing that they had been dispatched by the fiercest and most famous soldier the Crown Army ever produced.

Also the loneliest.

The Thames was Central London's highway, weaving through the city like greedy arteries. He rowed atop it in a wooden pirogue, six feet above what had once been Bricker Lane, in a light drizzle.

Rafe. The name still echoes.

He was, at that moment, the Rogue Army's most venerated captain. Broken inside—they all knew that—there was a coldness to him; in battle and out, his face was a stone. But he was a soldier's soldier, and had been for six years. Also a gifted strategist, his mind never still, his oars always seeming to move faster than everyone else's. Especially this morning. Word had come that one of his soldiers, a headstrong boy named Alger, was in danger behind Crown lines. And Rafe was rushing to rescue him.

London was the only home Rafe had ever known, the only place he'd ever *seen*—a wet and bloody chaos, much of it under six feet of polar water. Great buildings, once lions of commerce, soared into the sky above him. But their ground floors had no ground anymore. Eels swam through what had once been lobbies. And foliage wrapped around all those columns of glass and steel, entombing them in an embrace of vines and leaves and branches, so thick that no sunlight reflected off the windows anymore. The phantom towers were green and soft and tall. Happy birds nested in them, filling the rainy skies above with song. It was the year 2425; nothing was dry but the whistling of a chilly wind.

The West End was gone; Piccadilly was gone. The floor of

Parliament was a pool. So was everything else that wasn't hilly. Fins now sliced the water beneath what had once been traffic lights. The buildings were caverns, the light bulbs glassy ghosts. And battle was Rafe's daily bread.

Rafe hated the water and had all his life. He knew—in this, his eighteenth year alive—that it would kill him someday. Swallow him. But the river was London's only thoroughfare, so he muscled through it, his oars slapping the foliage that floated here—flowers, kelp, mosses—and the thin slick of oily film that clung doggedly to the surface. The smell on the water was fishy, fetid, unclean. He turned it all into froth with each new stroke.

On both sides of Bricker Lane were tall wooden poles, once the bearers of electricity and communication, each now marked with black strips of cloth. *Rogue territory.* To Rafe's right and left, handfuls of Rogue citizens sat on the rooftops of shops, casting fishing lines into the swollen river, which crested just below their dangling feet.

They recognized Rafe. One day, everyone knew, he would lead the whole Rogue Army; General Shapcott had been grooming him for years. A few of the roof-toppers saluted Rafe proudly.

Rafe had no time to salute back. A soldier was in danger.

Life was tribal violence: the spear, the knife, the mace, the bow and arrow, or precious sluggers fired from guns that had survived for centuries. Like everyone else on this benighted rock, Rafe awakened every morning trapped in a universe of battle, with no idea if wars like this one—or even life itself—existed beyond these shores anymore.

Death was fact. Truce was weakness. Peace was a fairy tale. And the entire city remained in the cross fire. His sworn enemy, the Crown Army, was tireless, its soldiers well trained and fierce.

Their finest, Rafe knew, was named Jule.

He'd seen her in battle once, gutting a close friend of his, her face half-masked in blood. She was famously relentless. And Rogue soldiers told stories about her, lionizing her.

Mostly, they *feared* her.

Rafe couldn't stand that. He hoped to encounter her again someday, just to show his colleagues that she was mortal.

The rain fell harder. He ducked his head as he sped beneath signage protruding from what had once been a seafood restaurant, a red-and-blue neon caricature of a happy flounder, so close to the surface it could nearly swim. Then Rafe reached his destination: the banks of Crown territory.

His fear stayed behind on the water.

TWO

A boy in a knit cap raced down Worthing Street, in Woolwich. The strips of cloth on the now-dead power poles here were gold, meaning Crowns claimed this stretch.

The raindrops didn't seem to know the difference.

The hungry river had claimed all but the rooftops of Woolwich's former shops. Crabs crawled across a few of them. Seals squawked. Again, that scent of rotting fish was everywhere.

But Worthing Street rose steadily as one traveled south, escaping the brine to become dry land at Owing's Hill. There, the skeletons of old buildings provided shelter to a cluster of sad wanderers who were neither Rogue nor Crown. Habs.

Habs lived in London's margins, a primitive existence. Most worked in fields, like serfs. They grew the food that fed the Crown and Rogue armies, so those armies allowed them to live. Their clothes were burlap. Their shoes were wood. Their days were sludge.

On this day, four rain-soaked Habs stood around a beech tree, stripping its bark with a military kind of vigilance.

Suddenly, the boy in the knit cap—Alger—raced past them in a blur, bolting for Eltham Common. The Habs barely noticed.

But Alger was about to die, and he knew it.

Eltham Common was a grassy square that had once hummed with quiet life. Now it was a ghost. A gallows stood in its center; an old abandoned police station marked its northwest corner like a hulking statue. Alger reached an alcove and hid himself there, huddling and shaking, trying to catch his breath. His boots had no heels. His leather jacket was tattered. The knit cap had holes in it.

Alger had always expected to die in this fight. But not today. Not *yet*, on Crown land, running and hunted and despised. He was deep in the Churn.

That was a soldier's term for the caustic acid fire that frothed in the gut when death felt near and adrenaline and cortisone were pumping too hard to hold back. The Churn was unrelenting and merciless. Hot vinegar in your veins. It galloped and raced and crept and crawled—scathing and scalding, cymbals and Klaxons, the sirens of suck, echoing. The Churn was a soldier's hell.

All Alger had ever wanted was a position of command. As a child playing war games with other children, he'd always been the general. He was the best wrestler of his age group, the best archer, the best shot. He ran the fastest, never whined or disobeyed.

Rafe had spotted Alger early and begun guiding the boy, teaching him. As soon as Alger came of age, reaching twelve, he was placed into Rafe's regiment.

Once there, Alger became a remarkable soldier. He volunteered for the most dangerous assignments, his ambition unstoppable. But *this* mission—to slip through Crown lines and sabotage the Crown forge—had been far too dangerous to support. Rafe had rejected it as soon as Alger had proposed it.

Alger had gone anyway. And now he'd been discovered, forcing him to run for his life . . .

He peeked out from the shadows of the alcove, rain hitting his face. But a stray dog, lean and hungry, the offspring of a thousand breeds, ambled by, spotted him, and barked loud enough to cut through the wind and rain.

In Alger's pocket was a corner of bread crust. He tossed it ten feet into the rain. The dog followed, a brief reprieve. But Alger knew that if he stayed in this alcove he would surely die. He had to keep running. Maybe all this rain would affect their aim. Maybe . . .

He exploded out of the alcove, sprinting lightning fast, heading for an old post office across the common, thanking God for all those foot-races he'd won as a kid.

An arrow instantly whizzed past his head. Then another, fired from windows that overlooked the square on all sides of him. He'd run right into a trap.

He kept going, trying to stay low. BANG-BANG. Sluggers tore past him, barely missing.

That post office was twenty feet away now. Refuge. Safety. Maybe. Screaming inside, he raced through the rain and wind.

Again, from those windows, from enemies met and unmet, death came at him. PHHFFT. PHHFFT. More arrows. Two of them grazed his arms. He kept running, leaping over two dead bodies on the weed-choked pavement, the post office just ten feet away now.

Get there or die. The door was in reach, but—

A woman popped out from behind the post office door, knife in hand, thrust his way. Alger turned . . .

The knife buried itself in his arm. Agony. And their eyes met, just a flicker. Then Alger saw a sword in her other hand and he fled onto the common again, zigzagging, his arm shrieking with every stride.

The dog was at his heels now, biting, barking.

This wasn't the Churn. This was feral. *Keep running. You're going to be a general one day, and this will be the story all your soldiers will ask you to retell . . .*

Up ahead, two more enemies appeared from inside a long-dead flower shop. One had a gun, the other a bow. Both fired. A perfect hell.

The slugger missed. The arrow hit Alger's shoulder and burrowed in. He reversed course and hurled himself at full speed toward the opposite edge of the common, a corner. He got to it, arms pumping and bleeding, and he turned . . .

. . . right into a spiked mace, swung at his head. And everything went black. He saw nothing, heard nothing.

His left eye opened, half-lidded, and he was supine, barely alive, rain pelting his face. His front teeth had been knocked out.

High above him was a water tower. A gold flag flew atop it, sagging in the pouring rain. Everything flickered.

Two men leaned over him, Evander and Paris. Evander was Jule's brother, a fifteen-year veteran of this war. His shoulders were wide and thick.

Paris was Evander's closest friend. They'd seen appalling battles together, one of which had cost Paris two fingers on his left hand.

The men were joined now by four more fighters, each wearing gold armbands: a young man and three women, one of whom had jammed that knife into Alger's arm. All were breathless.

Hunting was hard, and Alger's foot speed had exhausted them. But he was going to die now, and he knew it. Evander eyed him. "It's Alger, yeah?"

Alger just wheezed, absently noting the ring on Evander's left hand, a wedding band that had once belonged to Evander's father, making Evander the only soldier on either side of this war to defy his House's regulation about wearing jewelry. *All* metals belonged to the army. But Evander's father had worn this ring as a sign of devotion to his wife, just as Evander now wore it as a memorial to his parents. His answer whenever challenged about it was, "Anyone who wants to commandeer it from me is welcome to try."

Evander asked, "Who sent you to do this, Alger? Was it Rafe? Are you one of his lot?"

Alger just stared. Evander tried again. "Was that who ordered you here?"

Again, nothing. So Paris leaned in: "Hey, kid. What's it like to die as Rogue scum?"

At birth, every Rogue (and every Crown too) was inculcated into the life of war by anyone tall enough to look up to. The enemy was made hateful. The stakes were ingrained. We fight or we die. Sometimes we fight *until* we die. In other words: *Never surrender, even if you're flat on your back with your face demolished. Keep demonstrating resolve. Make even your death discouraging for them* . . .

So it must've given Alger a moment of satisfaction to mumble, "D'know yet. What's it like to live as Crown rubbish?"

He'd never get to be a general. But sod these Crowns . . .

Evander smiled, then jammed a dagger into Alger's chest. A great gasp emitted from the body as it expired.

None of them knew it—how could they?—but they had just doomed, and *saved*, their country.

The rain fell, washing Alger's lifeless face. The stray dog barked. And the war went on. Evander felt nothing.

Home was home. It had to be defended.

And this much was doctrine, the one thing they *knew*, repeated by the bivouac fires in the Crown camp every night: If Crowns governed this island, there would be no more war. If *Rogues* governed it, there would be no more Crowns.

And so they fought. And they killed. And sometimes they died.

Death death death death water water water water war war war war.

Rafe raced breathlessly up Worthing Street fifteen minutes later and arrived at the common, a Rogue on Crown ground, armed and prepared for whatever might follow.

He discovered Alger's body—now lifeless and rain-washed. That always landed hard—losing a soldier in his command—and it left Rafe with traditions to honor; one required him to return the body to Rogue soil. He knelt down to gather it. But then he paused... Something was tugging at him.

Grief. Landing right behind his eyes.

Alger was just a kid. Dead now. That shook Rafe; he couldn't say why. He pulled a kerchief from his coat and gently wiped the blood off Alger's face, then began to pick the boy up, when, suddenly—

BANG. A slugger, fired from a distance, suddenly tore up mud an inch from Rafe's right knee. He looked up.

And there she was, in a window less than a hundred feet away.

Jule. Famous Jule. Pistol in hand. Aiming right at him.

The miss had been intentional—he knew that—a shot meant as a warning. And ... a gesture of respect. It left him astounded. Not just because she could have fired again and did not.

More ... by her *face*.

He'd never really *seen* her before; she'd always been coated in battle blood and hidden by layers of protective gear. But not today. Today, she was herself. Unvarnished. Human.

And beautiful. It was shocking. A kindness in her eyes. Warmth. Was that possible? Her mouth, her skin ... lovely. Fierce, as always— but even from this distance, even with a gun in her hand, she was like gossamer. And he could see that there was a heart in there. It was deeply unsettling.

But hopeful too. Wonderful.

And she was, of course, sparing his life. That was treasonous. This beautiful warrior who had every reason and opportunity to kill him was simply choosing not to. His training told him to rise and flee, but he didn't move. He couldn't. His feet felt nailed to the earth. Instead, he nodded to her respectfully, gratefully, one soldier to another.

She half nodded back. That felt like hope too. A peaceful, unspoken promise. It was all utterly unfamiliar, un-military, and un-monstrous.

And Rafe was unafraid.

The moment hung forever—an unofficial truce. And though it was crazy to allow such an unholy thought, he'd never felt closer to another human being in his entire life. The air seemed like it was singing quietly to him. Humanity felt real. And it was all because of that soft, sweet face across the square. Madness.

Finally, Rafe grabbed Alger's body and stood. For a second, he remained entirely still, as if offering himself once again as a target.

Jule lowered her weapon and gestured for him to go. *I might kill you in battle,* the gesture seemed to say, *but it won't be today, not when you've come to retrieve one of your own.* Rafe breathed out a smile and carried the dead boy away from the common. Jule watched him go.

They both knew: a new kind of courage had just been born.

THREE

Rafe rowed through drowned streets, Alger's body at his feet. The roof-toppers barely reacted; death was a constant here.

But Rafe's survival had *not* been common. Today a Crown, *the fiercest soldier in the entire Crown Army*, had chosen to let Rafe *live*.

It made no sense.

This war was now in its fourth century. For that long, people on both sides had been born in it, fought in it, and died in it, as Alger had. Death. Water. War. That was London.

But not today. Today an armed angel had spared him. Why?

He rowed past Big Ben, which had been dead for centuries, having first frozen one fated day in the 2100s at 6:43, either a.m. or p.m. (no one knew anymore). Ever since, the great paralyzed clock had stood sentry over this swollen river and her land-starved city, its people unled and desperate.

Rafe rowed calmly, rhythmically, Alger's lifeless frame jostling with each stroke of oar to water. Just a boy. This dead thing, coming home for the last time, was just a boy. It made Rafe think about a history all his own, and a gray morning years before, when an old sailboat had entered this very same river through an estuary off the North Sea and made for London, settling near the Rogue camp, bringing death and disaster. April 2411, Rafe's sixth year on Earth . . .

Ever since, battle didn't frighten him. Guns didn't frighten him. Drowning did.

He paddled around a corner... and saw a surprise: an empty pirogue, floating idly. That was odd. He rowed toward it and discovered that it wasn't actually empty at all.

A boy had fallen asleep in this rig. Rafe thought about waking him, but that was complicated.

Because the kid had a gold armband around his bicep.

Which made him a Crown.

The child seemed too young to be on patrol; both Houses tried to keep kids out of the active fighting until they'd hit twelve, but young or not, he was carrying a sidearm. And it was entirely possible that the boy was a decoy. Rafe instantly scanned the nearest rooftops for signs of snipers.

He didn't see any.

Two choices. Wake the kid up, and Rafe might find himself in a gunfight with a child. Let him sleep, and the boy would almost certainly be captured by *other* Rogue soldiers patrolling this sector, which would mean imprisonment in a military brig in Paternoster, the Rogue fortress.

Rafe gently rowed closer to the child, until their pirogues touched. Then he reached across the boy's body—slowly—to get that sidearm.

The boy's eyes snapped open.

And in half a second he uncoiled and lurched backward in terror, grabbing his weapon and aiming it right at Rafe's head.

Silence. A man and a child. And a gun. Rafe didn't move. Instead, he said calmly, "Turn your boat around."

The kid was too scared to blink. Or breathe. Now he saw the dead body at Rafe's feet. Feral fear pounded. The Churn, amplified by adolescence.

Rafe tried again. "You fell asleep on patrol and you're nowhere good. Turn your boat around." He nodded to the black strips of cloth on two nearby poles. The kid gulped.

And *fired*.

The slugger whizzed past Rafe's face, then buried itself into a storefront across the street.

Rafe never flinched. Just asked, "You thirteen yet?"

The kid, hands trembling, didn't answer.

Rafe went on, "Best not to use that thing until you're a bit older. Next year, maybe."

The kid lowered his gun. Rafe asked, "You got a name?"

Again, no answer. Seemed like the boy might start to cry.

Rafe sighed, then: "Get back to Eltham. You'll die out here."

The kid finally spoke. "What's the difference where I die?"

Rafe didn't have an answer. The child grabbed his oars and rowed away.

The Crown camp wrapped around Eltham Lake and a leafy, tranquil field that had once been asphalt until grass had consumed it long ago. There had been a quaint village here before the water came; but once the war began and the village became a fortress to the Crown Army, its buildings were converted into dormitories and barracks.

Ringing the camp was a tall wooden fence of dense English oak, thick enough to withstand gunfire. Short watchtowers loomed behind its main gate, peopled by sentries.

More sentries walked the camp's rooftops.

Stacked up against one of the dormitories, like coal, was a three-story-high mountain of hundreds of thousands of ancient and useless "mobile phones." On Sundays, the kids in this camp would carry plywood sleds up the building's stairs to a third-floor window. Then they'd climb out and slide down the mountain of arcane devices.

But today was a weekday. The children were in school, learning to hate Rogues.

Each day, at noon, all Crowns shared a communal meal: stew prepared in huge cauldrons, 365 days per year. As Jule entered the camp, her sack slung over her shoulder, the great vats were heating. But her appetite was gone.

This morning she'd had a Rogue captain dead to rights—*the* Rogue captain, the one they all said would be general one day. And she had let him live. It made no sense. For years she'd heard whispers about him. Her own troops feared him.

So why did I fire into the mud?

She knew why: It was the grief she'd seen on his face. Standing over the body of a dead boy, hesitating before gathering it in his arms, wiping the blood from the boy's face—Rafe had seemed decent, kind, *human*. That was deeply unsettling.

And frighteningly familiar. Jule had felt it too, hundreds of times, standing over the bodies of the fallen, those moments when all the pain and loss felt too brutal to withstand.

And now she knew . . . a Rogue felt that too. She'd seen it. He had a heart. And eyes and lips and hands . . . and warmth. Was that possible?

She passed by the open-air classrooms and people mending things, workers fashioning and repairing pirogues, neighbors fishing the lake. And guards. Lots of guards. They all believed she'd be their general one day. Jule was famous here; no one had risen faster in the Crown Army or proven herself more fully in battle. No one taught the art of war more effectively or led more convincingly. No one did more and bragged less, a rarity in this army.

And Jule's generosity—to the wounded, to the children, to the down-and-outers in camp who took more than they gave—was a constant at Eltham. Some thought her a saint.

Private Eldrick Dorn was among them. Now he approached her in the center of the grounds.

"Captain!" he said, saluting.

Jule returned it. "Welcome back, Dorn."

Dorn tried not to sag. He was thirty, reporting to a superior officer who was twelve years his junior. Jule was sensitive to that; it's why she never called him "Private."

Dorn had been a failure in the infantry since his induction. Recently, morose and despondent, he had reported for duty intoxicated on home-brewed beer. Jule had given him two weeks of solitary for it. Today was their first meeting since he'd served his time.

Dorn smiled. "Just wanted to thank you for your deliberation in handing down my sentence, Captain. Solitary gave me plenty of time to reconsider my behavior."

"That's good to hear, Dorn."

"And I want to apologize, again, for my transgression."

Jule eyed him. "You don't need to apologize, soldier. You just need to do better."

"Yes, ma'am."

Moments like these, she knew that she did *not* wish to be a general. Generals, she assumed, would know how to transform someone like Dorn, but she'd been unable to do so, and did not believe she ever would. In her experience, laggards remained laggards, and cowards remained cowards, and pretending they could change just prolonged their humiliation.

"Your next patrol is posted," she said. "Be smart out there."

"Yes, ma'am." And off he went, leaving Jule alone with her thoughts once again. Not a peaceful place to be.

To her right was a merciless forge, where a smithy called Big Lil, so named for the breadth of her shoulders—she did three hundred push-ups every day—was melting metals into sluggers amid stinging, acrid fumes.

Jule ducked in to say hello.

"Cookie?" Lil grinned. On a splintery table were a few plain treats. Lil occasionally used her forge for baking.

Jule smiled. "You're too kind to me, Lil."

Lil grinned wider. "I like soldiers with good aim. Makes me think my work's not in vain."

Jule cringed a bit, suddenly imagining Rafe being struck by gunfire and falling. She grabbed a cookie and ducked out again, passing the Crown Dormitory Authority, where housing assignments were determined and overseen, and a human resources office where clerks took care to make sure that all the camp's necessary tasks were adequately staffed by teachers, knitters, cooks, rovers, janitors, nurses, orderlies, fishermen, scouts, messengers, latrine cleaners, hands at the granary, pirogue builders, candlemakers, undertakers. And soldiers. Did the army need more soldiers?

Art, and artists, were luxuries.

Jule's dormitory squatted two stories high, beside a sprawling strangler fig tree on the edge of Eltham Lake. None of the building's windows had ever been broken; Jule was oddly proud of that. She stepped into the lobby, headed for the door of Unit A, and entered without a knock. It was time to save a life.

FOUR

Paternoster Square was the Rogue fortress. Its elevation and topography were ideal.

The towers looming over it, like all the skyscrapers in London, stood tall and green, wrapped in relentless foliage. Atop them, around the clock, were Rogue sentries bearing guns, bows, and bullhorns—soldiers who climbed dank stairwells in darkness every day for the privilege of looking down upon a patchwork city: Rogues on one end. Crowns on the other. Water in between, dotted by farmland where the Habs worked and died.

The square itself—as medieval as it was modern—was home to family dwellings, tents, bivouac fires, forge, mess hall, knitting circle, and quarantine tent where Rafe paid nightly visits to cheer up ailing kids.

Soldiers were everywhere—black cloth on every arm; weapons of defense lined the parapets, black flags abounding—fighting a war that they believed in but didn't always understand. As everyone knew, both Houses loved children and battled illness and claimed to want peace. Each had its innocent martyrs, brave heroes, and righteous rage. Each had its own legend, its own *fable* about how the feud had begun. But this much was not in dispute: The cause of it all had been the twenty-first-century surrender of the ice caps north and south, an unstoppable torrent that flooded London and every other coastal city on the planet, followed by frantic global wars, nations battling over resources, days of pulse bombs and panic, destroying all grids and tech and transportation and communications. Billions froze and starved. Great cities went silent. Were they decimated? Evacuated? No one knew.

Then, The Event: In the middle of the lunch hour on a spring day in 2102, at the peak of the Great Soak, a biological weapon exploded in the middle of London. It was VX, a nerve agent. Fatal.

And so, panic. Terror. Mass casualties. No one ever tallied the actual number that had died on that day. In many ways, the whole *country* had; it was the last moment in which Great Britain had a functioning government or a royal family. They vanished, presumably to a castle somewhere drier.

Ten square miles instantly became unlivable, turning tens of thousands of Londoners into refugees searching for living space. These displaced souls formed a desperate alliance based on their shared and tragic geography, and sought shelter at Eltham, where the air was clean. But the people of Eltham, their own resources strained, turned the refugees away.

And it was born. Two Houses. One war. One side accused the other of theft, and called them Rogues. The Rogues accused the other side of imperiousness, and named them Crowns.

Soon, the great feud was everything. A death struggle over who would inhabit the Dry Ten. It spawned heroes and leaders—like Rafe and Jule—but also death and darkness and sluggers and scorn. It taught Londoners to fight and taught Londoners to hate.

They needed to be taught something else.

All Rogues, of course, insisted that they wished for peace. But each knew the same brutal truth: If Rogues governed this island, there'd be no more war. If *Crowns* governed it, there would be no more Rogues. And so they fought. And killed. And sometimes died.

Yet there was *one* man in London—one single clarion voice—who was determined to bring peace, to mend both Houses.

His name was Jameson. People believed he could see in the dark.

And his time was coming . . .

As the rain began to ebb, a warrior crossed Paternoster Square, knives holstered on both her hips. She was Maud, eighteen and fierce. Maud was Rafe's "intended." General Shapcott had announced his intention to "couple" them.

In both Houses, civilians could marry whomever they pleased. But among the military, coupling was an *order*, the army's means of repopulating itself. And a pairing like Rafe and Maud would produce spectacular soldiers. Maud often told people her name meant "powerful battler" in French.

As she strode past an open-air classroom where kids sat cross-legged on bare asphalt, she pretended to shoot one of them. The kid pitched forward, laughing. Maud was a hero here. The child's teacher scolded him, "Justin! Eyes front! This could save your life!" (Today's lesson was about poisonous plants.) The boy obeyed.

Behind the classroom, fifty Rogue citizens scraped out the carcass of a dead whale to make lamp oil. It was awful work. The stench stuck to their hands, hair, and clothing—no one ever felt truly clean here. But people needed light.

The whale carcasses always attracted cats, feral ones. Nothing tame could survive here. Outside London, animals roamed. The squirrel, the fox, the deer, the marten, the eagle, the bat, the owl, the horse, the boar, even the brown bear, living seamlessly in nature. But any creature who strayed inside the city was likely to become supper unless they were able to avoid traps and outrun arrows. Dogs were spared only because they sometimes helped with hunting.

Maud passed a lone woman playing a fife, while a nameless man absently tapped on a drum. That was music. It barely registered. She passed the Rogue med tent, where doctors and nurses toiled amid deep frustration. They'd studied all the medical books produced by the twenty-first century; the knowledge within was abundant. But they had neither the equipment nor the medicines necessary to implement it. CT scans, MRIs, arthroscopes, anesthesia—they were daydreams now. Doctors in Paternoster, like doctors in the Crown camp, had nothing but tinctures derived from the soil and crude ether. That felt medieval too.

Maud never looked in on the wounded and the sick; her superstitions prevented it. So she continued along, brightening at the sight of Rafe entering the camp at the main gate.

Then she saw the body of young Alger in Rafe's arms.

Maud froze for a moment. Everyone did. Death was commonplace here, especially among the soldiers, but Alger was not an ordinary casualty. So a dread-filled silence fell as Rafe carried the boy's body across the square, Maud wordlessly falling in at his side.

At the north end of the square stood a twenty-six-story building that had once been the grand Stock Exchange Tower. Rogue guards, manning the entrance, admitted Maud and Rafe without a word.

The building's lobby, once a gem, was now a relic. Mounted candles fought the darkness as Maud and Rafe trudged through, heading for what had been a trading floor; it was now a bunker, headquarters of the Rogue Army. Lamps of whale oil burned in yellow-orange.

On desks in here were centuries-old computer monitors, many still plugged into useless sockets. Once the water came, these machines became relics and were left in place, tethered now to a past no one could fathom anymore.

On Rafe's desk were thirty tiny toy boats he'd fashioned from random twigs and sap. A mini-armada. He and Maud walked past the little crafts and approached the Rogue leader, General Shapcott, whose staffers—captains, mostly—saw what was coming and went quiet. Maud mumbled, "General?"

Shapcott was something of an elder, having just turned forty-five. He had the bluest eyes in this whole doomed city, and the true loyalty of his officers and troops. Without looking up, he called out, "What say, Maud?"

Then he turned. And he paled.

Silence fell hard as Shapcott eyed the dead child. Alger had been many things to this House. An example to Rogue children, an inspiration to his fellow soldiers, a student to his captain, Rafe. But Alger had been something else too—

General Shapcott's only son.

Now, stricken, Shapcott tried to breathe, tried to clear his throat in search of speech. But he couldn't.

Rafe felt gutted. He'd lost many soldiers before, had delivered horrid news to many knee-buckled parents.

But this was his general. And Alger had been Rafe's responsibility.

"Rafe," Shapcott finally mumbled. "What do I do?"

Rafe paused, determined to shake any emotion from his voice, and offered a calm combination of kindness and clarity: "You take the Mark, General. So you never forget."

Shapcott nodded sadly and looked for the nearest candle. It was a few feet away, its flame dancing. He rose somberly and crossed to it as his officers watched: Rafe, Maud, a bearded veteran named Maddox.

And now Shapcott took the Mark, placing his hand, palm down, into the yellow flame. He held it there, his face contorting in pain, tears from those deep-set blue eyes beginning to trace his cheeks.

Ten seconds, twenty. A horrible hissing, and a smell they knew too well. Smoke curled up from Shapcott's flesh.

Then it was done. He removed his hand and mumbled, "Never to forget."

The rest of the room repeated quietly, "Never to forget."

As he dunked his paw into a jug of cool water, Shapcott's captains all raised their right hands. The Mark had scorched most of them over the years. Loss was life in this camp.

Steam rising from the water, Shapcott added, "And never to forgive."

They repeated: "Never to forgive."

And now, as was custom here, it was time to Blink-Tap-Reset. And await orders.

Each of them stood and found an object: a pencil, a mug, anything. And at once, as one, they shut their eyes and tapped those objects on desks and walls and said the name aloud: "Alger." Then opened their eyes again.

Blink. Tap. Reset. And await orders. It was all one could do.

Shapcott returned to his desk amid a silence that hung like a pall. Rafe quickly filled it: "General, I have a plan to retaliate."

After all, home was home. It had to be defended.

FIVE

The beech bark wasn't easy to work with. You needed just the right amount of water and the right level of heat. But if all that was calibrated properly, and if you were strong enough, you could mash the bark into a paste. Jule did that now.

Then, by light filtering in through the window, she fed spoonfuls of it to Nelly, a woman of sixty, once a soldier, frail now from disease. Nelly hated the bitter taste of the beech bark, but it was medicine, the only thing that could treat the Yellowing.

The disease had been around for a hundred years now. No one knew for certain how it had first appeared (each House blamed the other), but it had devastated the whole country in a contagious wave and then never left.

It debilitated people—too often fatally—by reducing their lung capacity and taking their muscles prisoner. Once one was infected, manual labor became impossible, and *all* labor in London was manual.

In soldiers, it was especially dangerous; they'd go into battle unaware they'd been infected, then find themselves unable to run or fight—utterly anoxic and breathless. That fast, they'd be wounded, captured, or killed.

In children and the elderly, people like Nelly, it meant terror. Their muscles weakened and atrophied. Their breaths grew shallow, and sometimes stopped altogether. Many such patients lost their ability to chew or swallow. Once that happened, they simply prayed to die in their sleep.

Its most visible symptom was a jaundice of the skin that served as a flag to all: *I am sick. Fear me.* Its victims looked eerie, corpse-like; Nelly's skin was the color of citrine quartz. And the scent of a Yellowing patient was distinct as well. They smelled oddly like rust.

The only answer was beech bark. It was a highly effective expectorant, and its tar was antiseptic. If you were strong, paste made from the beech bark could fend off the Yellowing's symptoms long enough to give your body a chance to fight back. The remedy had saved Jule at the age of fifteen; she was now immune. So Nelly swallowed the medicine without complaint, asking simply, "How'd you get it?"

Jule replied, "A brief and spirited negotiation."

"How spirited?"

"Eat, Nelly."

Nelly tried to wield the spoon for herself, but spasms in her hand made that impossible. She smiled bravely and surrendered the spoon to Jule, who promised, "You *will* get better."

Nelly nodded, a tear rolling down her cheek. Jule wiped it away and ordered softly, "Eat."

They had met when Jule was seven. Nelly had been relegated from the army to teaching by then, her body wrecked. Jule was her favorite student, bright and inquisitive.

Then, just before Jule's eighth birthday, in a span of three weeks, she and Evander lost both their parents in combat. Their uncle, General Chasen, supreme commander of this House, took them in—and turned Jule into a warrior.

But it was *Nelly*, every day in school, who nurtured Jule, making her losses feel cruel but bearable. Jule adored this woman and worried about her like family.

"Your breathing sounds better today," Jule offered.

"*Any* breathing sounds good to me," Nelly replied.

"Tomorrow I'll bring you a surprise. Something worth—"

Nelly interrupted, "Did you kill for me today?" There was a sadness in her voice. She ate another spoonful, waiting.

"Actually," Jule replied, "it's a very funny story. I was walking down the road when I saw two cows standing at an unguarded beech tree, licking it! Cows! Just standing there, looking like they were gossiping. So I shooed them away—they'd made the bark so soft I could pull it off without even using my knife! Kind of a godsend, actually."

Nelly eyed her, appreciating the effort. "Cows."

Jule nodded. "Cows."

Nelly smiled sadly. "Funny . . . when you pulled the bark from your bag I saw serrations on it. Knife marks."

"Did you?"

"I did."

"Hmmm . . . that is funny," Jule said. "Please eat."

Nelly obliged.

Rafe was on the water again, his pirogue slicing through the oily surface of the Thames, buildings to his right and left.

He had spent much of his boyhood devouring old history books, trading food for them if he had to, desperate to understand life before the Soak: how people had lived, how civilizations had functioned, how governments had helped (and hurt).

And the signs the world had missed. Rafe studied it all. Later, he made his troops—Alger among them—study it too. Of course, some pieces of history felt like fantasy now, utterly disconnected from anything Rafe or his soldiers knew:

> *Television, Tesla, text. Satellite, cell phone, sext?*
> *Blockchain, Bluetooth, bandwidth, barcode, Bitcoin.*
> *Voicemail. Microchips. Downloads. Uploads. AI???*

They all seemed like drunken fictions. Impossibilities. *His* London had long since been an urban sea, drowned in violence. He paddled to starboard . . .

A few moments later, at the north gate of the Crown camp, something unprecedented, stunning really, now appeared over the top of that wooden wall of dense English oak: a *white flag*. It seemed to be dancing in the air.

Two Crown guards were the first to spot it. They rushed up the ladder of the short outpost tower that abutted this gate and looked down in utter shock at what was standing on the other side of the wall: Rafe, black armband on, his eyes steady, his right hand clutching a stick with that white flag atop it.

Instantly, the citizens of the Crown camp reacted. Children climbed trees for a better look; many of them had never *seen* a Rogue before. Adults scaled the wall. And every soldier, including the two in the tower, drew their sidearm.

Rafe betrayed no reaction at all. Just stood there calmly. Behind him was the skeleton of a "Burger King" restaurant. He asked the Crown guards, "May I enter?"

Crown mothers wrapped cautious arms around their children, as if Rafe might suddenly (and impossibly) leap over the ten-foot-tall fence, produce unseen weapons, and slaughter them all. Who knew what Rogues might be capable of?

To his left, Rafe saw a familiar face—the kid who'd been sleeping on the river that morning, adrift in his pirogue. Their eyes met as the boy looked over the top of that fence, no other kids around him, and no mother or father nearby.

"Hello," Rafe said with a half smile.

Attention suddenly showered the poor kid; his eyes went wide from it. Rafe asked, "What's your name?"

"His name's none of your concern," the nearest Crown guard said.

Rafe replied, "He fired a slugger at my head this morning. Like to at least know who he is." Then, to the kid again: "Your name."

The kid reluctantly pushed out a single word: "Danton."

"Danton," Rafe breathed. "You're gonna be a fine soldier one day. Just mind how you go."

The kid swallowed hard. Then a murmur rose from the crowd as Evander made his way through the assembled to the gate and ordered it to be opened. The guards hesitated, so Evander flatly reminded them, "It's a white flag, mates, no matter who's holding it."

Soldiers tugged on a pulley rope. The gate opened. The whole camp held its breath.

Rafe nodded with military respect. "Captain."

Evander nodded back. "Captain."

They had watched each other from across battlefields for years, but this was the first time they'd ever been close enough to touch. Rafe noted the wedding band on Evander's left hand. He knew the history there. It made him grin.

Evander asked, "Any trouble getting here?"

Rafe answered, "None."

Evander smiled. "God bless a peaceful day on the river."

"It was less so at the Common," Rafe responded. "My general just lost his son there, boy named Alger."

Evander revealed nothing. Instead: "*My* general lost one too. Last summer. You were there."

Rafe knew that there were weapons pointing at him from all sides.

But he also knew that he was absolutely safe as long as Evander was in charge. So he kept his eyes forward and said, "He asked me to propose talks to you."

Evander reacted. All the Crowns did, shock on every face. There hadn't been talks—a proposal for a pax—in 120 years, and *that* negotiation had led to a horrendous three-month siege.

Evander asked, "A pax?"

"A *discussion*. At a place and time of your choosing."

"Where I and my cohort will be assassinated."

Rafe said, "*Jameson* will vouchsafe the talks."

Evander reacted with instant regard. "I'll take this to my general."

Just then, Rafe heard a metallic *click* behind him—the chambering of a round in a gun. He glanced over his shoulder, refusing to look alarmed.

It was Paris, his sidearm trained. The men eyed each other.

"None of that, Paris," Evander said.

Paris hollered, "Why not?" and declined to lower his weapon. A nervous energy rippled through the bystanders, especially Danton, who was, of course, armed as well.

"I should go," Rafe said, turning to leave.

"No one will harm you," Evander replied.

"Wish I could be sure of that." Rafe smiled. Then he nodded at Evander's adorned finger and added, "That's a nice ring."

Evander appreciated the jab. "Belonged to my father. He killed scores of you lot."

"Runs in the family, I see."

Evander paused for a long, pregnant moment. Then he said, "Walk with me."

Rafe was shocked but tried not to show it. "Here?"

"Outside the gate. No one will trouble us."

It was a challenge, a dare, a risk ... but an opportunity too. The whole Crown camp watched, awaiting Rafe's reaction.

Finally, he agreed. "Let's do that."

More murmurs. Evander stepped toward him. Rafe slung the white flag over his shoulder like a rifle, everyone breathless.

And the two captains—each responsible for untold numbers of dead and wounded in combat—now began a slow stroll along the edge of the hungry water.

At a window in Nelly's apartment, Jule's expression soured as she watched her brother walking with the Rogue captain she'd had in her sights this morning.

Rafe. Winner of battles, killer of Crowns.

"It's a trick," she breathed.

"White flag," Nelly observed.

"No. It's a trick." She hurried out of the apartment.

At the water's edge, Rafe and Evander addressed each other in respectful, professional tones, both taking pains *not* to speak of war. There would be time for that later.

Rafe asked, "The quarantine numbers are up in our Hab camp. Yours?"

"Slightly," Evander replied. "Can never seem to get enough beech paste to them. But we're not seeing a rise in any *serious* illness there. Just the usual lethargy."

He was more decent than Rafe had expected; that was troubling. Rafe replied, "That's true of ours too."

"And its worst symptoms seem to be seasonal."

Volumes were going unsaid here. And it was all being scrutinized—every step, every gesture—by the hundreds of Crowns watching atop the camp wall. A highly public summit.

Finally, Evander got to the point: "Where were you thinking these talks might occur?"

"The Gherkin," Rafe answered.

"Unacceptable," Evander said. "Fenchurch is *not* recognized as Truceland. Let's say the Tower of London."

"Fine."

"Number of soldiers per side?"

"Ten pirogues? Six to a boat."

"No," Evander said, "five pirogues from each House. No one to set foot outside of the boats except for one soldier per side, to moor the rigs."

Rafe knew *he* would be that soldier on the Rogue side. And he grinned. "Fine." Then he added, "And of course, no arms."

"Of course." But neither believed it.

Then they both heard, "HE'S LYING." And they turned.

Jule was ten feet behind them, a crossbow pointing right at Rafe. No smile at all.

And again, Rafe was struck. Breathless. Her eyes. Her lips. Her *voice*. It sounded like a beautiful breeze, even now. Good God. He had to force himself to mumble, "White flag."

"White flag," she said mockingly. "White lies. Whitewash..."

In truth, she was shocked by the way her body was reacting to *him*. Her skin felt like it was dancing; her throat felt tight. His eyes... they made the very idea of war and Houses feel preposterous. Good God... Yet she somehow shuttled it all to the back of her mind. At the moment, he was a danger to their camp.

Evander began to introduce her. "This is Jule, my—"

"Your sister," Rafe said. "I know. I'm—"

"Rafe," Jule said. "We know."

Rafe tried to settle himself, but his legs felt unsteady; the air no longer felt like air. So he feigned a casual bravado. "Since we're all so familiar, maybe you can aim that crossbow somewhere else. Your brother and I are talking peace."

"My brother trusts too easily," she said. "Always has."

Her face was flushing. Her fingers felt cold. And there was a flutter in her belly she'd never experienced before.

No there isn't, she told herself.

"I see," Rafe replied. He knew it would embarrass her—and endanger her—if he mentioned her great kindness in not killing him that morning. So he resisted. Jule showed no signs of appreciation.

Evander smiled. "She's our most decorated soldier."

"Yes," Rafe said. "Always figured we'd meet one day."

"Now we've met," she said. "You can row away."

Then the words tumbled out of his mouth; he would never know exactly why. "We can't fight forever, Jule."

It was sacrilege for a soldier to say that. Unthinkable. So she forced a grin and replied, "Maybe just until the last of you is dead?"

Rafe would never say so, but he loved that. Calmly, he breathed, "I'll return to camp now."

"Good," Jule responded.

"If your general consents to the talks, send word."

Evander nodded. "I will."

Rafe turned to go. Then stopped. "One other thing," he said. "General Shapcott will seek to know the name of the Crown who killed his son."

Evander asked, "As a condition of the talks?"

"As an aid to his grief. Come to that, so would I. Alger was one of mine."

"Then why'd you send him on a one-way mission?" Jule asked.

"I didn't," Rafe replied. "I ordered him to stand down. But he went anyway. Ambitious kid." He looked at Evander now. "Who killed him, Captain?"

Evander nodded, then, "I did."

A breathless silence hung as a look passed between them, mutual fearlessness. Jule betrayed no reaction at all, adding, "He did it to himself, spying like that."

Rafe said, "I see. Well . . . thanks for your candor. I'll take that to my general as well."

"Do that."

Rafe left Evander's side, brushing past Jule, the backs of their hands touching, every nerve ending in his body pinging, a jolt, a thrill—

"Here," he said, handing her the white flag.

She looked offended, almost flustered. "What's this for?"

That voice again—those eyes again. He smiled. "You might need it someday."

She dropped it to the ground and said, "Go."

Fierce. Resolute. Unshakable. Rafe admired it all.

He smiled and stepped into the pirogue he'd docked in front of that ancient Burger King, the watchful eyes of the Crown camp following him.

Jule felt a mild shiver in her legs. She stilled them as best she could, certain she'd feel better once he'd rowed away.

He shoved off, the fetid smell of rotting fish hitting him again. God, how he hated the water. For appearances, he waved goodbye to Danton, who chose not to wave back.

Then Rafe nodded to Evander. Then to Jule. No reaction.

She just stared.

And sighed.

The Windmere District of Hedgefield was quiet and dry. It lay outside the Crown camp, but Crowns patrolled it as their own. Hordes of feral cats ruled here, keeping it free of vermin.

The sun was high as Jule led a unit of ten soldiers through Hedgefield's abandoned streets. She was thinking about *him* again. Rafe. That was infuriating, constant, and preposterous. Better just to focus on her task. They rounded a corner and found one of those fierce wild cats sleeping in the middle of the street with utter confidence. Jule admired that.

Then, suddenly, nature happened. A huge eagle swooped down—from nowhere, it seemed. The great bird got its talons into the cat and lifted it off the pavement, spiriting it away as Jule and her troops watched in awe. The victim's screech tore through the sky as it fought and clawed, writhing in midair for purchase. But the eagle just kept flying. More screeches followed, audible for miles. Jule silently promised herself never to make such an undignified noise when *her* time came, no matter the terror. It just wouldn't do.

She joked to her troops: "Remember, we're the eagle. They're the cat."

Her soldiers loved that about her. She was always in battle. Or so it seemed. An hour later, she walked a dry patch of Albemarle Street as her soldiers scouted the buildings to her right and left; the tallest was ten stories high.

Suddenly, she heard glass shatter—

A window burst, ten stories above her. She turned, craning her neck as shards began to rain. Then—

A soldier suddenly leaned out of that empty tenth-floor window, as if about to jump.

Dorn. Shaking. Tears in his eyes. Afraid and hopeless. "Dorn!" she hollered. All that empty air between them.

"I'm sorry!" he shouted.

"DON'T MOVE! DO YOU HEAR ME?"

Dorn didn't reply at all. Jule tried again: "DORN, DO NOT MOVE UNTIL I GET THERE! THAT IS AN ORDER!"

He smiled at the irony as Jule raced into the building's lobby and found a door marked STAIRS. She climbed in darkness, two steps at a time, despite the weight of the gear she was carrying—her hand on the railing to guide her. Second flight, third flight . . .

Soldiers killed themselves now and then—"opting out," they called it—but no one in Jule's command ever had. She was *not* going to lose that record today.

Third flight, fourth flight . . . not a hint of light . . .

She went over everything she'd ever said to Dorn, every correction, every repeated order. She had been fair with him, she believed that . . . But she had certainly scolded him too. Had she humiliated him? Fifth flight, sixth flight . . . Throwing him in the brig had been necessary. A soldier cannot drink beer while on patrol! No captain in either army would have countenanced that.

Seventh flight, eighth flight . . . Blood pounding behind her temples, breaths shallow and short, legs burning . . . Ninth flight, tenth . . . She had to reorient herself to guess which apartment he was in. Dorn had been facing east, so the correct door must be . . .

This one. She burst in, her chest heaving. And there he was, leaning out the window—fully armed (knives, guns, ammo, a nightstick—"battle rattle," they called it). Sobs wracked his body.

"I'm sorry to do this on patrol," Dorn cried. "It isn't you. It shouldn't reflect on you in any way."

"You're one of mine," she said.

"You didn't train me. You weren't *even born* when they started training me!"

Dorn leaned too far and began to fall. Jule's breath stopped. He caught himself and regained his balance. Ten floors down, the rest of Jule's team had now gathered on the sidewalk, shouting to him: "Get back inside, Dorn! We can work this out!" That made him sob harder.

Jule said, "I'm sorry I had to punish you like that. I didn't like doing it. It was just regs."

"I deserved it," Dorn said. "I'm a shit soldier."

"You're not," she lied.

"It's so perfect you'd be the one to try and save me . . ." His words were wet. "You were always the one I tried to be like. Isn't that sad?"

"Come back in. We'll talk about it. I can help you through this."

"No," he said ruefully. "I just don't have it. In here." He pointed to his gut. "Never did."

"Let me help you, Dorn." But she could see that he'd decided. He was done. The pain had simply become unbearable.

"Captain . . ." he replied. "I'd consider it an act of mercy if you'd push me out. I'm kinda stuck."

Yes. He was done.

"You know I can't do that," she said. "I went out with ten troops, I plan to *return* with ten troops. And we're going to handle this, you and me. I'm coming over, okay?"

She took a first step.

"Don't!" he pleaded.

She halted. Dorn was shaking. He went on, "You'll just have to punish me again. And I can't go back in that brig."

He was right. But she lied, "No one needs to know."

"THE WHOLE UNIT KNOWS! THEY'RE DOWN THERE WATCHING!"

Jule paused, then tried again. "Then we'll assign you to a labor detail and call it punishment."

"With the Habs?" he asked.

"With the Habs," she said.

Dorn began to sob again, squeezing his eyes tight. Jule seized the moment and took another two steps.

Then his eyes opened again. And she froze. "The army wouldn't miss me," he said.

"Of course we would."

It was another lie. They both knew it. Yet she just couldn't make it sound any truer.

"You wouldn't," he said. Agony behind that.

"Dorn, we—"

"And I'm in love with you," he added sadly.

And he *jumped*. Just like that. Private Eldrick Dorn.

Jule stood in silence for a stunned moment, then raced to the window to alert her troops below. "COVERRRRRRRRR," she yelled. They scattered.

Then *impact*, Dorn's body hitting a stone bench on the pavement, a crash as loud as if a car had fallen the same distance. Jule shut her eyes, gutted. When she looked out again, she saw nine soldiers, men and women in her command, standing over a big broken doll.

Dorn was her failure. She knew it. Tonight she would assemble her regiment to blink, tap, and reset. And someone (she assumed) would take the Mark for him. She couldn't recall if he'd had any friends.

She leaned out and shouted to her unit, "Carter, stay with the body. The rest of you finish your missions."

They dispersed. No, she did not want to be a general.

She turned from the window again and began a search of the apartment. Her breath felt unsteady. Her hands were twitching. This one would stick. *I'm in love with you.*

She exhaled hard and entered the kitchen. It had been stripped long ago. No metal appliances left. The cupboards were empty.

Her hands were still shaking. She hated that. *I bet no one in* Rafe's *command ever opted out.* She hated that even *more*.

She pushed herself into a bedroom. Hardwood flooring. No

doorknobs or handles. Big sunlight pouring in through a curtainless window. She pulled open a closet door.

That's when she spotted the box.

It was hiding in the back of this closet—old, very old, but sturdy. And big. A box made of thick dark wood, square in shape, with a black metal handle on one side, a crank.

What was this thing? What was it for?

Then she opened it and looked inside, and she knew, that fast. She had found a revelation.

Hope itself lay inside that box. She felt that to her core. The Habs would see it too, she was sure. She gathered it in her arms, sent up a silent prayer for Dorn, and headed for the lightless stairwell . . .

SIX

Ab's day never ended. And never really began.

On this endless day, Habs reaped and threshed rows of barley as toddlers played beside them. The elderly sat on stoops at the edge of the fields, weaving baskets or mending clothes. Bored Rogue soldiers supervised the laborers like overseers of old. It was eighteenth-century work, tough on the spine—a cruel agrarian dream.

Twenty-six-year-old Byron Biggs pushed a grain-loaded cart right through the heart of it.

Byron had spent his entire life on this land. Here, he'd been robbed of a childhood, had buried loved ones, had read by firelight, taught children, set broken bones, mended souls, absorbed punishment.

And here he had toiled. Endlessly. Exhaustively. He had planted and nurtured crop after crop, feeding the very people who oppressed him. And he had done it without cease, without complaint, out of sheer self-respect and a desire to show the Rogue guards overseeing the place that Habs do not shirk. It had made Byron a favorite among those overseers, the only Hab they trusted. And it had made him a leader among his peers.

One day that would matter; he was sure of it. One day he'd lead these serfs *off* this land, to somewhere better. Until then, there was just effort . . . and encouraging those who worked beside him in the fields, and doing small kindnesses for the old ones who couldn't work any longer, and caring for his collection of books—centuries old—that he so loved to share with others. Like Rafe, he had plenty.

Grief was fuel to him. He had plenty of that too.

Pushing the grain-loaded cart past a Rogue foreman, Byron asked sarcastically: "Tell me again what we get for this?"

The foreman shot back with a playful grin, "You can sleep each night beneath the benevolent protection of the Rogue House and its tireless militias."

Byron answered, "Must be why I feel so safe."

The guard laughed. "You are salty! How's your winepress coming along?"

"Very well!" Byron said, referring to an apparatus he'd been tinkering with. "I'll be serving you spirits soon."

"Good."

Byron fashioned a pleasant smile and moved to the granary, where all the hauls were weighed and recorded. The place had its own dull smell, its own haze in the air, and a particular feeling underfoot from unswept grains. He wheeled his load to the scales, where a Rogue clerk waited. Byron's hauls were always the highest, even though he often tried to slow his production so as not to eclipse his fellow field hands by too much.

The Rogue clerk jotted down the total. "Number one again, Byron." The clerk grinned.

"You finish that book I gave you?"

"Yeah, *Of Mice and Men*. It was good. Sad. But good."

"Try this one," Byron said. He handed over a small bound volume of *Uncle Tom's Cabin*, the copy so old and worn that the pages felt like lint. "Careful with it," Byron added. The clerk nodded. And Byron left, pushing his now-empty cart.

He felt he'd just struck a small blow for freedom.

As he trod down a dirt road toward his quarters, he saw a row of children filing in from the field, some with carts, some with sacks over their shoulders. They called out to him, "Byron! Draughts tonight?"

"You know it."

The children entered the granary for the weighing of their hauls, a nightly dose of shame. Byron continued on, nearing a row of wooden cabins. To his right, he heard the familiar sound of a goods-laden cart approaching. Pushing it was a peddler named Mean, purveyor of oddities from long ago. He was fifty but looked older, his back hunched, his knees sore, his voice scratchy. "Eve, Byron."

"Eve, Mean. Anything new tonight?"

Mean smiled. "This!" From his cart he produced a globe, hundreds of years old, its stand broken. Byron examined it.

It had been made somewhere around 2100, a grisly still life of the world as it had been in that moment, when the tragedy had begun but not yet ended, when half of Greenland was still above water, parts of northern Siberia too, and much of Canada. Byron stared at it, running his fingertips along its curved face. It felt foreign, in a good way, a product manufactured and finished by machines, from *back then*.

Mean knew he had a sale. "Meals for a week?"

Byron countered, "Five days. Follow me." He was a soft touch. Mean could count on that.

That evening, Byron's mother, Lynn, stirred a pot over a strong flame. She'd been Byron's rock since birth, their loyalty to each other total. Whenever Byron had complained about being a Hab—as a child, as a teen, as a young man—Lynn always had the same ready reply: "Rogues and Crowns just hate all day. You get to be *loved*. By me. Would you trade that?"

The answer—at six, sixteen, and now—was, "No, Mama."

A lone lantern hung overhead; it too had been purchased from Mean's cart once. No one knew where Mean found all these relics. He just *did*.

A few Hab children, having drifted over after their suppers, sat on the floor, staring at the globe. Byron headed out. "Night, Mum."

Lynn threw him a look: "Where're you going?"

"Trucelands."

Lynn eyed him disapprovingly. "Now?"

He answered, "Flags're down tonight. Read to the kids before they go, okay?"

SEVEN

There *were* moments of joy in the Rogue camp, now and then. Children played at night, inventing games, chasing one another, making things, sometimes with nothing more than mud and stones to work with. The rhyme was "Mud and stones and ANIMAL BONES!"

There were the smells of dinner cooked in open pots over flame. The simple grandeur of an English sycamore tree growing untroubled near the river. And the tenderness of couples returning to each other at the end of another day. People looked after the very old and the very young, crafting rocking chairs for one and toys for the other. Community and love had found purchase here, despite the suffering. Love had not drowned. Family still mattered. People breathed and greeted each day with resilience and belief. And some days, when soldiers returned and the Yellowing claimed no victims, felt graced.

Jameson was a part of that. He was revered here.

He'd come to London fifteen years before, tall and broad, having crossed a hundred miles on foot from the Midlands with a single purpose: to *save* London from the Yellowing.

It was Jameson, a student of both botany and medicine, who'd first guessed that a paste made from beech bark might help tame the disease. He used it to treat hundreds of patients in his native Midlands, and then brought it to the city.

Because he was neither Rogue nor Crown, neither House paid much attention to him at first. But the Habs did. The Yellowing had ravaged their numbers, and they were grateful to volunteer as Jameson's inaugural patients.

The first was Lynn, Byron's mother, her lungs badly weakened. Jameson saved her, the paste quickly easing her symptoms. More ailing Habs soon stepped forward. Their conditions improved as well.

That fast, *both* Houses were courting Jameson. Each had hundreds of ailing soldiers, and his paste quickly returned them to fighting form—not cured, but healthy enough to contribute again. Jameson was a hero. But his paste had also created a new kind of chaos: Both Houses quickly laid claim to every beech tree in London. And battles over the trees erupted all across the Dry Ten.

Jameson was mortified; his creation had become the cause of *death* instead of life. At a battle in Whitehall, where beech trees lined what had once been busy streets, he rushed to the scene to try to get the Houses to cease fire. But at the Rogue front, he stepped into disaster.

The first soldier he reached was in the process of feeding an imperfect slugger into her rifle. When she fired it, the weapon simply exploded, killing her.

And blinding Jameson instantly.

The news shocked soldiers on both sides. The battle actually stopped long enough for the Rogues to carry Jameson to the safety of their medical tent. But no available treatment could return his eyesight.

Londoners in both Houses sank in shame. He had come here in peace, had eased tremendous suffering, and had paid for it in a monstrous way.

Yet he never complained. He just thanked his doctors for their care, left the Rogue camp, found himself a place to live, and learned how to navigate the river sightlessly, with such dignity that Londoners young and old began to regard him with awe—especially the Habs. He was the only person in the city who literally could not see the difference between gold and black. People admired that. Soldiers came to revere him. And soon he was regarded as untouchable by both Houses; no other Londoner had ever enjoyed such a singular status. One night he'd drift through Paternoster, pausing to greet people, sharing stories. The next night he'd visit the Crowns in Eltham and do the same there, without a hint of fear or favor.

He was, in that way, a symbol of possibility. People believed he was an emissary of goodness, or promise.

Tonight he sat by a bivouac fire, listening as Rogue mothers and fathers sang tired songs.

At that same moment, Rafe stood at a window in his quarters in St. Paul's Cathedral, looking out at dark streets below. *Jule* was on his mind tonight. That troubled him deeply. She was in the air, in the walls, everywhere. Damn it. He grabbed a book from his shelf (his collection ran into the hundreds, centuries old, their dust jackets badly faded) and left.

In the camp, guards kept watch as families huddled around fires. It wasn't an especially cold night, but the swollen river always left the air feeling damp. Rafe ducked into the quarantine tent for his nightly visit to the convalescing kids there, making his rounds, getting them to smile. They liked knowing a famous soldier, and they all wanted stories. Rafe was happy to oblige—he had plenty of them to share.

Some of these kids would get better. Some would not. The Yellowing was a relentless thief; the smell of rust hung like dust in here.

Each night, the last cot he visited belonged to an ailing six-year-old named Willa. The disease had hit her unusually hard. Her breaths were rattles, her muscles were failing, and her skin was so lifeless it looked more purple than yellow. Both her parents were soldiers, fearless. But they spent their days in terror now. She was their only child.

"Hello, Willa." Rafe grinned.

A smile fanned her face, utter joy. "Machines! Machines!"

"Machines," Rafe breathed, opening up the book he'd brought along. "Yes."

The books he shared with her each night were always manuals, technical books, about *machines* . . . machines that went places. Willa loved them.

Rafe had books about boats of all kinds and sizes. Dinghies, sailboats, yachts, luxury liners. Warships too: destroyers, cruisers, battleships, aircraft carriers, submarines.

And *cars*. The first ones ever built, or the first to be churned out on an assembly line when such a thing was possible . . . big cars, little cars, trucks, race cars, jeeps. And tractors. Anything with a motor.

And planes. Oh God, the planes. Rafe loved them; so did Willa—the military planes: the Flying Fortresses that had saved the world once, fighters, bombers, stealth bombers, planes that somehow fueled *other* planes mid-flight. And commercial aircraft, jumbo jets that had connected the globe. The freedom that represented—*leaping from one continent to another*—it dazzled them.

He opened his book to a large color photograph of a jumbo jet from centuries past, a Boeing 747. Willa's eyes went wide. Sheer wonder, almost disbelief.

And Rafe began, from memory: "It was built in the biggest factory ever constructed. The first model took eight years to complete; it had six million component parts. Each wing alone needed forty thousand rivets. It could carry six hundred people and had ten bathrooms!"

"No!" Willa whispered.

One photo showed a full 747 cabin, mid-flight. Row after row of ordinary citizens. Life as it was then lived. Strangers Rafe would never meet, leading lives he'd never know, in lands he'd never see, captured by a technology he'd never understand. Paper ghosts. Printed.

People didn't *need* memories then. They had proof, on paper, that they'd been here. That ate at him now. Rafe knew he would die unphotographed, and it suddenly felt cruel.

He kept turning pages until fatigue overtook Willa and her eyes began to close, the smile never leaving her face. Then he rose, leaving the book on Willa's cot beside her. That was a first, parting with a volume of his. He departed the tent.

In the square, Maud sat at a wooden table, carving a branch into a spear. Opposite her were Beckett, a captain, and Rafe's dear friend Maddox, who was stretching his legs as if about to run a hundred-meter dash. It was how Maddox kept himself battle ready, ten sprints per day, every day, in all kinds of weather. He was, without doubt, the fastest runner in the Rogue Army. Speed had saved his life more than once.

They saw Rafe passing by, and Maud asked, "Where're you going?"

Rafe replied: "Patrol."

Instant suspicion in her eyes. "You're not on watch tonight."

"When've I ever given a damn about lists?"

With that, he was gone. Beckett joked to Maud, "Man o' yer dreams, eh?"

Maud shot back, "Least he's not boring."

Beckett and Maddox laughed.

Maud didn't. "Piss off," she said, and returned to carving that spear.

Maddox grinned. "Hey, Maudy, I'm beginning to think your name *doesn't* mean 'powerful battler' in French. I think it means 'salty'!"

Maud retorted, "Go make one of yer stupid dashes, Maddox."

Maddox smiled. "God of speed!" Then he raced away in a sprint, fast as hell. Beckett wisely remained silent.

Maud felt a shiver. She despised the part of herself that loved Rafe; it felt unsoldierly and weak. Worrying about his safety was torment.

And knowing he didn't love *her* . . . was misery.

Outside the Paternoster Wall, pirogues were stacked by a barren shop that had once sold mobile phones. Rafe grabbed one of the boats and carried it down the street, which sloped gently until it met the water. There, he saw a woman a few years his junior, armed for patrol.

Breena, his sister. She was tall and slender, her hair shorn tight. Breena's pridefulness was well-known. Rafe loved her for it. She asked, "You outside the line tonight?"

Rafe answered, "Yeah. You?"

"Patrol. The Hump."

"Careful there."

Breena shook her head, mildly offended. "Don't you worry."

Rafe smiled. "It's my duty to worry, little sister."

"Not so little," she said. "You remember that."

"Noted." Rafe grinned as he pushed off, putting his oar to the water. Breena watched him row away.

He liked the feeling of starting out. It made his shoulders feel strong. And Ludgate Hill was quiet and untroubled, Rogue territory.

But two strokes in, a Bloat swam alongside his pirogue.

Bloats hadn't existed before the Great Soak. Back then they were simply adders, the European common viper, living on land in deep country. For millennia, no one from a city ever saw them or gave them a thought.

Then the water came, and centuries passed, and they evolved, learning how to swim and hunt in rivers. And they grew, earning their new name. Now the Thames was filled with Bloats that were as long as Rafe was tall, but heavy enough to topple a pirogue and throw its occupant into the river. Then one poisonous bite, instant paralysis, drowning... and dinner. Feeding was the only time they ever made a sound.

Yet another reason to despise this river.

Rafe slammed an oar into the water, enough to frighten the Bloat away, then paddled on. Once he'd cleared the sight lines of the Rogue guards, he removed his black armband and paddled to starboard, heading for the Trucelands.

The Trucelands had never been recognized by any formal agreement; they'd just been left alone by both Houses as sectors too hopelessly drowned to fight over, dozens of square miles—a wet and unloved city all their own—home to Bloats, drunks, and not much else. Rogues and Crowns alike had ceded them to the Habs in a somewhat-empty gesture of humanity. No fighting ever occurred there.

Now Jule headed toward them, guided by moonlight and a few distant torches, with the box at her feet. To her right, the fronds of an aquatic tree unfurled across a rooftop where a drunken Hab splayed and snored. Jule paddled to starboard—

And there it was, the top of the Victoria Memorial, poking out of the water to herald the appearance of Buckingham Palace—or most of it, anyway. Eight feet of water consumed the great mansion's ground floor.

Once, with the Great Soak underway, the royal family had ordered a watertight wall built around the palace. Two days after the wall was completed, an angry mob tore it down. Never again would the place be any safer or drier than the rest of London.

Tonight, dozens of pirogues were secured to its open windows by rope. Habs had come here to drink and forget. Jule hoped tonight's entertainment might make them feel less like Habs, at least for a while. She tied up her pirogue to the top of a first-floor window casing and stepped inside . . .

Miles away, Breena and a fellow Rogue soldier named Glendon patrolled "the Hump," a tiny urban park as wildly overgrown as all the other parks in London.

Centuries ago, the first full-scale battle between the Rogues and Crowns had been waged on this spot, the Hump, mere weeks after the terrifying VX attack had carved all London into two skittish Houses. The casualties in that first fight, astounding as they'd been, were dwarfed by the bloodbaths that followed—hundreds of years of uncivil hatred and slaughter.

But tonight was calm. Tonight was just patrol. Glendon filled it with idle chatter, as he always did when bored. "Someone must know," he groused. "Somewhere."

"Believe it when I see it," Breena answered.

"World's a big place, Breena."

"Not mine. Not yours. Keep your eyes front." She was serious about patrol.

But Glendon went on, "People were smart enough to build all this. *Someone* out there has to be smart enough to power it."

Breena shrugged. "Maybe all the tech just drowned—"

. . . which was when—THUMK—a javelin suddenly dug into Glendon's ribs, hurled from the darkness. A gasp shot out of his mouth, and he was dead before Breena had time to spin around. She heard rustling from a thick branch above her.

Suddenly, a lasso wrapped around her, tightening sharply. Someone in the black night pulled hard, yanking her off her feet.

She hollered. It didn't matter. They dragged her away, her Rogue armband coming loose and falling to the soil.

The walls of Buckingham Palace were unpapered, and there were holes where light sconces had once been. As Rafe strode down a hallway that monarchs had once walked, candles flickered on the floor, lighting his way. Water lapped at the walls outside as he passed by empty rooms. In one of them, beside a window, a man and a woman clawed at each other with furious energy. In the opposite corner, two men did the same. Not an armband in sight.

Rafe reached the end of the hall, where Byron waited: "Glad you could come, Rafe." This was a perk Byron received for working so hard and never frowning, the trust of the Rogue House to do as he liked in this palace. It was his domain.

Rafe smiled thinly. "Good to see you, Byron. I always wondered what Habs did for entertainment."

"Sleep, mostly. But tonight's different. Tonight's a first."

"Any Crowns around?" Rafe asked.

"There's more to life than Rogues and Crowns, my friend."

No other Hab would dare to be so familiar, but Rafe just smiled, turning to enter a room to Byron's left. Byron stopped him gently.

"Rafe. Respect the Trucelands."

Caught, Rafe grinned and removed a dagger he had hidden on his ankle. Byron appreciated it, but he was still waiting.

. . . until Rafe removed the dagger secreted on his *other* ankle as well and handed it over.

No Hab but Byron could have gotten away with *that* either. He nodded. "Enjoy."

Rafe entered a room that felt musky and stale, the air hanging visibly in front of him. It was a grand study, candlelit, its massive floor-to-ceiling bookcases emptied long ago. Fifty or so Habs relaxed here, men and women, drunk on gin from an old and shaky still. They turned as Rafe entered—and they tightened, as one.

Behind Rafe, Byron said, "He's all right." The Habs swallowed their resentment. Rafe scanned the study for Crowns and didn't see any. It *almost* made his fists uncoil. Almost.

Gin burbled from that shaky still. Someone handed Rafe a glass of it, thin and clear. It had a stench, but he knew better than to refuse. The others were all gulping theirs. Rafe sipped. In a corner, the old peddler, Mean, did magic tricks, making a playing card vanish. His Hab audience applauded. Mean nodded at Rafe and declared, "If only I could make *Rogues* disappear!"

The Habs laughed. Rafe breathed out a smile. Byron looked to Mean with a soft reproach: "Respect the Trucelands, Mean."

The old peddler grumbled, "I like this room better without gold or black in it. Must be hard for you, Captain, seeing us outside our toil."

"Not a bit," Rafe replied.

Just then, Byron moved to the front of the room, ready to start the show. The Habs fell silent. He announced, "Welcome to the Un-Club, my friends!"

Their hands full of stinky gin, the Habs stamped their feet on the floor.

"The Un-Club," Rafe muttered. He liked that.

Byron went on, "Something special for you tonight. Very new—but very old too, discovered by someone you'd least expect. Are you ready?"

More foot stomping. Rafe found himself becoming mildly intrigued. Then a door behind Byron opened and . . .

In stepped Jule, carrying the box. And it happened again—

Rafe was staggered. *That face.* His throat tightened; his cheeks flushed. His heart thumped; he couldn't stop staring—and it was all happening automatically, involuntarily. His body simply reacted to her, every cell suddenly famished. It physically *hurt* not to touch her, and to know he never would.

The room hushed. Everyone here knew who she was, *what* she was. Mean called out: "Bloody *Crowns* here too, Byron? You trying to get us all killed?"

Jule pretended not to hear it. And Byron answered: "Quiet, Mean. We all know the rules . . ."

The crowd parted for her as she moved through the room. Confident, centered, *certain*—just as she'd been certain this afternoon while pointing a gun at Rafe's head. In the center of the room stood a table. Jule got there, and upon the tabletop she placed the dark wooden box—a great golden funnel poking out of it. No one had any idea what it was. She eyed the crowd calmly.

Rafe wanted to be alone with her, wanted everyone else to leave.

Unthinkable. Everything he was thinking was unthinkable.

Jule waited for quiet and attention. Got both. Then she cranked that black handle on the side of the wooden box. A small black plaque on its front said one word: VICTROLA.

Mean crossed his arms, refusing to be intrigued, but everyone else in the room was leaning forward.

Especially Rafe.

Jule finished cranking the handle and opened the top of the wooden box. Rafe moved in closer . . .

Jule noticed. Their eyes met. Mortal enemies.

Inside the wooden box, a circular platter spun around. Maybe it'd been powered by that hand crank; Rafe wasn't sure.

Then Jule grabbed an odd square of cardboard and pulled a strange round black vinyl disc from it.

What is that thing? Rafe didn't know. He'd never seen anything like it. Jule placed the black disc on the spinning platter, then lowered a thin metal arm onto the rotating disc. Lord, she was a mystery.

From the box, silence at first. Then a weird crackling sound, coming from its big funnel.

Rafe waited. They all did. So strange. Then he was stunned—by what he would later learn were the first four notes of Beethoven's Fifth Symphony.

DUN-DUN-DUN-DUNNNNNNNNNNNNNN.

The sound knocked everyone back. Some fell. Rafe was poleaxed. They all were. A moment of astonishment . . . then the next four notes knocked them back again.

DUN-DUN-DUN-DUNNNNNNNNNNNNNN.

Music. Recorded music. Emanating somehow from that box. It was overwhelming. Sensory shock. The sounds exploded, ricocheting off the paperless walls, Jule enjoying the wonder on all the faces in here. Byron too. Even Mean was moved.

Rafe forgot how to breathe. This wasn't some Rogue kid badly blowing through a fife in camp while another kid badly played a drum. This was a miracle, hundreds of musicians at once, conspiring to feed one another, their precision perfect. And all of it *recorded*, somehow, on that disc. A lifetime without real music and then *this*—the sound, the newness, vibrations hitting his chest—and again, *her face*. That was a miracle too. The floor felt fluid beneath his feet.

Their eyes met again. The moment was full, perfect, impossible. Again, he couldn't move—yet everything *inside* him was moving. *This*, he thought, *must be what electricity felt like.* The sounds kept coming. She was *making* them, somehow. And they were as beautiful and impossible as she was. A *symphony* . . . and her lovely face. Both masterpieces.

This was elation. Tempo, melody, harmony. Even the water outside looked like it was dancing. In mere seconds, Jule had changed everything. She'd made war feel juvenile. Rafe couldn't believe how quickly and completely that had happened.

Now and forever, Jule was music.

Byron smiled. "Beats killing each other, doesn't it?"

Rafe stayed silent. Across the room, Jule continued to soak up the exhilaration around her. It all felt new. And *no one* seemed more moved by it than this Rogue captain who'd suddenly become the focus of her day. *Rafe.*

Today he'd borne a white flag, which she'd been certain was a ploy. Could this be a ploy too? The joy on his face?

She didn't think so, and it was hard to be cynical amid all this euphoria. Many in the room were in tears. There were no guns here, no *hate.* She looked into Rafe's eyes and saw . . . herself. Impossible, but there it was.

Beethoven continued to soar. Jule decided to soar too.

The show had ended now. The air was the air again. Habs filed out, still intoxicated by the sounds they'd heard. Jule and Byron remained. "Brilliant night, Jule."

Jule smiled, eyeing the Victrola. Such promise in there. She asked, "See you home?"

Byron grinned. "I'll be okay."

Jule nodded, her fondness obvious. "Night, Byron. Thanks for the room."

"Thanks for the religion." And out he went.

Jule remained, preferring to stay in this room and remember. The water and the war could wait.

Then, a sound, which didn't surprise her a bit. A closet door, slowly opening. She turned.

Rafe. He'd been hiding inside. Now he tried to look soldierly, but his face was reddening.

The next second took an hour. Both of them staring. Holy hell, this captain was handsome—a word she'd learned long ago but had never actually used before. Jule settled herself and grinned casually. "Had a feeling you might loiter."

Neither felt like a stranger; it was as if they'd grown up knowing each other. In a way, they had. But Rafe was shaking. Breathing felt like an accomplishment. All he could mutter was, "Those sounds . . ."

Jule cut him off. "They are pretty."

Rafe replied, "Never heard anything like— Never heard anything that powerful before . . ."

"You've heard a lot of Crowns take their last breath. That wasn't powerful?"

Rafe let that go. "That box. When is it from?"

"They were called Victrolas, long before the water. Five hundred years ago? Six? I found it in a closet. Took me a second to figure out what it was for."

"That disc survived six hundred years?"

"They were called records."

Rafe eyed the Victrola, awed. "Maybe we followed geniuses."

Jule asked, "Geniuses who drowned the world?"

"Whoever made those sounds was a genius."

Jule held up the album cover. "Beethoven."

A silence hung. Rafe filled it. "Thank you, for not killing me at the common."

She breathed, "Maybe I'm just a poor shot."

Everything felt fraught. And unprecedented. Neither of these two had ever flirted before; there'd never been a reason to. Soldiers were coupled, and that was that. Yet the war suddenly felt like a distant bell.

And for the first time ever, no one was watching them. There was no crowd, no one to lionize or scrutinize them. That felt utterly new, and liberating, like being reborn.

"Do you have more?" Rafe asked.

"Many," she said. "But this seems like a terrible idea."

"I think it's brilliant."

"Why? So we can have pretty songs in our head next time our Houses meet in battle?"

He wanted to say, *No, no, no. That's all over now. There won't be battles anymore. Tonight you put an end to all that.* But he knew how absurd that would sound.

Instead: "I wasn't going to come here tonight. Byron had invited me before, and I'd always said no."

"Me too," Jule replied.

"Always felt like he was trying to trick me into seeing the Habs in a different light, and he never needed to. But today I said yes, and I couldn't figure out why. Now I know."

"I just thought they'd like the music."

"Can I hear more of it?"

She asked, "The talks you proposed. They're a trick, right? An ambush?"

"No." That suddenly felt entirely true.

"No," she repeated.

"May I hear more of the music, Jule?"

She surprised herself. "It's the Trucelands. Why not?"

She grabbed a candle and added, "If you would," indicating the Victrola. Then she drifted into a room off the study. Rafe lifted the Victrola and followed her. None of it felt real. The walls were rushing past him.

The room off the study was smaller. "Put it here," she said, pointing to the floor near a cabinet. Rafe obeyed cheerfully. Jule opened the cabinet, revealing hundreds more "records," standing in a row like impossibly narrow books.

Rafe's eyes went wide. "Can we hear them all?"

"Not in a night. Sit down."

He sat. "We have a drummer in our camp. And a kid with a fife. But—"

"—and shut up."

He *loved* that, loved her armor. She grabbed another record, removed it from its sleeve, put it on the Victrola. "This one has singing," she said.

"How many of these have you heard?"

She didn't respond. Needle touched vinyl. Scratch, scratch . . . then—

Four young men singing a single word: "HELP!"

The sounds knocked him back. Were they real? It was too much to process. *What was this?* Joy itself was in that box. The sounds of electric guitars, "rock and roll," such a departure from Beethoven and yet somehow a worthy *child* of Beethoven. It made him feel like a kid, and the shock on his face made her laugh.

Good Lord, her laugh. He loved that too. His head was exploding. Rafe stared at the black vinyl disc as it spun. What a mystery. Impossible. *Jule* seemed impossible too. He began, "Were you—" "Sssssshhhhh," she whispered. "We can talk after."

Yes. That was right. The music deserved the fullness of this room. *Just do what she tells you*, he thought. *She's smarter than you are.*

He looked at the cardboard sleeve. The Beatles. Four lads. Funny hair. Looked like they'd never killed anyone, or had to run for their lives or row across a street. *Thank God*, he thought. His fingers tapped in rhythm on the floor.

Jule noticed now that hers were doing the same thing. It made her cheeks red. She could feel the moment etching itself into a forever file in her memory, *everything* about this room: the texture of the walls, the dust on the floor, the rotation of the record, the sharpness of the needle. The feeling of her bottom against the hard floor, the tingle in her arms, the exquisite thrill in her chest, the numbness in her throat. Rafe wasn't pretty at all, but he was beautiful. The line of his jaw, the frame of his shoulders, the worn-down heels of his boots, the half-healed cuts and scratches on the backs of his hands, his voice, his skin, his nose—she could see it'd been broken a few times. And he had soldier's arms. Even under a shirt she could tell. She wanted to touch them. It was all just . . . *handsome*.

But the real magic was the wonder in his eyes. There was no bitterness in them, no coarseness at all; he almost seemed guileless. Years of battle, countless deaths—yet he was utterly open, unguarded, joyous, and willing to be wounded. *He's braver than you are*, she thought enviously. It was all a deep shock. Yet she felt calm in a way she'd never experienced before. Rooted.

The sounds danced around her. She felt like she could taste them. And in that moment, Rafe *was* music.

"I have one of my soldiers to thank for this," she said, nodding to the Victrola.

"Shhhhh," he said kiddingly. "We can talk after."

She blushed, then smiled and went on, "I found it in a closet after he jumped out a tenth-story window."

"That's terrible."

"Thought I'd gotten to him in time. Turns out I was a few years too late."

"It's hard, losing someone in your command."

"Someone like you would've killed him anyway, before long."

That armor of hers again. He moved right past it. "Still hard. I'm sorry."

The record ended. He asked, "Can we hear another?" She reached back into that cabinet. Rafe waited.

This was a fulcrum moment. He knew that. From now on, *everything* would be sorted into one of two categories: *his life before the palace* and *after*. She changed the record. Someone named Ray Charles. Then other sounds followed, over the course of hours. People called Etta James, Frank Sinatra, Edith Piaf, the Rolling Stones . . . Rafe and Jule could feel their ears getting drunk.

"More," he asked. Mysteries named Diana Ross and Stevie Wonder (who had written his songs' lyrics on the back of that cardboard sleeve). Rafe and Jule took turns cranking the handle on the Victrola, hoping it wouldn't break.

Their eyes were locked. Their skin felt taut. Violins swelled. Drums pounded. Guitars buzzed. Voices rose. The air was filled with tempo. Muscle. Fury. Love. Magic. *God?*

"I could stay here all night," Rafe said.

"Might be the gin talking," she shot back.

"It's not the gin," he answered.

She smiled. "Really? I had vats of it."

"You are so salty."

"Seems only right, considering I might have to kill you tomorrow."

Rafe eyed her. "I think you've killed me already."

Jule refused to be charmed, reminding herself to think about Eltham, where the Crowns lived and toiled and suffered. The forge, the med tent, the quarantine tent, her tiny room, the paste she fed to Nelly, the endless training of the young as they entered the army.

None of it rhymed with tonight, none of it fit with this man. Her enemy. Sitting here meant doom. She knew it.

Yet she wasn't running away.

Rafe smiled. "Smelled awful, that stuff." Jule just shrugged. He asked, "Didn't bother you?"

She answered, "I didn't notice."

That threw him. She pointed to the tip of her nose and said, "It doesn't work. No sense of smell."

"Really?"

"Really. Never had it."

That was the truth. She'd been born without it.

"Maybe that's why battle doesn't bother you. The smell is really pretty awful."

She swallowed a single thought: *Doesn't bother me? How can he think battle doesn't bother me?* But she'd never said that it had. That armor again . . .

Rafe added, "Play me more."

Another song pounded. It was called "The Chain," but what the hell was a Fleetwood Mac?

She said, "Found *this* too."

She handed him a small leather-bound book. It said HYMNAL on its face. He opened it and saw page after page of musical markings on five-lined rows. Notes, chords, clefts. He'd seen these symbols before, but he didn't understand them.

And he asked, "How does *this* become *that*?"

"I don't know," she said.

He returned the hymnal to her, but she said, "Keep it."

A gift. From a Crown. He stuffed the book into his jacket, right over his heart.

The song ended as faint sunlight began to creep through the nearest window. Rafe wanted to touch her, but he knew better. She was the enemy.

But her face . . . and the morning quiet as it floated around her, and a soft scent rising from her shoulders . . . It was all too much.

"Tell me something," he began. "You find this box. You find the records. You realize what they are . . . but you bring them *here*, to the Habs. Not to your own House. Why?"

"What makes you think I didn't share them with my own House?"

He eyed her knowingly.

She shrugged. "The Habs never get anything first."

"No, they don't. But why didn't you share this with your own?"

She thought about that for a while. Then she admitted, "My House wouldn't know how to hear it."

That touched him. "Mine wouldn't either."

She smiled. "So God bless the Habs . . ."

He nodded. "I'm glad you're a captain and not a general. If you were in charge, your House would've won by now."

She wished she could breathe him in; it felt unfair. "We should go." She smiled.

They both stood. He leaned in to kiss her.

She sweep-kicked his legs. He landed hard on his back, looking up at her, his spine sore.

"Now I'm in love." He smiled.

"That was a warning," she replied.

"Tonight? Back here?" He was still on the floor.

She didn't reply. Just closed up the Victrola and put it in a cabinet. The records too.

"Put out the candles before you go."

"But—"

"Flags won't stay down forever." And she left. He got to his feet and crossed to the window, watching as Jule climbed into a pirogue, rowing away without a look back.

EIGHT

Morning light poked through slats in the side of a wooden barn. There, Byron toiled, exhausted. His life's work was before him.

It was a giant machine, a press: large circular wooden slabs, valves, knobs. He'd built it by hand during stolen hours, late nights, early dawns. Three years' worth. The press was too big to hide, so he'd told his Rogue overseers its purpose was to make wine, and they left him alone. Its true purpose was to save souls from the Yellowing. The disease had killed Byron's wife three years before.

Grace and Byron had met as children, then worked in the fields together, connecting like twin flames and marrying at eighteen. She was joy. They read books together, made plans together. He slept beside her in utter awe.

Then Grace fell ill. The Yellowing. She couldn't work. Her skin turned to mustard. She swallowed beech paste and tried not to complain. Byron nursed her and worked extra shifts to make up for her absence.

One Saturday morning, bored of resting, Grace decided to venture off the Highlands in search of good fishing. "Air will be good for me," she'd said. An hour later, she was trudging through a forest grove, aware of the shallowness of her breathing, when she was spotted by two Crown soldiers on patrol. They instantly gave chase.

Their names were Pritchett and Boggs.

Later, they would brag to their colleagues that Grace had sprinted to get back to the fields where Rogue soldiers would protect her—that was the agreement, toil for safety. But her weakened lungs failed her . . . and she was theirs.

The next two days were sheer hell for Byron. He couldn't find her. No one could. Fieldwork simply stopped as every Hab went in search of her. Byron didn't sleep or eat. Then he found her. Her body had been secreted inside a hollow tree trunk, fifty yards from a riverbed. Byron fell to the earth.

His fellow Habs carried him—and her—back to the Highlands. Friends maintained a strict watch over Byron, to keep him from harming himself.

Burials were illegal in this world; there wasn't enough land to spare. So the law dictated that Grace would enter the afterlife as all Londoners did: in a compost pile amid wood chips, straw, and alfalfa—becoming mulch after thirty days.

Sod that, Byron thought. And in an open and unapologetic violation of that statute, he buried her beneath the same barley field they'd worked together since childhood.

The next day, he began to build the press.

Maybe, *maybe*, the machine would do some good. Maybe it would produce the medicine on a vastly larger scale, and curb some of the suffering. Maybe the loss of Grace would become less excruciating. Byron needed to believe.

Of course, if the Rogues ever discovered the press's actual purpose, they would commandeer it. Byron wasn't sure how he'd manage that. Perhaps an appeal to their humanity. Or maybe he'd just fight back and die . . . and his mother would bury him alongside Grace beneath all that sun-splashed barley.

And his fatigue and grief would end.

He sat down to finish the press. Just then, the barn door opened behind him. A fellow Hab—her name was Dawson—entered. She wore a thin white band around her neck, the mark of a minister; Dawson's sermons mattered in these fields.

"Morning, Byron. How's the work?"

"Near ready."

"Haven't seen you at services lately."

"No."

"Planning to join us this morning?"

"Hadn't been, no."

"I thought as much." Dawson opened the barn door wider. Outside it were thirty more Habs—Byron's neighbors, friends, partners in toil. They drifted in now with warm smiles for him, finding seats on the floor. Dawson had brought her church to this barn, for him.

She stood in front of the press, removed a small Bible from her thin coat, and breathed, "Let's begin." Byron didn't know if God was in that barn, but the yearning for God certainly was. He closed his eyes and tried to believe . . .

Jule arrived at the main Crown gate, unfolding from her pirogue and pulling it to dry land. Her sack, slung over her shoulder, was filled once again with beech bark, acquired this morning without a fight. That felt like a blessing.

Sentries opened the gate for her, and she drifted in to find camp life unfolding as it always did: The forge roared with flame. The huge cauldrons of stew bubbled. Chores were performed. Fish were caught. Laundry was hung. Battles were planned. Two Habs passed her with an empty horse-drawn cart, having just made their morning deliveries. Their wheat filled a granary deep inside the grounds.

But the previous night—and the music—had changed everything. There was a Rogue, his name was Rafe, and he was beautiful. That made everything feel new, made all that had once been true now feel *untrue*. She now knew—in the same way that she knew about war and work and the wetness of water—that life *wasn't* always poison.

Joy, and love, were possible. Delight danced on her lips. She knew now, more than ever, that she *couldn't* be a general. Commanders cared only for victory; that was no longer her true north. She neared Eltham Lake, where Crowns gathered to wash their clothes and their bodies. The water had been Jule's enemy all her life. But today, she eyed it fondly, remembering that children often splashed in it, and citizens old and young fished it for all its gifts. It swelled in rainstorms and made things grow and moved in tiny whitecaps when the winds howled, as they often did. It didn't *want* to be feared. It just wanted to dance.

She waved to her neighbors as she passed, eager to see Nelly, who always worried extravagantly whenever Jule was out all night on patrol. She entered their lobby.

But an oddity stopped her: a twelve-year-old Crown girl named Madeline, sitting on the second step of the lobby stairway, absently beating drumsticks against its metal railing. It was a tinny, ugly noise, but what caught Jule wasn't the sound. It was the kid's face. The blank stare.

"Madeline?" Jule asked. Madeline didn't answer, just kept beating out a tuneless rhythm with the sticks.

Jule calmly stilled the child's hands, and silence fell... until another sound now evidenced itself. A *human* sound, coming from a few feet away, muffled and strained. A pained whimpering. Jule followed it under the stairs. And there she saw—

Breena. A stranger to Jule, lying on the floor. Hands tied to a radiator with rope. Her bloodied mouth covered with a gag. Her eyes, one of which bore a gash over it, blindfolded. Shaking from fatigue and dehydration. And moaning.

Jule was horrified. Repulsed. Ashamed. That surprised her. Yesterday she might've seen this same thing and shrugged it off as another act of war. But now it all just felt so tragic, so ugly. *Must it always come to this?* She threw the drumsticks to the floor. Madeline began to run for the door, but Jule grabbed her wrists. "Who put her here?"

Madeline hesitated. Jule rushed under the stairs and removed Breena's gag and blindfold and yelled again, "WHO DID THIS?"

The child was silent, but *Breena* spat out, "Their names were Pritchett and Boggs."

Jule sighed hard. Pritchett and Boggs were in her command. She'd heard rumors years before—everyone had—that they'd once bragged of killing a pretty Hab girl in a forest and leaving her body in a hollowed-out tree. But no proof ever existed, and they'd denied the charges when she asked.

Now, disgusted, she looked to Madeline. "Is that true? That's who it was?"

Madeline nodded. "They said you'd wanna interrogate her. Is that the right word?"

Jule sagged, shame rising up again. Breena tried to stand, but could only get to her knees as Madeline asked, "Can I watch? They said I should watch, so I could learn."

"Go home," Jule breathed. "And the next time those two ask you to do *anything*, you say no, understand?"

Madeline nodded, frozen. Breena hollered, "Run, little drummer girl!"

Madeline gathered her sticks and ran off. Jule untied Breena's wrists, which were deeply bruised. Seemed every part of Breena's body had been beaten. "I'm sorry," Jule said.

Breena knew who Jule was; every Rogue did. So it was hard for Breena to believe the kindness she was seeing, even when Jule asked cautiously, "Did they . . . ?"

Breena shook her head no, then rose slowly to her feet. Jule nodded, relieved, and said, "Come with me."

Breena stiffened. "Sod off. Let's just fight and die here."

Jule exhaled hard. "No. I'll show you how to get out of here, and back to your camp."

Breena emerged from beneath the stairs now, her face bruised and bleeding; one eye was bloodshot.

Jule sighed. "Did they give you water?"

Breena eyed her sarcastically.

"Do you want some?"

Breena didn't reply.

"Okay," Jule said. "Listen, to get you out of here, I'll need to put this back on you." She stepped toward Breena with the blindfold.

Breena's reaction was feral; she exploded past Jule, all adrenaline and elbows, knocking Jule aside and vanishing around the stairs into a hallway. Then heavy footsteps, and a back door blowing open. Jule knew that giving chase would get Breena caught and killed. Nothing to do now but hope she made it home.

That seemed unlikely. Breena would probably be captured by Crowns whose lives were just as ugly as hers, and they'd kill her. Then they too would die at the hands of Rogues, because here, life *was* death. The ugliness was everywhere.

But life had not felt ugly last night. The music had not felt ugly. Her hands had not felt ugly, even though for so many years they had done ugly things. And it felt good not to hate. New and unfamiliar, but good. It felt like a gift.

She reminded herself to tell Rafe that, next time they met.

He docked his pirogue and strode through the Rogue camp, trying not to look as weary, or as gleeful, as he was.

Another night of privation and war had passed here—and nothing had changed for the civilians around him. No one had gotten appreciably worse or better, happier or sadder, healthier or closer to death. Hours had simply slogged past.

But for Rafe, everything had shifted. His bloodlust had left his body, replaced by Beethoven and Jule. He kept hearing those impossible sounds and seeing *her* inside them—the two things wedded now, forever. The music, that symphony. DUN-DUN-DUN-DUNNNN. And her face. She was *all*. Just like that—notes, chords, magic, *joy*. And he knew she always would be. It felt impossible in a way, unreachable. But he was grateful for it.

It told him what to do.

As he entered the trading floor, a quiet tension hung—Shapcott and the captains were arming themselves with great urgency. They stopped when they saw him.

"Jaysus!" said Beckett. "You're not dead!"

A collective relief filled the room, everyone heartened—except for Maud. "Where the hell were you?"

Maddox grinned. "Not his wife yet, Maud."

"Was I talking to you?" she snapped. Then she asked Rafe: "Did you see Breena or Glendon out there?"

"Saw them when they set out," Rafe answered. "Why?"

"They haven't come back from patrol."

That fast, Rafe sank—utterly certain that his sister had been captured or killed. Or maybe she'd drowned.

... while he had been listening to records. It was crushing.

A candle burned nearby. He knew that soon he'd be sticking his hand into its flame, taking the Mark ... "Have we sent out a search team?" he muttered.

Shapcott answered, "We were just about to. Thought we'd be looking for you as well."

"I'm here. I'm fine. The team should've been *sent* by now!"

Shapcott let that pass, watching as Rafe crossed to a hand-drawn map of the city to point out where Breena had been patrolling. He added a precise description of where Crown pockets remained—the details of each block, shop by shop, which ones had basements, which were accessible from rooftops. His mastery was awe-inspiring, especially now.

This too was why they followed him.

Briefed now, they all headed for the door. As Rafe brushed past Maud on his way out, she muttered, "You never did say where you were last night."

"Fighting."

"With who?"

"Next time I'll bring you a few heads. Can we go find my sister now?"

Across the city, his sister was in fact running for her life.

NINE

A dense fog hung heavy in that same wood where Byron's wife had been murdered. It settled between the trees.

Breena raced through it.

After she'd fled the Crown camp, hopping over that wall of dense English oak, she'd been spotted by three Crown soldiers on patrol and had been running ever since. Now, her ribs aching, one eye so bloodshot she could barely see through it, she forced her legs to keep pumping. The three Crowns were slower than she was, but they were armed. Their footsteps fell noisily across the leaves.

The fog quickly thickened as only English fog could, and an odd silence fell.

The three Crowns stopped, suddenly unable to see anything before them but a heavy white mist and the bottoms of damp trees. They stood still, blind, their chests heaving.

One had rank, a female sergeant. She held up a hand, indicating to the others, *Don't make a sound.* But they were panting noisily, unsettled—and blind. Then—

THUMP. THUMP. THUMP.

Fist-sized stones, hurled from the dense whiteness with breathtaking precision, hit each soldier in the back of the head. None fell, but all staggered.

Breena was instantly upon them, grabbing a club from the wooziest of the three and cracking him in the skull with it. The others, both women, got the same. Now all three were on the ground, helpless. Breena could have killed them easily.

So she did, walking away without a hint of remorse.

"Morning," Jule heard. It was Paris approaching.

"Morning, Paris."

Behind him, Eltham Lake looked clean and clear. "General's looking for you."

"Oh?"

Paris nodded politely, his face blushing a bit. It was common knowledge at Eltham that Paris had been in love with Jule for years. But he had never said so aloud because he knew—as did everyone else—that Jule had no time for romance and no interest in anything except killing Rogues. Besides, they were both soldiers. Their marital fate would be decided by General Chasen. Paris joined her as they marched to Chasen's command post.

It was a vast bunker, lit by oil lamps, its ceiling supported by wooden struts. Two centuries ago, Crowns had fashioned this redoubt by hand, an astonishing achievement given their limited tools. It was stocked with enough food and water to last ninety days if Chasen and his captains ever had to isolate in wartime, thirty days if they had their families with them. Everyone hoped that would never be necessary.

But the Rogues were such lawless animals, one never knew . . .

Jule entered, unsettled. Her general asked, "Long night?"

"Hello, Uncle." She smiled thinly.

She was his favorite. She was also, in a secret that wasn't a secret at all, the captain he'd chosen to be his successor one day, despite her distaste for the idea.

"You didn't report in, Jule. And when it's you, I don't sleep."

"I was up to no good," she said. "Sorry to have worried you."

Chasen said, "You haven't told me your thoughts on talks with the Rogues. Although I suspect I know."

All her life, she'd been the hardest of hard-liners in this House, the fiercest in battle, the least tolerant of the idea of peace. "No, I haven't," she said mockingly. And everyone chuckled.

"Well?" the general asked.

"The idea of a pax troubles me for all kinds of reasons. Mostly, what would we soldiers *do* all day?"

More chuckles, from Chasen too. Her faux breeziness seemed to be working. She continued: "Truth is, I don't know how seriously to take the offer. Shapcott lost a son; that wouldn't make *me* seek peace. And the messenger he chose, Rafe, is in line to lead that army someday. You achieve that by *fighting* wars, not ending them."

The turn followed: "But Jameson is a serious man. And if he is guaranteeing our safety . . ." She allowed that to hover, allowed herself to look as though she were processing it, then: "It can't hurt us to hear what they're thinking."

Chasen eyed her. They all did. Never before had Jule referred to a pax with anything but contempt. The general nodded. "I agree."

Sold. She stopped her face from betraying a hint of relief.

Chasen went on, "Send two of yours under that white flag to say we'll meet."

"I'll see to it immediately, General."

"Thank you."

She headed for the exit. Chasen called out to her. "Are you ready to be coupled yet?"

Coupled? Jule froze—then turned—replaying the words in her head, hoping she'd heard them wrong.

Chasen went on, "I was thinking of you and Paris. You'd make tall soldiers together."

That fast, Jule felt herself gag with revulsion and panic, her head swimming. Paris, however, was thrilled. A smile erupted across his face.

"Were you?" Jule managed to say. The bunker felt airless.

"Yes, I was," Chasen said. "And he certainly seems amenable."

Everyone laughed. Evander beamed. "My sister and my best mate! A wonderful pairing, General!"

"I think so too." Chasen smiled. "Unless Jule would prefer someone she could give orders to all day!"

More laughter. Jule forced a smile, but she felt herself sinking. Her stomach dropped and her face felt flushed. She had to get out of here, soon, and she knew it. "I apologize for worrying you last night," she said mechanically. "It won't happen again." And she left, as fast as she could, climbing rough-hewn wooden steps by oil light in search of morning air.

She reached the top of the steps, pushed through a door, and emerged into bright sunlight and the normal flow of foot traffic, the calm chaos of the Crown camp. Air danced around her, but she couldn't manage to draw in a breath.

Coupling. With Paris. It would be hell. Years of hell. A life without *Rafe*. She bent over and sucked in dusty oxygen. Then—

From behind her: "What just happened in there?"

Evander had followed her out. Jule turned. "Nothing."

"Nothing," he repeated, studying her. He pressed: "And where were you last night? Where'd you go?"

She tried to steady herself. "If you must know, I was in the Trucelands. They throw some interesting parties, those Habs."

"What kind of parties?" he asked.

"Singing, gin. It was a long night, Vander. I'm tired. And I have to track down my men to deliver that message."

"You look pale. Are you all right?"

"Fine. Just tired," she said, heading for her dormitory.

Evander loathed being lied to. "It's a dangerous time, Jule."

She didn't reply.

Across the city, Rafe stood in silence as a search team assembled to look for Breena. Beside him was Maud, his future bride. That felt intolerable now.

"You should prepare yourself," Maud said. "Your sister's likely dead."

"I know," he replied.

Shapcott was among the search party; he'd always despised generals who led from a bunker instead of the field. "Ready, Rafe?"

Just then, the Rogue main gate swung open.

And there stood Breena, her face bruised and bleeding, fresh blood smeared on her knuckles.

Elated, Rafe raced toward her from a hundred feet away. "Breena!" An exhausted relief.

Shapcott was far closer—and more stern. "Were you followed?"

"No," Breena said. Speaking was painful. *Everything* was.

"And Glendon?"

"Glendon's dead."

No one seemed surprised. Rafe reached her, embraced her. "What happened?"

She half lied through those bleeding lips, "We got jumped by two Crowns. One put a javelin into Glendon. I killed them. But I must've passed out. Woke up this morning."

It was easier than admitting that she'd been captured and held captive—and then freed by Jule. A debrief on that kind of thing would take *weeks*. Besides, everyone seemed convinced by her story.

Except Rafe. And perhaps Maud.

Shapcott said, "See the medic. Then we'll debrief."

"Maybe she could rest a bit, sir?" Rafe asked. "And debrief in the morning?"

"Very well. Sunup."

Breena nodded, grateful. The search team disbanded. Rafe remained by his sister's side. "Breena, the blood on your knuckles is fresh."

"My lip opened again this morning. They could fight a bit."

"Ah." There was no point in pushing it further.

"See you at the debrief?" she asked.

He nodded. Breena walked away. Then she turned back and added, "One thing?"

Rafe waited. Breena went on, "If we ever capture a Crown named Pritchett or Boggs, make certain they're brought to me."

"Why?"

"No reason." Then she was gone.

The service was over now, and the barn was cleared. Once more, Byron worked on his press.

Behind him, he heard Mean's cart again and turned to find the peddler struggling with a heavy load that was covered by a stretch of crude burlap.

"Morning, Byron."

"Morning, Mean."

"Special goods today. Wanted to make sure you were the first to see 'em."

"Okay." Byron smiled, expecting little. "What've you got?"

"Meat!" the peddler announced, pulling the burlap away. In the cart were six human legs. Hours ago they'd been running through a wood, chasing Breena.

Mean grinned. "Disease-free. Died of entirely unnatural causes."

Byron just stared. "Thanks. No."

"Protein, Byron. Good for your mum."

Byron paused for a moment, then—"You can ask her yourself if you want. But no, not for me."

Mean shrugged. "Cost of principles, I suppose."

"I suppose."

Mean sighed, turned his cart around, and left the barn. Within minutes, all six legs were bartered to Habs who had filled this very barn with morning prayers.

In the Crown camp, the legless remains of those three dead soldiers had been identified. Their loved ones took the Mark. Then their colleagues found a stick or a pencil or a rock or a mug and tapped it on the nearest surface.

Blink. Tap. Reset. And await orders.

That night, the hymnal was in Rafe's pocket, over his heart, as he ducked into the quarantine tent for his nightly visit. He entertained the children on his rounds—stories and more stories—and found Willa where she always was, delighted to see him. The gift he'd left for her, the book about planes, was in her arms.

He smiled and opened it to a new page, a photo of a British Spitfire from World War Two, centuries in the past. He told her about the Battle of Britain, waged in the very same sky that hung above this tent, recounting the bravery and firepower that had saved this island and freedom itself. Her eyes, as always, were wide with awe. "I hope I dream about flying tonight."

Rafe wanted that for her. He hugged her and left the tent.

As he exited the main Rogue gate to secure a pirogue, he noticed Maud following him to the edge of the water. She asked where he was going.

"Patrol," he muttered.

"Mm-hmm," she replied.

Captains rarely did patrol two nights in a row; both of them knew it. He rowed away with a soldierly wave.

In the quiet, he was greeted by the thoughts that always hit him on the water: It wanted to drown him. It wanted to fill his lungs and live in his death.

Not yet, he thought. *Not tonight.*

He pulled his oars through the river as night birds flew overhead in a cloudless sky, goldfinches and starlings, darting around buildings. Occasionally he'd see vague outlines of human shapes behind a second-story window, framed by candlelight, and he'd wonder: Who was in there? What was their life like? What did they fear? What did they prize? How had they suffered? He'd never know.

He reached the palace, where the music had freed him, then climbed inside and sat on the floor beside the Victrola and a few records. He wouldn't play any of them until Jule arrived. The sounds belonged to her too.

So all that was left was the waiting. He lit candles and stared at the flames. And time passed.

And he began to doubt . . .

She might not come. She'd never actually said she would. And it wasn't ridiculous to believe that she had died today. Soldiers died all the time.

Or she might've been discovered by her fellow Crowns. This room had been packed last night—by Habs, to be sure—but information about a Crown and a Rogue fraternizing would be worth a great deal. And highly lethal. It was easy to imagine a desperate Hab selling such news to either side. Or both.

And Rafe would be to blame.

Or perhaps she'd decided this was too dangerous. The voice that had told her to sweep-kick him to the ground, perhaps it grew louder today. They were sworn enemies.

Yes, she'd obey that voice.

Or maybe she just hadn't felt as much as he had. She'd said nothing romantic, or even vaguely encouraging. It was possible he'd imagined the whole thing. And here he was, sitting on the floor with a wooden box, like a fool. He rose to leave.

But at that same moment, Jule was sitting in a pirogue just outside the palace, eyeing her own reflection in one of the few panes of glass that had survived the dark centuries.

Mirrors didn't exist in this world; they'd all been shattered long ago for the metal they hid. So she'd caught glimpses of her face bouncing back at her from surfaces of water—lakes or the river. But the water was never still, and Jule had never really *seen* herself before. She'd just assumed the worst.

Tonight, though, the woman looking back at her in that solitary pane of glass seemed lovely. Even beautiful. Jule absently traced her own profile with the tip of her forefinger, the contours of her nose and lips.

She *liked* them.

That was new; that was a gift. She climbed out of the pirogue and into a long hallway.

The bare walls surrounded her. The ancient flooring creaked beneath her feet. She could hear her own breathing and the gurgling of her stomach. Nerves. Anticipation. She felt bare.

Ahead, at the end of this hallway, was the faintest wisp of light coming from the study, where a candle was obviously burning. The glow was comforting and terrifying, all at once.

Jule kept moving toward it. She reached the end of the hall and turned into the study, which was empty, save for that one candle. She crossed the floor to the smaller room they'd shared before.

And there she found Rafe, just about to leave.

His face flushed. So did hers. Another one of those seconds that felt like an hour. Her mouth suddenly felt desert dry.

"You're here," he said.

"For now," she replied flatly.

Again, he smiled at her bravado.

Her hope since noon—as she had worked, and helped others, and rowed here, and walked down that long hallway—had been that she would step into this space, and see him . . .

. . . and feel nothing.

Instead, it all hit hard—this room, Rafe, the shape of him, the sound of the air itself, the thundering in her chest—even harder than it had before. She'd seen hundreds die. Their faces escaped her recall. But *this* face, this moment, this room . . . felt permanent. Damn it. A bit unsteady, she asked, "How was your day?"

"I can't remember. I'm not sure I ever left this room."

"Maybe you banged your head when I took your feet out from under you this morning."

"Yes. That must've been it."

All the while he was thinking, *She's definitely smarter than I am.* He knelt down and began to crank up the Victrola.

"You move right along, don't you?" she said.

Flatly, he said, "Jule, we only have a few hours. Give in a little."

That knocked her back a bit. She nodded silently, well rebuked. *Yes,* she thought, *far braver than I am.*

He grabbed a random record from the top of the stack. Down went the needle. Bach filled the space. A piece called "Air."

There was heaven in that sound; it climbed inside her, overwhelmed her. Rafe overwhelmed her too. Jule stared at him without wanting to, everything suddenly feeling floaty and unreal—his shape, his worn-out clothes, his face. Something told her to move, to act—*anything* but standing here and feeling lightheaded.

So she crossed to him. And his eyes went wide. She drew closer, and he felt his breath catch. Hers did too. There was a line they hadn't crossed yet. It could still stand, if—

But she crossed it . . . and kissed him.

His legs nearly buckled. Nerve endings that had stayed so calm in battle now began to ignite.

The kiss ended. "What possessed you?" he asked.

"We talk when I want; we kiss when I want. That's the rule."

"Fair enough."

Bach wrapped around them. Strings and reeds and ether. "It's strange," she said, "watching myself make a mistake."

Rafe shook his head as they sat on the floor. He saw his future and saw her in it. So, "There are boats, in Peterborough. Real ones, sturdy enough to sail to the Continent."

"It was just one kiss, Rafe."

"But it was a good one." He smiled. "And it'd be enough to get us killed if anyone knew."

She knew that. It terrified her. And yet she was here. She kissed him again.

"Y'ever think about that?" he asked. "Leaving?"

"It's no better on the Continent. It's no better anywhere."

He took her hand. "But no one would know us there. Or hate us on sight."

It was absurd, talking about the future. They'd just met.

"It's not so bad," she said, "being hated. Keeps you sharp. And don't you want to *command* someday? Everyone thinks you'll replace Shapcott. Isn't that what you want?"

"It was. But I think now I'd rather decommission the whole army."

That sounded impossible—as if he'd never fought in the war that had defined and destroyed them all. Hope was so alien to her that she asked, "What would you do without battles to fight?"

"I dunno," he replied. "Surrender?"

An involuntary smile spread across her face. But then, just as quickly, it vanished. "I'm never leaving England," she said flatly. "We have to *save* this place, not abandon it."

"Save it from what?"

"What do *you* care? You're sailing away."

His fingers were tapping on the floor again. His head was nodding again. His shoulders were perfect again. She felt parts of her swaying. "Yes," he said. "Right now I am sailing away."

She hated how good that sounded. "There's a woman I look after," she said. "Nelly. She lives right beneath me, used to be my teacher. I don't know if she'd die without me, but she might. I'm pretty sure I'd die without her. Don't you have people like that in your life?"

He smiled. "A couple hundred."

"You would just leave them?"

"I would now. Now there's you."

Impossible. Childish.

"Until the next battle," she said. "Then there might not *be* a me anymore. Or a you."

"I don't wanna hear that," he said.

He tried to take her hand. She crossed her arms.

The night was spent like that—Jule would push away and then come back again; she'd challenge, provoke, disbelieve . . . and then embrace. Military stiffness followed by tender silence. Closeness, distance, openness, caution, then great care. The music soared and stirred and then calmed. Theirs was a dance—

Battle. Truce. Reconciliation. Battle. Peace. Revelation.

They knew it was madness. But the music somehow made it all seem fated. Inevitable. Unstoppable. It filled them, dared them, and made promises that felt true.

It was home . . .

At about two in the morning (they couldn't be sure), seated on the floor together, he muttered absently, "Do you have a favorite color?"

"You're a funny one," she answered.

"I want to know you," he replied.

"Green," she said. "Forest green."

"A favorite animal?"

She exhaled hard. Then: "I like foxes."

"How come?"

"They adapt. They can see at night. They're shy. They're the one thing I won't eat."

"Then I won't eat them either."

She breathed out a smile. But it was hard not to think, *Yes, I am indeed watching myself make a mistake, a life-changing mistake*. It shook her.

He asked, "And a favorite song? Of all these?"

"Yes."

"Tell me."

She cranked the Victrola and put another record on it. The Beatles returned. A guitar playing.

"Can you sing?" Rafe asked.

"Passably," she replied.

"Will you?"

"I want you to *stop* this," she said flatly.

"Stop what?"

"Acting like *any* of this is normal! Or even *possible*. It's going to get us killed. Just *being* here could get us killed."

"We were dead before," he replied.

"You have an answer for everything."

By then, the song's vocal had begun. It was about the sun. Here it came...

Jule wasn't singing; neither was Rafe. It didn't matter... Their whole *lives* had been a long, cold, lonely winter.

Her face began to redden, in a wonderful way—every sense but one heightened. Sound, sight, touch, taste, all peaking. The pull toward him was tidal. So she revealed a bit: "I've been surrounded my entire life, and I've always felt alone."

"Me too," he replied.

Not anymore. Not on this night. They were *breathing* each other now. It was a good kind of drowning. And Jule, without making a sound, felt *heard*.

The song ended. Another began. She said, "I had a chance to kill someone this morning. One of yours."

Rafe paused. The song continued. "Who?"

"Two of my men had beaten and gagged her and left her under my stairwell for questioning. A Rogue soldier; I let her go."

An alarm went off between Rafe's ears, but his face betrayed little. He lifted the needle, stopping the music, then asked, "Did she have a name?"

Jule seemed a bit thrown. "I didn't ask."

"The soldiers. Did they?"

"They did. They do." But she said no more.

"Maybe Pritchett and Boggs?" Now alarms went off for *her*. Rafe added, "She's my sister."

Jule sagged. They both did. And she sighed, "Then we really are doomed, aren't we."

"Not if we get on a boat."

"There's *no* boat," Jule said sharply. "No running away. This is where we are. We have people to protect."

"Let's *bring* them. My sister. Nelly. Whoever you want."

"Doesn't matter what I want. I'm a soldier."

"But you *can't* protect them, Jule. Not really. The Yellowing could get them, or the Bloats, or the war. And for what?"

She didn't have an answer. Love suddenly felt cruel, capricious, impermanent. Rafe took her hand again.

They stayed there, fixed, each in a dreamless sleep until the sun rose once again. Her eyes opened first. The record on the turntable had long since stopped rotating. The room was the room. The water was the water. The war was the war. And Rafe was beside her. "Have you been coupled?" she asked.

His eyes were slits. "Don't Crowns say 'Good morning'?"

"Have you?"

"Yes."

"I see."

He was about to ask *Have you?* but Jule quickly rose to her feet and asked, "What's her name?"

"Does it matter? I'm here."

"I'm not asking out of jealousy."

"And I can't reveal the name of a fellow soldier."

"No. You can't."

Rafe sighed, irritated. "There *could* be a pax."

She answered, "That sounds like a wish."

"My general is an honest man."

"So's mine. What of it?"

Her hostility was wearing on him. But he swallowed it. "You're cynical. I understand."

"Anyone who isn't is a fool."

"I'm just saying, it's possible. No one wants to keep fighting forever."

She eyed him, almost sorry for him. "I think maybe you'd better find that boat, Rafe."

"Would I be sailing alone?"

"I fight alongside my *brother*," she protested.

"I fight alongside my *sister*. The one you found beaten."

"Point is, this is a betrayal."

Rafe answered, "Then why's it feel like the truest thing I've ever done?"

That caught her. *Damn it.* She needed some armor again: "*I've* been coupled too. So that's our lot."

"You have?"

"Oh my, yes. Another captain. We're expected to produce lots of tall baby soldiers."

Wounded, Rafe replied, "You *should* be a general, Jule. You know just how to devastate the enemy."

She pushed him away and walked to a window, staring out at her waterlogged city. He sighed hard, then crossed the room to meet her there.

She looked right through him. "Never speak of it again," she began. "The future. Us. Being together. Just don't. It's cruel. We'll see each other because there's no way *not* to see each other. And then it will fade, or one of us will die, but it will be behind us. Understand?"

"No," he answered. "I'm gonna say it whenever I want. Why would I *pretend*? I—"

She cut him off. "We're attracted to each other. That's great. Let's not make any more of it than—"

"STOP DOING THAT!" he shouted. "Please."

She was silent, surprised. He continued, "I'm betting *everything* on you, Jule. I *need* this."

Yes, she thought, *far braver.*

He thought he saw a tear in her eye . . .

TEN

The smithy in the Rogue camp was frail, almost delicate; when his shirt was off you could see the ridges of his ribs. But his strength was legendary; he could lift anything. And the sluggers he produced were perfect. Honus was his name. His mustache was long and thin.

When alone, Honus lived in his head, giving every piece of scrap metal that went into his forge a rich personal history. A centuries-old shopping cart? Honus could imagine its happy travels down the aisles of a grocery store. He could hear the rattling of its wheels, even though that was a sound he'd never heard in his life, from back in the days when England was still dry, when it all could have been saved.

In it went, into the furnace.

An iron rod from a gate? Honus saw the knuckles of crazed protesters wrapped around it, outside a government building—human beings, screaming, begging the officials inside to DO SOMETHING about all this water and death. It went into the furnace too.

He had a secret, this smithy—weapons he'd been working on for three years, unbeknownst to anyone else. To develop them, he'd worked endless hours, using materials he'd hidden away, even metals. Once finished, he was sure, they would change warfare forever and earn him a hero's reputation.

He called them Canners. And they were nearly ready.

In the Crown camp, Jule approached the forge where Big Lil was liquefying scraps with great pace. Another plate of plain cookies awaited. "Cookie?" Big Lil offered again.

Jule took one and nibbled its corner.

"You are the genuine article." Big Lil smiled. "Unlike some you serve with."

"Now, now, Lil . . ."

The smithy pantomimed a gun-toting soldier with shaky hands: "I seen 'em in battle. They'd have better luck *throwing* my sluggers at the enemy! But *you*! Bull's-eye, every time." Jule swallowed hard. Lil went on, "You're a true Crown."

Jule breathed out a false smile. "You could've been a baker."

Lil laughed. "Waste of God-given talent."

"The world always needs more cookies," Jule said. Then she left the forge.

Her eyes burning, she passed the medical tent, where battle wounds healed, or didn't, and a quarantine tent, where there was never enough beech-bark paste to meet the demand.

Everywhere Jule looked, life hummed with its usual rhythms. A row of woodworkers carved out new pirogues. Unnamed Habs dropped off food stocks as knitters knitted and menders mended and builders built. It all felt routine—the unhappy but grooved reality she'd known her entire life, the one she'd never even *contemplated* escaping. Until now.

She and Rafe couldn't stay in this limbo, she knew that: hiding from the world, living with longing, living with *fear*. Moments of bliss, moments of terror. They'd be caught eventually, and the punishment would be death. Betraying one's House was the ultimate sin for a soldier.

But she couldn't *end it* either.

There was a *third* future . . . in which she and Rafe might somehow be together in the open, unafraid, embraced by all—in a different kind of London.

Each of these futures was possible. Each was ridiculous. One of them—or none of them—would happen. The reality could be far worse and just as unknowable. That made her uneasy. Her whole *life* had been about knowing. Leading. Certainty. She found herself missing the days in which all she'd thought about was battle. They were simpler.

She walked past an open space where a few children made music with sticks, while others played tag. To her own surprise, she joined in the game for a moment. They couldn't believe it. *Jule! The hero! Playing with us!* They giggled; they shouted. So did she.

She was changing. Rafe was making that feel possible. She decided to tell him so, to thank him—maybe the next time they met.

Then, a distraction in the corner of her eye: Pritchett and Boggs, grabbing apples from a cart. *Reality*, just like that. She howled their names aloud. They turned. "Ma'am?"

She reached them and leaned in close: "Next time you capture a

Rogue, if I can't be found to interrogate her, you *stay with her*—you don't leave her in the care of a child."

"Yes, ma'am," Pritchett replied.

"She escaped, and most likely killed three of our ranks in the forest. I consider you responsible for that."

"Yes, ma'am," Pritchett said, his eyes at his shoe tops.

"Boggs, do you understand?"

"Yes, ma'am."

"Dismissed."

They turned and left. Jule felt murderous. She headed for her dormitory, leaving all those children at play . . .

In Paternoster Square, schoolteachers taught and children struggled to sit still. Doctors tended to their patients. Stitchers sewed. And a stiff breeze put a chill on the tip of every nose, reminding people that nature would always have the last word. A sixteen-year-old boy, irrationally full of himself, challenged Maddox to a footrace and was quickly humbled. Maddox's status as Fastest Rogue Alive remained undimmed.

Rafe spent the day in a romantic daydream, where there was no war—just a boat, a destination, and Jule's lovely face. *Impossible.*

No. It wasn't. He could do this, create it, will it into being. Belief was fuel. Faith was wind. Love was enough.

Doubt crept in: *You're going to be discovered and you're going to be killed. And so will she. Selfish bastard.*

But then he remembered it all. Her eyes, mind, spirit, voice. And the *music*, the way it shook him and stuck to him. And her hands. He kept thinking about her hands. The way her touch felt.

Impossible. Yes. But only if they stayed *here*. Not if they fled this soggy, war-torn country. He began to hum that song about the sun ending the lonely winter . . .

He just needed a sailboat. And that wind. And her hand.

And a pax between the Houses.

ELEVEN

On the agreed-upon day, at something close to the agreed-upon hour, two flotillas of pirogues rowed from opposite ends of the city to the castle at the Tower of London. In the 1200s, King Edward's masons had built stone walls on these fabled grounds to keep out invaders and peasants; no one had ever thought to make the gates watertight. And a thousand years later, the water came, ten feet of it.

Now ten pirogues bearing the guardians of two great Houses were approaching this hallowed place to discuss a pax. As hapless Habs tossed lobster traps from shop rooftops into the ghost of the Thames, Chasen's flotilla of five crafts arrived from the south. Shapcott arrived from the north. All the warriors remained in their pirogues. The lead crafts were secured by each House's finest soldier—

Rafe and Jule. Both armed. Their eyes met.

Rafe put a hand to his heart, where that hymnal remained in a coat pocket. Jule acknowledged the gesture, but only briefly. She wanted to say something, but everyone they knew was watching: Maud, Maddox, and Beckett; Evander and Paris. Jule needed to be steel today, needed to do *anything* she could to bring a pax to these two Houses. That would solve everything.

From one pirogue, Maddox nodded toward Jule and muttered to Beckett, "*That's* the bitch we'll be fighting one day."

"Guys," Maud said, grinning, "don't you believe in *peace*?" The three shared a knowing smile.

Breena had been granted a place in Rafe's pirogue. Her face was still battered and her quiet rage shone through as she glared across the water at Pritchett and Boggs. Neither man would meet her eye . . .

Shapcott and Chasen held up a hand to each other. On Shapcott's right palm was that fresh burn mark. Chasen had one too: older, better healed. Their pirogues bobbed in the water, dozens of warriors neither eyeing one another nor looking away. If things went well, perhaps a handshake or two might be exchanged. Maybe.

But first, silence. Jameson was arriving.

He appeared in a pirogue rowed by aides, disembarking onto land without help. Every soldier here regarded him respectfully; they knew no one but Jameson could possibly broker this pax.

Jule sent up a silent prayer. Rafe tried not to look in her direction, tried to pretend she was just another enemy.

Impossible. She had become everything.

"Welcome," Jameson intoned. "General Shapcott, my condolences on the death of your son. May such losses end here."

Shapcott said nothing, nor did his captains.

"It has come to this," Jameson continued. "Two Houses, fighting over beech bark. Prolonging a war your *children* won't live long enough to finish."

Paris blurted, "We've never sought anything from their House but to be left alone!"

Jameson shot back, "You shut your bloody maw, Paris!"

The Rogues loved that. Maddox shouted at the Crowns, "YOU brought this war on, not us!"

Jameson erupted again. "*Yours* needs shutting too, Maddox!"

Evander grumbled, "It was a Rogue war from the first."

The blind man erupted, *"I gave my* EYES *to your war! It's a pox on* BOTH *your Houses! And it stops now!"*

Silence. He added, "Just know this: The Habs haven't grasped it yet, but they outnumber you. If I give them arms and direction, *you'll* be working the fields for *them* before long, as will your children. Oughta consider that." He turned toward his youngest aide, just fifteen. "Boy?"

The teen held a long stick in one hand. With the other he led Jameson ten feet to the underside of a bridge, where the soldiers in the flotillas now saw markings on the wall. Jameson announced: "We track the water. Do you?"

No one replied. The boy pointed with the stick, and Jameson added, "This is where the water was six months ago. *This* is where it is today."

The lowest marking was six inches *above* the top of the water. The soldiers stared, bobbing up and down on a fickle river.

Jameson said, "The water is receding, you idiots. All over the city. Might take years, but if this rate continues, the river will go back inside its banks, and London will be livable again. And what will you fight about then?"

Rafe saw hope there. So did Jule. If the water receded, maybe . . .

Jameson continued, "You've come to discuss a pax. Its rules are simple: You stop fighting. Today."

Unimaginable. A few soldiers laughed without meaning to.

Jameson went on: "Flags down PERMANENTLY. No more patrols. No more ambushes. No more 'protection' of Hab farms. They can grow what they like and *keep it* if they like. If either side violates this pax, I'll arm every Hab on this island and turn them loose on you. Is that understood?"

The soldiers paled. No more patrols? That would be suicide. Beckett mumbled, "We are following the blind. Literally."

Jameson didn't hear that. But the other soldiers did. Chasen spoke up. "Jameson, it is . . . antithetical to us to expect a Rogue to keep to a pax."

Shapcott fired back, "I don't know what *antithetical* means, General. But if it's an insult, sod you too."

Shapcott's captains chuckled. Chasen answered, "It means 'against our nature.' Means having to ignore everything we've ever known about you."

Shapcott replied: "And we of you."

Paris spat out, "Rogue scum."

Maud shot back, "Crown rubbish!"

"*You* brought on the bloody Yellowing."

"It started in YOUR camp! And everyone knows it!"

Rafe and Jule could feel themselves sinking. Paris shouted, "Let's just end this once and for all!"

Maud barked, "I'll take *all* your fingers! Your hands too!"

Rafe looked to Jule. Jameson stayed silent. In each pirogue, soldiers began to stir, to grasp weapons reflexively.

Chasen barked, "Shapcott, mind your soldiers!"

Shapcott barked back, "General, mind yours!"

Evander shouted. Beckett answered in kind. Others followed, Captains hollering at one another from boat to boat. Curses, warnings, threats, promises. Sixty voices, like children. The only ones who stayed silent were Rafe and Jule.

"Screw your pax!" from Evander.

"Screw YOU!" from Maud.

It all was erupting now—rage and contempt, three hundred years of war, Jameson helpless to intercede.

Then, in a single and shocking instant, the world changed.

Above them, suddenly, was a noise none had ever heard before—it sounded like the air itself was being torn in half. The captains stopped shouting and looked up, but couldn't believe their eyes. Every jaw simply dropped.

Thousands of feet in the air, a *machine* roared through the clouds, ripping the sky apart. A nameless monster of thunderous sound and impossible propulsion and power, hurtling metal at an ungodly speed, white smoke blasting from its tail, rocketing past in the straightest line anyone had ever seen—real, here, *above* them, somehow. Terrifying.

Then the sky shook with a loud BOOM. Every pirogue shuddered. Big Ben did too. And on every face, the terror and disbelief grew.

Everything they'd ever known, gone. Jule's wiring suddenly melted; she forgot every word she'd ever learned.

They all did. Even Jameson seemed awed. Those SOUNDS.

It actually did have a name, this machine, yet none but Rafe knew it. *MiG-35*, he thought breathlessly, a Russian Miyokan fighter. Hundreds of years old. He'd stared at the image a thousand times in the manuals. *Supersonic.* Now, just as impossibly, the MiG was gone and the sky was the sky again, save for the vapor trail the beast had left behind, cruel proof that their world was no longer their world. The boom had left no fingerprints behind, but it had happened. They knew it. The sky had opened . . . and roared.

Miles away, Byron and every Hab in the fields stared at the sky, slack-jawed and terrified. Minister Dawson was among them, unable to explain what they'd all just seen and heard. It had not come from God. They all knew it. But this much was certain:

There was in fact a world out there.

It had recovered. It had reclaimed technology and harnessed power. It had rebuilt its military. And it had found London, a centuries-long Stone Age simply ending, ceasing to be true.

All of that, in a single unfathomable moment of shock and awe. At the Tower, Rafe looked to Jule—astonished, breathless.

Jameson's aides flanked him, whispering into his ear to describe what they'd just seen. But words failed them too.

Ten pirogues jounced on the water, soldiers on both sides trying to process what they'd all just witnessed. But none of them could. And now what? Surely, a pax would follow. This feud had instantly become trivial, silly.

Rafe and Jule waited... yet Chasen merely stiffened, abject fear rocking him. He mumbled absently to his lifelong foe in black, "No pax."

Shapcott, just as unnerved, nodded helplessly in return, almost gratefully. "No pax."

Rafe sank. Jule too. A chance for happiness bombed from above. And perhaps from below. Instantly, the other soldiers descended into tribal corners. Maud howled, "To hell with every Crown that ever breathed!"

Evander fired back, "To hell with *you* soon enough, Princess!"

A tear rolled down Jule's cheek. She now knew—as Rafe knew, as Breena knew, as Byron knew, as everyone in London knew...

Death was fact. Truce was weakness. Peace was a fairy tale. The future had come to this city and flown headlong into the stone wall of the past...

TWELVE

Shapcott sulked in silence as his flotilla rowed from the Tower to Paternoster. He was quieter still as he led his senior staff across the stunned square.

Everything had changed; people now stared at the sky, deeply shaken. Yet the general would not acknowledge what had roared overhead, as if the jet *simply hadn't been there.* Once he'd crossed the square, Shapcott ordered, "Double the guards on every building; double the scout teams on the perimeter."

Rafe wanted to scream. Breena too. *Scout teams? To fight a supersonic jet?* Breena's look said, *Say something!*

Rafe tried: "General. The plane."

"What about it?" Shapcott asked.

"Isn't *that* our enemy now? Isn't that our greatest threat?"

"Our *enemy*, Captain, is right in front of us, as they always have been. And we're going to destroy them now, before they can make a pax with whoever put that thing into the air. We attack at first opportunity."

Shapcott was terrified—they all saw it—but no one would say so aloud. Rafe tried: "General, that was a Russian fighter. They call them MiGs. Three times the speed of sound, eighty-nine-thousand-foot ceiling, carrying missiles and cannons. And we've got sluggers from melted-down shopping carts. We need to be preparing our citizens for an attack from the air."

Shapcott yelled, "'No pax!' Those were Chasen's words. He will now attack us; it's his nature. So we're going to hit first—and eradicate them, forever."

"I see." Rafe asked, "*Where* do you plan to attack them, sir?"

"At Eltham," the general replied. "We'll go over the wall."

Rafe paled. A frontal assault on a heavily guarded fortress was madness—yet the captains were silent. Rafe tried, "That gives them the advantage of defensive fortifications, sir."

Shapcott snapped, "And gives *us* the advantage of surprise. Send out every rover in camp. We're going to the furnace!" With that, he stormed into the Stock Exchange Tower. His captains followed.

Rafe looked to his sister. She seemed lost. "This is how armies die," she breathed. Then she drifted away, untethered.

Rafe went inside, to the trading floor, where he found Shapcott surrounded. He tried again: "General, we have to assume that MiG was part of an air force of some kind, and they now know we're here—"

Shapcott cut him off. "Captain, you're not to mention that aircraft again until the last Crown has fallen. Is that understood? And tell the sentries: Anyone seen leaving camp without authorization is to be shot on sight."

Rafe nodded dutifully. "Yes, sir."

In the Crown camp, the same unspoken panic simmered. Chasen too had rowed home in silence. Now Jule and Evander strode wordlessly through the grounds, where every shocked Crown civilian was thinking the same tortured thought: *What the hell was that horrifying beast overhead?*

This is why I can't sail away, Jule told herself. Great leaders didn't flee. They stayed, and they *led.* She and her brother descended into Chasen's bunker, each hoping that the general would now address the new reality imposed by the MiG. But the first words he uttered were, "We're attacking Paternoster Square at the earliest opportunity." His hand shook. They all pretended not to see it.

Jule had to respond. "General," she began, "I believe that is an unnecessary risk."

"How so?"

"First, an assault on a heavily defended fortress gives the Rogues several tactical advantages."

Chasen answered testily, "It also gives them *civilians* to protect. That's a huge *dis*advantage."

"Second," Jule continued, "I believe that right now Shapcott is planning to attack *us.* Here. Soon."

Chasen asked, "What makes you think so?"

Jule told a dangerous truth: "For the same reason *you're* doing it, sir—he'd rather fight an enemy he understands than confront the unknown that just flew over our heads."

Utter silence. No one could believe she'd just said it. But Chasen's expression never wavered.

"Captain," Chasen replied, addressing her by her rank for the first time in her entire life, "there will be no more mention of that aircraft. By anyone. It is a distraction to our main purpose, which has always been to protect this House from our rival. We are attacking Paternoster."

"Sir—"

He cut her off. "I expect battle plans by morning. Until then, send out the rovers and alert the forge. And tell the sentries that anyone seen leaving the camp grounds without authorization from me personally is to be shot on sight. Is that understood?"

Madness. But orders were orders, and Jule was alone in her objections. She nodded. "Yes, sir."

The Habs had always believed.

Water and war had nearly chased religion off this island in the 2100s. ("God isn't just dead," people had said as the reality of the Great Soak began to take hold, "he *drowned*.") Most Rogues thought it folly to pray to the same God that Crowns prayed to. And vice versa.

But the Habs had always worshipped. And now, a mechanical beast having torn up the sky overhead, the Habs needed God more than ever.

There were too many of them for Byron's barn. So Minister Dawson stood on a table at the edge of the field, delivering an improvised sermon in the open air. Byron took his place alongside awed parishioners.

Dawson began, "Well, now we know. Now we know. At least one of the world's nations has recovered. Perhaps others have too. Hard to say. The bigger question is this—"

Just then, a new face appeared in the back of the crowd—battered and swollen, with puffy, scabbed lips. *Breena.* Unarmed. And unsettled.

No one knew why she was here. They knew only that she was a Rogue soldier. So a familiar tension quickly spread.

Dawson addressed her: "We have the right to congregate. You have no call to make us disperse."

Breena spoke slowly, haltingly. "I came here to worship."

"You did?"

"Yes," Breena replied. "The sky stopped being the sky today." She closed her eyes for a moment. No one knew what to do.

Except Byron. He made his way through the crowd, got to Breena, then stood beside her. Her eyes opened. Byron looked to Dawson and said, "Minister?"

Dawson nodded and went on. "Yes, some nation has rediscovered machinery. The question is . . . *what does it matter?* Is that machine any deadlier to us than guns, or soldiers, or disease, or drowning, or overwork? Heaven doesn't care how we die. Heaven cares how we *live.*"

Breena now knew that she had been right to come here. She needed God. She was ready. Dawson continued, "That thing overhead tore our sky in half. And yet the sky recovered. God knitted all that blue back together, for *us*, to remind us that no machine made by humans could ever be more powerful than the Almighty." It was registering.

Dawson added, "Machines are temporal. They can frighten none but the godless. Are we godless here?"

"No" came the faint joint reply.

Dawson repeated, "ARE WE GODLESS HERE?"

A loud "NO!" from the crowd now. Breena breathed it out too. And she smiled, a feeling of grace passing through her.

Soldiers needed to be led sometimes; she knew that.

"Going to the furnace" meant a sweep for metals, *any* metals. And Rogue children, "rovers," now combed the city excitedly. The awesome spectacle of that thunderous, wondrous MiG had ignited their imaginations. And though they didn't know the details of the upcoming offensive, they knew *something* big was afoot, and they were excited to be a part of it.

Two Rogue ten-year-olds, Liam and Portia, explored the river itself in an old leaky pirogue, diving into the Thames two blocks from the Stock Exchange. The water was cold and fraught with dangers. Liam did the scavenging as Portia treaded water, looking for Bloats—a long stick in hand, useless as it was.

On his third dive, Liam found a four-hundred-year-old appliance. It was metal, with slots for putting something inside, and a dial that said DARK and LIGHT on it. Who knew how many sluggers it might yield?

Shivering, he pulled it from the water and they headed back to camp. Without paddles, the children hand-rowed, their faces close to the water, eyes peeled for Bloats.

"I'd like to fly," Portia said.

"Me too," Liam agreed.

"Fast." She made a roaring sound, imitating the MiG. Liam repeated it. Both laughed.

Just then, a CRASH from above toppled their pirogue. Two Crown rovers, also children, had just jumped off a rooftop and onto the leaky boat. The four kids and the appliance now spilled into the water. That fast, Liam and Portia were fighting for their lives against fellow kids trying to drown them—as the appliance sank.

Liam's head went under twice, but he clawed and kicked and bit his way to safety, then dunked his Crown foe. Portia was bigger, stronger—but so was the Crown opposite her: Danton.

He pulled Portia under, and she quickly began to choke on old, cold water. Then she surfaced, and fought, and got pulled under again. They wrestled for minutes—breathless, desperate, exhausted—adrenaline pumping through them, until Portia went under for the fifth time and swallowed too much, the Thames filling her chest and fogging her brain.

Danton was atop her now, his grip fierce, holding her down. A feral death. Gagging, panicking, Portia's eyes began to roll. So the next thing she saw seemed dreamlike . . .

A red cloud, billowing out of Danton's shoulder, in the dim dance of the water.

Suddenly, his grip lost its power and his body stiffened, nearly convulsing as he pushed off, half swimming away with one good arm, that cloud of red following. Stunned, Portia breached the surface in time to see the other Crown child swim off too. Fight over.

Danton dragged himself to a rooftop—not easy because he now had a bloody bullet wound in his right arm. His fellow Crown pulled him along anxiously. Portia turned quickly, to see who'd fired the shot . . .

It was *Maud*—floating ten feet away, on a pirogue, gun in hand. "Go," Maud barked at the little Crowns. "Go!"

Danton and the other one ran—or tried to—hopping rooftop to rooftop, often falling, Danton howling in pain and fear, a clumsy and anguished retreat.

Maud eyed Liam and Portia. "What were ya fighting over?"

"A metal box," Liam breathed. "I dropped it."

"Well, go get it. We need sluggers."

Liam dove down again. Portia treaded water in silence. Bloats circled. They were always circling . . .

Later, at Eltham, Jule and Evander passed the forge, where Big Lil was again liquefying scraps with great pace. Lil had always loved the eve of a big battle—the tension, the promise—and *this* battle would be huge. Everyone in camp was moving with purpose. No Crown army had launched an actual offensive in nearly a century. The air felt charged with dangerous opportunity. And patriotism.

The MiG, all had decided, had been a collective illusion.

Jule and Evander passed the medical tent, where Danton, having been shot by Maud, had now been made tranquil by a dose of liquid henbane. He sat quietly as the camp physician pulled a slugger from his thin arm. A war wound, at twelve.

"Where'd that happen?" Jule muttered.

"On the water," Evander replied. "Got ambushed by some Rogue rovers. I'll see you in a bit."

He split off. Jule passed the quarantine tent with its quiet aches and groans. There was no one she could talk to except Rafe. The enemy. She longed to see him, feel him, warn him . . .

Impossible.

Rafe, at that moment, was part of a group fashioning battle plans for the suicidal assault on Eltham. The chatter focused solely on logistics, as if they were planning a picnic.

Rafe could barely hear them. All he could see was Jule. He longed to see her, feel her, warn her.

Impossible.

As night fell, Jule sat in the Crown medical tent, rolling gauze bandages. It was mindless work, usually meditative for her.

Not tonight. Tonight she was in the Churn, filled with dread. For the first time ever, she felt an impulse to mutiny—to replace her general. How else could she save her troops?

Across the tent, she saw Chasen talking to Danton as the kid sat on a cot, his arm in a sling, suddenly looking tiny.

"Never forget," Chasen said. "And never forgive." Danton nodded, dazzled by the attention of a general.

Evander and Paris entered the tent now, looking for Jule. She waved them over, handed them some gauze. Evander reported that five soldiers with the Yellowing who'd been quarantined had now been cleared to join the fight again. "They're at fifty percent. But they'll be able to make a contribution."

"It's suicide," she replied. "You know that. Attacking the Rogues when the *real* war is coming for both Houses."

"It's an order," he replied.

"It's like trying to burn the water! You *can't* burn the water!" She threw her bandage down and pushed herself away from the table. "I'm going out."

"You heard the general," Evander said. "We're in lockdown."

"Tell him if ya like," she said. "He's right there. I'm going on patrol."

Evander felt himself reddening. "We're in *LOCKDOWN*, Jule."

"I'll be in the Trucelands."

Evander eyed her sternly. "There *are* no Trucelands now."

She sat again . . . and resumed rolling the bandage.

THIRTEEN

All that mattered now was getting to her.

That shocked him, the suddenness of it. He'd lived a life caring about just one thing—this House: defending it, training its young, killing its rival, bleeding black.

Now Jule was the world. His House didn't matter, the war didn't matter, becoming a general didn't matter, even the goddamn *MiG* didn't matter. She was *everything*. Seeing her. At any cost. How was that possible?

He had to warn her, somehow, about the upcoming attack. He slung his rifle over his shoulder and left his room.

Soon he was walking the perimeter of the Rogue camp, looking for a weak spot on the fence line to escape through. Between two of the square's tallest buildings was an alley he knew well. There stood an eight-foot-tall wooden barrier, known to everyone as the Cadbury Wall because this alley had once boasted a billboard for a chocolate company. The billboard had long since vanished, but the name had stuck. Guards occasionally patrolled here, but none were visible now. Rafe stood, facing the wooden wall, eyeing the spot that would be easiest to scale, when, from a few feet away, he heard, "Where the hell d'you think *you're* going?"

Rafe turned. Maud was behind him, Maddox beside her. Christ.

She had remarkable instincts; Rafe had seen them in battle. Maud could *smell* when an enemy was about to make a move.

"This is where I'd attack," Rafe replied, as if he'd been on a scout. "If I were a Crown, looking for a weakness in our line, this is where I'd attack."

Maud fired back, "It feeds an alley, which is a choke point. We'd slaughter anyone who breached here."

"Not if they surprised us," he said, firm and credible. "Which is what I think they're now planning to do."

Maddox jumped in. "Then let's reinforce it."

Rafe climbed the wall nimbly and straddled it. Then he turned and looked back at them. "Yes. Let's do that."

"Okay," Maud grumbled. "You made your point. Climb down."

"Nah," Rafe replied. "Going out on patrol."

"General gave an order," she said. "No one outside the line."

"I'm not no one." Rafe grinned.

"Bit of sleep wouldn't hurt you, mate," Maddox said.

"The night before a battle?" He hopped down to the other side, disappearing from their view, his footsteps hastily tracing away.

Maud hollered, "I hope the Bloats get you!"

Outside the main gate, he grabbed a pirogue and pushed off. Across the watery city, Jule did the same thing . . .

It was in the quiet that the Voice grew loudest.

There wasn't a soul on the water—no sound except her own

rhythmic rowing. And into that void stepped the Voice, the one that tormented her:

It told her she was a traitor.

Yes, there was the palace, and the music, and the wonder. And his face and his touch. And in another world, it all might have been perfect, legal, even celebrated. But *this* world, the real world, was one of Houses and rules and laws. Wasn't it? She fixed her eyes on the distant horizon and kept rowing, a pistol by her side. The Voice did not relent: *He's fooling you. He's tricking you. You should slit his—*

She kept rowing. Two strokes per side. Tension in every tendon. She had to see him before the attack, before another plane tore the sky in two. The water was her roadway to get there.

But a hundred yards from Buckingham Palace, sounds on both sides of her craft told her she wasn't alone. Three Bloats now swam alongside her pirogue. Jule kept up her pace—two strokes per side. Her body knew where to go. Then, suddenly, the water moved—

One of the Bloats *struck*—breaching the surface and slamming its upper half onto her pirogue in a blur. The craft listed hard to starboard, about to submerge.

But Jule grabbed her pistol and fired so fast that the Bloat's head was off before the pirogue sipped a single drop of river water.

The corpse slid lifelessly into the black. Its mates peeled off and slithered away. They had more evolving to do.

Rafe stood at a window inside the palace, having seen it all, his wonder for her growing. He watched her row up to the building and secure her pirogue to a window casing. Then he waited—almost breathless—for her to appear in this room, where candles burned and Mozart played.

There it was—the sound of her footsteps echoing faintly in the empty hallway. His face got warmer. Then she appeared.

"Here comes the sun," he offered. "Nice shot."

"It's what we'd do to each other if we had any sense."

"You knocked that out of me," Rafe replied.

She envied his hopefulness. "You're relentless," she sighed.

"I can stop, if you like," he said. "I can leave and we can go back to hating each other. Is that what you want?"

She felt like she was coming to life—and *killing herself*—all at once. He crossed the room toward her. And the part of her screaming *yes* grew louder than the part screaming *no*.

"The world has found us," she sighed.

"I know," he answered.

But it didn't matter. Skin was touching skin now. Lips were close enough to graze one another. Eyes were full. And there, with the magic of Mozart bouncing off every atom in the room, Rafe and Jule fell into each other, helpless and hopeful—love and water clashing for the first time in centuries. The war would indeed wait . . .

Later, they lay in silence, a perfect stillness in the room. The army of each was soon to attack the army of the other, but neither could say so. That would be unforgivable. Instead, Jule whispered, "There's this mountain of old mobile phones in our camp, three stories high. The kids slide down it. Mobile Mountain."

Rafe breathed out a smile. "People used to talk on them all day. They could *see* each other through them."

"Just to say hello," Jule breathed wistfully.

He pulled her closer. "I think I would ring you a lot." A wonderful fantasy. They imagined it fully.

Then she said, "Chasen won't let us talk about the plane."

"Same."

"He's decided it didn't happen. But it *did* happen. There's a world again. And it's armed. What do you think they want?"

"I don't know. What do we have?"

Neither could come up with an answer. But the MiG was inside these walls now, roaring and soaring. "We could be invaded," she said. He didn't disagree; there were a million ways in which a well-equipped force with fuel and firepower could easily end life on this island, and reduce the mighty Rogue and Crown armies to dust. It made Jule want to race back to Eltham and build its walls higher. It made Rafe want to barricade the doors of this palace and stay inside with her forever.

Instead they just lay quietly for a few more hours, in and out of sleep. Every second made things better. And far worse.

Too soon, sunlight warmed his face, and he awakened to find himself on an old sofa. Jule was at its opposite end, wide awake, dressed, her dagger on her hip.

"Good morning," he said.

"Is it?" Her eyes were cold.

Hostility. Again. He knew not to overreact to it. "Something wrong?" he asked. She didn't reply. He tried again. "Jule?"

"Do you know who my parents were?"

That surprised him. "No," he admitted.

"Why would you? They were Crowns. Dead Crowns."

He shot back, "And mine were dead Rogues, since I was ten. Shapcott took me in, or I'd've died too."

"Boo-hoo," she said.

He studied her until she looked away, grief in her eyes. The Voice had been hammering at her since dawn. Rafe knew that.

"I should go," she added.

"Why?"

"House rules."

He took her hand. "Jule—" She yanked it away. He eyed her. "We're gonna sail away from here. You and me."

"You're doing it again. I really want you to stop."

"No. You're *not* going to take that from me." Real anger there, surprising them both. He added, "We're sailing away from here."

"No one who does ever comes back, ever notice that?"

He mocked, "What do you think is out there? Dragons? Pirates?"

"I just know that everything I care about is *here*. Running away won't help."

"But here is where the *fighting* is—and I don't want it anymore."

No reply. "I don't believe in it now. I don't believe in my House. I think I just believe in Beethoven."

She laughed without meaning to. But the sadness was palpable. "I believe in him too," she offered.

Again, each knew an all-out assault was coming. Rafe couldn't say so—just couldn't—but, "Whatever happens next, I want you to know . . . I'd die before I'd let anyone hurt you."

"Who's gonna hurt me?"

"No one. That's my point. And I'll be back here, waiting for you, when it's over."

"When *what's* over?"

He paused, his face working. "I dunno. Whatever tomorrow brings. I just want you to be safe. *Bunkered.*"

"You talk too much," she breathed. He pulled her close and kissed her.

"I told you," she objected, "we do that when I—"

"No more rules," he replied, kissing her again. She allowed it. After a moment, he whispered, "I love you."

He'd never said it before, ever—had always wondered what it would feel like. Now he knew. It felt joyous and frightening. It felt naked. Mostly, it felt true.

But she couldn't say it back. Couldn't *fathom* saying it back. Instead: "You keep acting like we *deserve* to be happy. I've done terrible, horrible things. Evil things you should *hate* me for."

"I could never hate you."

It was all too grim. She started for the door with a casual, "Mind the Bloats."

He called to her back, "I don't understand."

"No?"

"No. Why're you always trying to kill this?"

She stopped. Turned. "You say these *huge* things. 'I love you.' 'Let's just sail away!' But you don't even *know* me. And I don't know *you* at all."

He exhaled hard. "I know you. We've lived the same stupid life: Everyone looks up to us, and we can't *feel* anything. If we didn't both want more, we wouldn't keep coming back here."

That unsettled her. She shook her head sadly and confessed, "I really have been coupled. His name is Paris."

"He's a fair soldier, hardly worthy of you though."

She went silent. It felt like forever. Then Rafe went on, "Tell me about them."

"Who?"

"Your parents."

The air hung heavy again. She sighed. "I was never afraid before. Of anything. Now I am. *You* did that."

"Tell me about them," he repeated.

She kept studying him for signs of falsity; it all had to be a trick, an ambush of some kind. Didn't it? Yet he never wavered. "I want to know."

"It's a long story," she said. "You'll be listed overdue."

He crossed toward her. "Tell me."

She shook her head. Trusting was so hard.

"TELL ME."

And for reasons she herself didn't entirely understand, she did. All of it. Her life.

And he listened. That touched her. Soon, she was telling stories she'd long since forgotten. Some were funny, and laughing took some of the pain away. One story was about her late father, Talbot. "He was a mountain," she said. "And a great soldier. Wore that wedding ring and no one would ever tell him he couldn't."

Rafe smiled. Jule continued, "He took us to the lake a lot, me and Evander. And we'd play."

She went on, telling Rafe about one such afternoon, when Jule had been six . . .

Talbot had sent her to the lake's edge in search of stones for skimming while he and young Evander slept on the shore.

She patrolled the banks, putting flat rocks in her pocket, then she waded into the water, looking to the lake bottom for more. There were plenty. But the lake had a steep drop from one shelf to another, and as Jule stepped off it, she sank, the weight of the rocks in her pockets tugging her down.

The water was in her mouth before she could even holler.

And there she stood, her feet on soft silt, water over her head, six years old. She coiled her legs and pushed off as hard as she could, breaching and hollering, "DADDY!" Then she sank down again. No idea if he'd heard her.

She tried it again—coiling, springing, breaching, yelling. This time she caught a glimpse of him diving into the water. By the time young Jule's feet had hit silt again, Talbot's hands had found her and pulled her up. She sucked in the air, her tiny body shaking, a cry on her lips, hiding in him. He waited, smiling calmly. "Well now. We just learned something about the weight of rocks, didn't we?"

Young Jule nodded, not letting him go.

"Okay," he said. "Give them to me and go back to the bank. You frightened your brother."

"I'm sorry," she said.

"It's all right, Jule. Nothing bad happened."

Talbot kissed her on the forehead. That helped. She handed him all the rocks. "Good flat one there," he remarked. They all went into his pockets. Then: "Go. I'll find a few more."

"No," young Jule replied. "I don't want you to!"

"Why not? Got a big contest planned for the three of us!"

"They're too heavy! You'll go under!"

"I'll be fine."

"No, Daddy! Please don't!"

"Back to the bank, you."

"I don't want you to!"

"Julie, I'm fine."

"Daddyyyy!" But he stood there, waiting . . . until she began to trudge her way out of the water. When it was at the height of her knees, she turned back. There were tears in her eyes. He smiled, pure warmth.

"Don't worry, baby," he promised. "Daddies don't sink."

BURN THE WATER

Rafe was silent, tracing his fingers along her lips. Jule added, "Turns out, daddies *do* sink. All the time. Sometimes they sink a whole *army*."

That was a clue. Rafe knew it. But he didn't push. Instead he breathed, "You are fierce."

"Not fierce enough," she said.

Rafe had a story too—a reason why he felt a lifelong debt to the water. She asked to hear it. He obliged, relating a story—*the* story—from his sixth year on Earth, and a boat that suddenly appeared alongside the Rogue camp.

The craft, once sleek, looked like it'd been through hell. So did its sailors—four Belgians—two male, two female, in their fifties, lean and hungry. Their arrival was news—someone from the Continent! *The whole camp was instantly riveted.*

The boat's "captain," named Ella, asked for permission to come ashore and the favor of some drinking water.

General Shapcott granted it.

Ella reported that they'd fled the Belgian city of Evergem, on the banks of the swollen Lys River. "Nothing but war there," *she said. Patched-over bullet holes in the hull of her boat testified to that. Shapcott allowed them to stay docked for the night.*

That evening, young Rafe was introduced to true evil.

Ella and her cohorts kidnapped six Rogue children who'd been playing tag by the river, unsupervised. In silent seconds, the kids were thrown into the hold of the boat. Rafe was one of the taken.

The boat sailed away, Rafe huddling in that hold in shocked silence, hearing only the whimpering of his fellow captives, none older than seven.

Then he heard a sound that made him shudder—his name, *cried out with utter desperation and terror by his mother. His parents had jumped into a pirogue and were now rowing as hard as they could in pursuit of the sailboat, both shrieking his name. "Rafe! Rafe!"*

Suddenly, gunfire erupted from the deck above him. Rafe's bladder emptied and his eyes filled with tears, terror seizing hold of him; his parents were about to die.

He screamed. All the children did. The gunfire continued, and with each round fired, the screams grew louder.

Yet the sound of his parents cut through. "Rafe! Rafe!" They sounded close, maybe right off the stern, close enough to be shot. God, no . . .

It was then that young Rafe spoke to the water—a plea: "Don't take them. Take me."

And the water spoke back: "Yes."

That fast, the gunfire stopped.

The boy couldn't know it, but Ella's team had run out of sluggers, her final shot burying itself into the forehead of a desperate father whose pirogue now drifted into the bank.

At the same time, on the shore of the river, General Shapcott and six captains ran along the bank and raced across a low bridge on the river just as the sailboat passed beneath it.

Shapcott's team made the leap, landing hard aboard the sailboat's deck, and—with knives, guns, and clubs—quickly slaughtered Ella and her cohorts.

Shapcott dropped anchor and rescued the kids from the hold. Shell-shocked, the children emerged onto the deck, running to the stern of the sailboat and looking to the river.

Five sets of parents had been hit and killed.

Rafe's had been spared. They were unharmed, their eyes wide.

At the sight of him, his mother collapsed with relief. And Rafe dropped to his knees, his head spinning. He had saved their lives. He and God. Their pact.

Forever after, he would owe the water.

Now Jule took his hand. He went on, "I don't want to be in a House anymore. I want to be in a family."

"Family," Jule breathed. In truth, it sounded wonderful. She reminded herself to *tell* him so, someday.

Maybe the next time they met.

FOURTEEN

Shapcott and his inner circle stood on a rooftop on Ludgate Hill, overlooking St. Paul's Cathedral and what had once been a Thameslink station. Four stories below was an empty but dry street, sitting just outside the Rogue walls.

Honus, the smithy, was here, bearing a cloth sack and a huge grin. He liked being among such rank.

Rafe arrived late. Shapcott swallowed his frustration. "Apologies," Rafe said. "What's in the bag, Honus?"

Honus bragged, "It's *victory*, my friend." Not a small claim from a guy who'd be miles from the actual fighting.

The general nodded to Honus. "Show us."

From the sack, Honus produced an old tin can. Centuries ago, it had contained corn or beans or carrots. Now its contents were a mystery. A thin white string stuck out of the top. The other captains looked deeply unimpressed.

"It's a can," Beckett snorted.

"No, sir," Honus replied. "It's a *Canner*. Observe." He strutted to the edge of the roof. The others followed.

"CLEAR BELOW!" Honus hollered toward the street. No one was visible there. Just a stray cat, looking for scraps.

"Prepare yourselves, gents," said Honus grandly. Then he pulled the string and tossed the can off the roof. The can plummeted without event.

Until, a foot before impact, it *exploded.*

A huge blast, spraying shrapnel everywhere, blowing the back off a wooden bus bench and liquefying the stray cat while sending up a hot wave of compressed air that knocked the captains back. Rafe's ears rang. Smoke filled his nostrils with the acrid smell of cordite. He regained his balance. Jaws dropped. Maud laughed without meaning to, thrilled.

And Honus could not stop grinning. "*Canner.* See?"

Silence. Rafe had read about grenades in his books; soldiers had carried them into battle since World War One . . . But nothing close to them had existed in *this* war before. This wasn't a knife or a pipe or a handmade slugger. This was as fatal as the VX. This could wipe out a company in a flash.

Jule's company.

That's all Rafe could see as he gawked at the wake left behind by this terrible weapon. It could kill her in an instant. He looked to Honus. They all did, hushed.

Never before had the smithy enjoyed such status. He boasted, "I found a way to heat grain alcohol into a powder. Metal scraps and a fuse inside. Ya toss it over the wall. Pretty big pop, as you can see. Should kill anything within ten yards, and daze everyone else. Then you're in."

The thick smoke had settled around them now. Honus inhaled it proudly. Shapcott asked him, "How fast can they be made?"

Honus answered, "Few days. The fuses take some doing. They're delicate."

The general asked, "How many empty cans do you have?"

Honus half smiled, a bit chagrined. "Fifty. Been working on this for a while. Saving things. The shrapnel too."

The general said, "We need them *tomorrow* for the attack."

Rafe began to panic. But Honus answered, "Can't do that, General. Only have two hands."

"Then use theirs!" Shapcott ordered, gesturing to his ten captains. "*No one* rests until we have *fifty* of these. Is that understood?"

The captains were silent. They thought the task impossible—all except for Maud, who let out a cheerful, "YESSIR!"

Another captain, Maud's half sister, Gillian, called, "Absolutely, sir!"

The men were silent, Rafe among them. Honus offered, "That many hands, we can get a lot done, sir."

Shapcott nodded. "See that you do. And fine work, Honus."

"Thank you, sir. It's the fuses that were the hard bit."

Shapcott headed for the rooftop door, hollering, "We're killing them all!" Then he was gone.

Maud and Gillian eyed their male counterparts, everyone trying to digest what they'd just experienced. They all saw a clear path to victory now—a means of breaching Eltham, finally.

But Rafe saw only Jule, killed by a ruthless blast.

"Honus," Maud began, "get us set up in the long hut with all the materials you can. We'll be along."

"Yes, ma'am," he said, leaving the rooftop.

Just the captains remained now. Maddox looked to Rafe. "Whaddaya think?"

Rafe shrugged as if unimpressed. "Big bang. And it's hell on cats. But can it knock a Russian fighter out of the sky?"

No one had a reply. All the answers had drowned long ago. But Maud offered, "Like he said, Rafe. One war at a time."

The captains left the rooftop and headed toward camp again. They had weapons to build . . .

Recovery was not a straight line, and on this day Nelly felt her body rebelling. She tried to cross from one end of her room to the other, but had to pause and catch her breath. She hated that—loathed the weakness in her hands and the smell of rust that clung stubbornly to her body. This disease made you forget what it had ever felt like to be well.

Jule was by her side for each step, but her every thought was *Rafe*. Seeing him again.

"Is it love?" Nelly asked.

"What?"

"You're daydreaming."

The door flew open behind them, and Evander charged in, "You disappeared again last night!"

It was then that Jule noticed it: a faint yellow color in the skin beneath Evander's eyes, spreading through his cheeks. He knew she could see it, but neither commented on it. Instead, she lied. "Patrol."

"Patrol. Again. With a standing order forbidding anyone from leaving camp."

She eyed him. "Can you fight? Can you run?"

"Well enough," he replied.

"And your strength?"

"I could lift this building. And my troops need me. Let's get back to y—"

Jule cut him off, "The moment the battle is done, you'll go to the Q tent."

"I promise," he replied.

"Here," Nelly said, offering Evander a spoonful of the beech-bark paste.

Evander grumbled, "Bloody do-gooder Jameson." Jule breathed out a laugh.

Evander swallowed the medicine.

Rafe spent the rest of the day making bombs at a long table in the long hut, alongside the nine other captains. It was hard work—tedious and terrifying. Heating the alcohol. Gathering the powder. Building the fuse. Marrying it to the string. Inserting the assembly into the can. Arranging the shrapnel just so. And then sealing it, stacking it. Carefully . . . while trying *not* to imagine such a weapon detonating anywhere near her.

But death was coming for her. He knew it. He was *building* it. *Fifty* of these damn things were going to be hurled over that wall of dense English oak—and they would obliterate anything close, changing this war forever. Maybe killing her... And all because Shapcott simply could not acknowledge what had flown right over his head.

Flanking Rafe were Maddox and Beckett. Across the table from them was Gillian, who'd been competing with Maddox all day to see who could build the bombs faster. Gillian was winning handily. And chatting. "This is what I'm talking about," she said. "*Competition*. It makes people more productive."

"Go on," Maddox replied. Maud listened intently as well.

"Ten Rogues go out to fish," Gillian began. "We want them all to give their best so the camp will have more to eat. But we don't give them any *incentive*; the one who catches the most isn't rewarded any more than the one who catches the least—and yet she's clearly more valuable to the House than the other. Why would she keep working harder?"

"Pride?" said Maddox. "Devotion to the House?"

"But catching more fish requires more *effort*, more time in cold water, more strain on your back. She should be rewarded; it would make the others work harder. It's an unfair system."

"So what's a better one?"

"Habs have their haul weighed every day. The most productive of them get benefits. More food, better socks, *something*. It makes people do better."

"We aren't Habs."

"But look at *us*, right now. I'm gonna build four Canners before you've built three. And look at Rafe here! He's still on two!"

Rafe turned at the mention of his name, suddenly wondering if his pace had unmasked him. Maud was watching him closely. He returned to his labors, failing to notice—as they all did—that Beckett had just placed a finished Canner too close to the edge of the long table . . .

Gillian went on, "Maybe you'd work harder if I got rewarded and you got docked. It'd be far more fair."

Rafe smiled. "Never knew you for a capitalist, Gillian."

"They built the world," she answered.

"They built airplanes too," Rafe replied. "Like MiGs."

There it was—the unspoken, spoken now. Silence fell. Gillian shrugged. "I'm gonna stretch my legs. Bye, slowpokes."

She started to rise just as Rafe finally spotted Beckett's Canner on the edge of the table. He shouted, "Beckett!"

Too late; Gillian's rise had shaken the table. The Canner toppled toward the floor.

Beckett gasped. Rafe threw his arms over Maddox. Maud screamed, "COVER!" Gillian froze. The Canner hit the floor . . .

And nothing happened.

A dull thud, a few ingredients harmlessly spilling. Then silence, save for some loud breaths, filling the room. Beckett gulped hard, mortified. Gillian eyed him. "Slow *and* dim-witted," she said.

Beckett retorted, "You're the one who jostled the table."

Rafe leaned down to put the Canner gently back together.

"Godsakes," he muttered. "Let's stack the finished ones on the floor, in the corner."

And they did, carefully. Twenty-three devices. Gillian nodded to Maud. "I see you built four too, Maudy! Maybe it's just *men* that need extra incentive!"

Maud grinned. The Canners were now wedged carefully into the corner. Everyone returned to the long table except Gillian. She grabbed one of her own Canners and smiled. "Gonna show this to my father so he can have the pleasure of saying, 'We didn't *need* those in my day!'"

They all laughed knowingly, except Rafe. Gillian headed down the length of the long table, chuckling, "Try to keep up, what?" She pushed open the hut door, then merrily kicked it shut behind her.

And her Canner *exploded*.

A pop of concussive white light, shrapnel ejected with demonic force, the door becoming a million splinters. Rafe flew into a wall, then fell to the ground. He looked to all those Canners stacked on the floor. None had detonated. A miracle. His next thought was to rescue Gillian.

But Gillian was gone, torn in two. And six Rogue civilians, hit by propulsive shrapnel, now lay where they'd stood just a moment ago, in varying degrees of emergency. Rafe howled, "MEDIC!!! MEDIC!!!" while crawling, then running out the doorway to the street, where he saw the full horror. Gillian was splayed in a half circle, that familiar smell of blood and flesh. "MEDIC!!! MEDIC!!!"

Horrified citizens tried to help the injured. Mothers pulled their children away. Doctors raced out of the med tent. Honus peeked out from his forge. Rafe found that infuriating. "Honus!" Rafe hollered. "Get over here!"

Honus gulped, then emerged. Trailing behind him were several children who'd been watching him work. Together they stepped around prone bodies and busy doctors doing grim triage.

Rafe wanted an explanation, an acknowledgment. But Honus simply mumbled, "I told you to mind the fuses. I said they were delicate!" Rafe was too angry to reply. Honus eyed those children, hoping to retain his status among them as a hero, and muttered, "Failure so often comes from carelessness, kids."

That's when Rafe erupted, grabbing the smithy by the neck—"She's DEAD, GODDAMN IT!"—and barking at the kids, "Go!" They obeyed, slaloming through bodies to get away.

Honus tried, "I *warned* everyone about the fuses!"

Rafe yelled, "You'll take the Mark for this!"

Maddox stepped in, firmly pulling Rafe away. "Got wounded to tend to," Maddox said. Rafe released the smithy.

Nearby, citizens stared at the halves of Gillian's body. Thirty days from now she'd be soil. Tomatoes would grow from her. "Bloody war," one said. "It never ends. Damn Crowns..."

Shapcott strode past them, eyeing the carnage with dismay.

This was the moment. Rafe turned to him. "General?"

A horse-drawn cart was backed in to carry Gillian's body away.

"General," Rafe went on. "You have to stop this. The Canners aren't ready."

"The Canners can end this war," Shapcott replied.

"They're as likely to kill *us* as our enemies!" Rafe shouted. "The weapon hasn't been sufficiently tested. Today is proof. We cannot carry them into battle."

Shapcott asked, "Maddox, do you agree?"

Rafe prayed that his friend would support him. Instead Maddox said, "I think Gillian built hers too quickly and got careless. For that I accept full responsibility. I'd challenged her to see who could go fastest."

Rafe tried not to sag. It was an effort.

Shapcott asked, "What do you say to that, Rafe?"

Rafe replied steadily, "Sir, I will *not* ask my troops to carry these weapons tomorrow, even if you order me to do so."

That was insubordination. Rafe continued, "Battle is hard enough without blowing ourselves up. Especially during a frontal assault on a heavily defended position."

"Captain," Shapcott replied, "you are testing me."

"Sir, I'm *begging* you. On behalf of my troops."

Behind him, Gillian's severed body was hoisted in two parts onto the cart. Shapcott exhaled hard, then went inside . . . and ordered his captains to halt production.

At that moment, in his airless Hab barn, Byron gave his invention its first test, loading five pounds of bark onto a platter, then lowering the press.

It worked. The paste was consistent. He gathered it into a bowl and brought it to five Habs who were suffering with the Yellowing. They found the taste more bitter than usual. He promised to add honey to the next batch.

But within hours, something miraculous happened.

Their symptoms were gone. Not improved—*gone*. His remedy was far more effective than any beech bark had been before. And Byron now revealed why:

This wasn't beech bark at all.

For three years, he'd been testing a theory, a hunch, that the bark of *English sycamores*—not beech trees—might provide the long-sought cure for the Yellowing. Sycamore bark was coarser, denser, harder to mash. But the press had solved that. And now the results had confirmed his fondest hopes. He began to picture a London in which no one—Hab, Rogue, Crown—would ever again suffer from the Yellowing. Grace would have loved that. Tears filled his eyes . . .

That night, Rafe was outside among the bivouac fires and the low murmuring of the Rogue citizenry. The bad fife and drum played tunelessly. The feral cats roamed.

The blast that had liquefied Gillian and injured six others this afternoon was history now—just like the MiG. She'd been mourned with the usual ceremony—blink, tap, reset—and Honus had been forced to take the Mark. Then life had rolled on. There was a battle to fight tomorrow, a heavily defended wall of dense English oak to scale.

And on every face, Rafe saw the same dread. He walked past soldiers so certain of death in tomorrow's fight that they were stitching their names into their shirts so their dead bodies would be identified even if mangled.

He walked laps inside the perimeter of the camp, thinking too much—not of his own survival tomorrow, but of Jule's. At one point he saw a fox slink by.

A sign. Jule was *everywhere*. He kept walking. Nearby, Maddox sprinted from one spot to another, his speed unchallenged. On Rafe's next lap, he saw a commotion at the main gate, where Rogue guards were yelling at someone seeking entry.

It was Byron. Over his shoulder was a burlap sack, which the guards were trying to wrestle away from him. Rafe approached.

"Let him go," Rafe ordered. They obliged, and closed the gate behind Byron, who nodded a thank-you to his champion. Rafe led him from the gate.

"What's in the sack?" Rafe asked.

"A cure. For the Yellowing."

Huh? Byron opened the sack to reveal *five pounds* of paste, sitting inside a wooden bowl. Rafe stared, dazzled by the quantity. But he said, "There's no such thing as a cure."

Byron replied, "Until now. It's sycamore. And it *cured* the patients I tried it on. This is enough to treat your whole camp, twice over."

Rafe mumbled, barely audible, "How did you . . . ?"

"I built a press. Here." He handed Rafe the sack.

Rafe asked, "What do you want for it?"

"I want *peace*. For my people. Freedom."

Rafe was silent. Byron went on, "And I want to be left alone by the guards to make as much of this as I want, for *whomever* I want, without them commandeering it for your House."

"I will see to it."

"I want you to see to it *tonight*. Your goodwill won't do me much good if you die tomorrow."

Which meant that somehow Byron knew about the attack. Rafe admired the candor. "I'll go to your camp tonight and issue the order. You won't be disturbed."

"Then we have a pax," Byron joked. Rafe smiled and headed toward the quarantine tent. Byron called out, "One other thing. I'd like to speak to your sister."

Rafe stopped. Turned. "What about?"

"*She'll* know."

"What about?" Rafe repeated. No Hab had ever paid a *social call* to a Rogue before.

Byron replied, "God. Music. Death. Airplanes. Does it matter?"

It mattered. Or maybe it didn't. Truth was, rules felt silly tonight.

Armageddon was approaching. Rafe called a guard over and ordered her to summon Breena.

Then he entered the quarantine tent and began feeding the suddenly plentiful sycamore paste to the soldiers recuperating there. A half hour later, certain now that it hadn't killed any of them, he spooned it into the mouths of the sick children in his care, among them Willa.

Meanwhile, Byron and Breena sat on a curb inside the gates. Rogue citizens tried not to stare, but a centuries-old taboo was vanishing before their eyes.

"Did it help?" Byron asked. "Coming to church?"

"It did," she said. "I don't know why. But it did."

"How? How did it get *in*?"

Breena didn't know how to reply, so Byron continued, "They killed my wife, three years ago. Crowns. Left her body by the water. How do you find God after that?"

Breena breathed out a sigh, the air frosting. "I don't know, Byron. I just know we both need to feel something *else*."

She took his hand. It made him gasp. "Breena, that's a dangerous thing to do."

"But it's what you came here for, isn't it?"

He reddened a bit. "I really hope you don't die tomorrow."

"A God-fearing woman like me!" she mocked. "I'll be fine."

In the quarantine tent, Rafe stared in utter astonishment. The patients—some of whom had been hovering on the edge of death for months—were improving demonstrably. Most of the soldiers were on their feet. The children were sitting up. And Willa seemed *fine*, almost healthy. A normal hue was returning to her face. Her breathing had stabilized. It was all miraculous. Rafe stared, struggling to integrate this new and impossible result. Death had been cheated, this child had been saved . . . and he had been witness to it. Willa's parents, both soldiers under his command, entered the tent to see the change for themselves and instantly began to cry thick tears. Rafe embraced them and kissed Willa on the forehead. "Will you still read to me?" she asked.

Through tears of his own, he answered, "Always."

He emerged from the tent, stunned, looking for Byron and Breena, who hadn't moved. Rafe stumbled over. "Byron," he sputtered, "you've changed the world."

Byron exhaled a big smile and replied, "Not yet."

Rafe tried to calm himself. "I have to tell Shapcott about this. Who else knows of it?"

"Just the patients I've treated."

"Good."

"I feel an obligation to share it with the Crown camp as well. There's a lot of suffering there."

"I know," Rafe replied. "Just don't share it with them yet, all right? That will actually *save* lives, maybe thousands."

"Okay." Byron nodded.

"Thank you," Rafe returned. "I'll go to the Highlands tonight and make sure the guards know not to bother you."

Breena asked, "Is that smart? Going out tonight?"

"I made a promise. Thank you, Byron."

"Happy to help."

Rafe hurried to Shapcott's quarters. He had his solution now, a way to stop tomorrow's battle, saving *thousands*, saving *Jule*—simply by reporting a truth.

He rushed up the stairs of a building overlooking the square. The general lived there in a second-floor apartment. Rafe navigated the dark hallway and knocked urgently.

The door opened. He began, "General, we can't attack Eltham tomorrow."

Thrown, Shapcott paused. "Why not?"

"Because we've just been given a great opportunity. And we have to act on it, immediately." He entered, closing the door behind him. Shapcott waited.

Rafe went on, "A Hab has just found a *cure* for the Yellowing."

"My God," Shapcott breathed.

"A different kind of bark, sycamore, turned into paste by a giant press. I saw the results myself. It cured our entire Q tent. Ten were soldiers, completely recovered now. No more symptoms, no more illness."

Shapcott could barely believe what he was hearing. Rafe continued, "So what matters now, for the health of our citizens and the strength of our military, is to secure every sycamore tree we can find, *before* the Crowns can. Wouldn't you agree?"

Shapcott was a quick study. "Yes," he agreed.

"And you know where the largest concentration of sycamores is. Right, sir?"

"Yes," Shapcott breathed. "The Bloody."

The Bloody. Blood Park, so named by soldiers for the ferocity of the battles that had been fought there over the centuries. No one could remember the park's actual name; it had always just been the Bloody.

And it was replete with sycamore trees. Thousands of them.

Rafe said, "We need to call off the attack on Eltham and instead lead the troops to strip those trees. May I do that, sir?"

"Yes," Shapcott said. "Make all the necessary arrangements."

"Yes, sir. Thank you, sir."

No attack. Jule would live. Rafe left, thanking God along the way.

That night, a thick tension choked the Crown camp. No one could sleep, even the children. The soldiers looked stricken. Paternoster, with all its defenses, awaited.

Jule sat in Big Lil's forge, honing knives on a hand-cranked sharpening stone. It was monotonous work that made her eyes sting, but there was a ritual satisfaction to it. The night before every battle, she always gathered the knives of her entire company and sharpened them personally. Her soldiers loved her for that.

The wheel turned. Sparks flew. Screeching sounds cut through the night. Battle was just hours away, a frontal assault on a fortified position. But there was only Rafe in every thought. She finished a blade and eyed its perfect edge, hating what it might do. He had brought her to life.

Jule began to hum that song about the sun, almost unconsciously... She picked up another knife and placed it against the rotating stone. Just then, Mean, the peddler, approached her, accompanied by two soldiers.

Jule knew him well enough. "Not looking for any goods right now, Mean," she said.

Mean smiled. "I'm not selling goods tonight. I'm selling your survival."

That got her attention. She nodded to the soldiers. They left. Then she said, "Go on."

"First, price," Mean said. "I expect to be compensated."

"Maybe you should tell me what you're offering first."

He pressed, "I want a place to live, inside this camp."

Jule replied, "No Habs have ever lived here."

"No Hab has ever offered anything this valuable."

"Mean, my time is short. Say what you're offering or leave."

"A fellow Hab has found a way to cure the Yellowing."

Not a small claim. Jule gulped. "Say more."

"He built a press to make the paste. But it's *not* beech."

Seconds later, Jule was running across the Eltham grounds, to Chasen's bunker; she pushed through the door and raced down the rough-hewn steps to find Chasen quiet and alone. "General," Jule began urgently, "we have to call off the attack on Paternoster. Every available soldier needs to be moved to the Bloody."

"What's at the Bloody?"

"The cure," she answered. "The *future*."

Rafe rowed to the Highlands by moonlight and let the Rogue overseers there know that Byron and Byron's press were not to be disturbed. Then he rowed home again, inhaling the quiet on the dark water. No Bloats troubled him tonight. No fighter planes streaked overhead. No enemies struck.

There was just Jule—her face, that face—and the happy knowledge that Eltham would be spared. The moon lit Rafe's way back to Paternoster.

Around midnight, Maud heard a familiar knock at her door. "Yes?" she said.

Rafe stepped inside. No hello. He simply said, "I'm going to speak to Shapcott to make it official, but I wanted you to know first—I won't be coupled with you, Maud."

"I see."

Silence hung. Rafe added, "Would be bad for both of us."

Maud was hurt, angry. But she smiled as if offering friendly advice. "Ya know, Rafe—soldiers don't *get* to decide who they're coupled with. It's the general that does that."

"I speak for the general," he said.

"Maybe not on this," she insisted.

"I'll desert if I have to. I'll join the Habs."

"To avoid coming to my bed?" she asked.

"To avoid a lie," he replied.

Maud digested that. Then, "Shame about the Canners. I was hoping this might be the battle to end all battles, once and for all."

"Maud, our battles don't make sense anymore."

"What the hell has happened to you?"

The truth was an option here, might've even been a kindness. Instead he said, "My mistakes are mine to make. I'm sorry."

She fired back, "What're you *sorry* for? I don't care. Childbirth sounds awful."

He nodded. "Get some sleep."

She shot back, "Sod off."

FIFTEEN

Dawn broke clear and cold over the waving greenery of Blood Park—the Bloody—a sprawling meadow at its center.

The grass there, too tall to stand, bent lazily at the hips and drooped down everywhere. Once, this meadow had been home to paved walking paths and metal frames for soccer goals. But no more. Grass got one, and rovers got the other—long ago.

On all sides of the great meadow lay forest, thousands of suddenly indispensable sycamore trees providing shade and shadow. If you were standing in the center of that grassy field, you could be surrounded by *thousands* of soldiers on all sides, and you'd never know it—the foliage was that thick. This morning, it was the domain of calm birds. Their songs were full of promise.

On the other side of the city, as the sun rose over Eltham Lake, Crowns huddled anxiously. Today, Crown troops were to occupy the Bloody; one soldier joked that it would be "the largest bark-shaving operation in military history."

Jule had insisted that they be in full battle rattle. "There is every reason to believe," she'd said, "that the Rogue army will be as interested in those trees as we are."

So they armed themselves. Jule was never wrong.

Now they assembled, thousands of them. And Chasen sent out

every rover in the camp to scout the environs of Blood Park. Each youth was given a blade and a sack.

Sixty kids, none older than twelve, ran or rowed or waded toward the Bloody. Big Lil watched them go as she finished her last batch of sluggers for the day, ammunition that was still warm when eager Crowns, assembled in the center of the village, fed it into their handguns and the odd rifle.

In their backpacks, the Crown soldiers packed knives, swords, maces, clubs, sluggers, bows and arrows, plus provisions: canteens, hardtack crackers, cotton gauze, compasses, signal mirrors, extra socks, tourniquets, and shovels.

Battle rattle.

"Jesus," one soldier griped. "How much gear do ya need to strip trees?"

Chasen gave the order to move out. Now 5,342 Crown soldiers headed for Blood Park. Jule led an entire regiment.

In the Rogue camp, a quiet calm hovered. The paste had healed the sick, and now the Rogues were going to secure more of it, forever. The mood was light, almost jovial. Soldiers wagered on who would secure the most bark. But Rafe sensed that the likelihood of encountering Crowns today was high. "There's every reason to believe that word of Byron's work will reach Eltham before long," he now told Shapcott. "And Chasen will see the military implications just as we have." Rafe had sent rovers to the park to scout it. Each bore a sack and a knife.

It was time to move out. Now 5,647 Rogues headed for Blood Park, in search of trees.

Nelly sat at her window, stacking small square wooden tiles. They'd once been part of a board game, but the board and its box had vanished long ago—and all she knew about the squares, or the game, was that a *Q* was worth ten points and a *J* was worth eight and all the vowels were only worth one. This was her ritual when nervous, stacking them into a tower, as if *forcing* her hand to be steady.

Today it was impossible. Today she was terrified; dread had been knotting her belly all day, a fear that Jule was about to die. To push the thought away, Nelly started a new tower. But after just six tiles, the shaking in her hand brought it all crashing down. A knock on her door startled her further.

"Yes?" she asked. The door was opened, gently.

There stood Jameson. "Thought you might like some company," he said.

Nelly began to weep. They'd known each other for years, a friendship built on moments like this, when Jameson just seemed to know she was in need.

She rose and met him in the doorway, taking his hands. "Is she in danger?" Nelly asked.

"I think they all are," he replied.

Nelly felt her face go cold. Jameson added, "Jule sees things. She'll know what to do."

"But she *cares* too much," Nelly sighed. "She'll endanger herself to save her troops." Jameson couldn't deny it. Nelly went on, "She can't die. We need her. She has to lead us all *out* of this someday."

He felt the tiles on the table. It made him grin. "How tall has it gotten today?" he asked.

"Not very."

"Maybe I can help." He began to build a tower—slowly, by feel alone, with the same great patience he brought to all his endeavors. Nelly watched him, marveling at his kindness. "Thank you, Jameson."

He smiled. "Don't distract me. I'm aiming for the ceiling." Nelly laughed. Jameson added, "And yes, we need her."

The bloodiest battle in the history of this war began with two ten-year-olds. As that huge grassy field lay quiet and slack—its silent reeds awaiting the arrival of eleven thousand unknowing warriors—the sycamores surrounding that field were now the province of dozens of children, rovers from both Houses, looking for one another in dense vegetation.

Liam, of the Rogues, sprinted from tree trunk to tree trunk, bush to bush, eyes up and darting. His diving partner, Portia, was nearby but unseen. Stealth was Portia's great gift; *no one* was better at hide-and-seek. On this day it made Liam feel alone.

The sycamores around him were wide and closely packed. A Crown rover could be ten feet in front of Liam and still remain invisible—an unsettling thought. So Liam spun in loose circles as he walked, afraid that someone would sneak up behind him.

But the blow that felled Liam came from *above*—a red brick, centuries old, dropped on him from a branch fifteen feet overhead, thumping the top of his skull, then bouncing down to the forest floor. It staggered him.

And just like that, a ten-year-old Crown named Hollis hopped down from that branch to the forest floor and began punching Liam into submission. Liam dropped to a knee, then fell face-first to the leafy ground. But Hollis did not stop. So he never saw the great ebony club that Portia swung with all her might into the back of his head.

She had just become a soldier. Hollis pitched forward, his skull cracked.

Portia dragged Liam away and got him to his feet, walking him through the dense forest toward the wide-open meadow. "You're gonna be fine."

But *his* head was bleeding too, his gait unsteady; he needed a doctor, which meant she'd have to get him to Paternoster Square somehow. She placed Liam's arm around her shoulder, ready to half carry him as far as she could.

But then she saw a horror—no, *thousands* of horrors—entering this grove of trees from the north. The *entire* Crown army, a hundred yards away, gathering in the trees that lined the eastern edge of the fallow field. Portia's heart stopped.

This wasn't a scout unit. This was over five thousand troops. A massive offensive force. The Rogue Army needed to be apprised. Immediately.

"Liam," she whispered. "Are you all right?"

He nodded, which was a lie, blood trickling from his scalp and face.

Portia whispered again, "I need you to *say* it. I have to get to everyone. Are you okay?"

"I'm okay."

She sat him against a thick tree: "Say it again."

"I'm okay." Barely audible, but it would have to do.

Portia handed him a canteen. "Drink!" she said, then she left him there and sprinted across that still-empty field, disappearing into its western edge for Paternoster. She was as fast as she was stealthy, and her pace got her to the square in mere minutes, where she sought out Rafe.

Breathless, she panted, "Their *whole army* is in the grove."

Rafe paused, his face calm. "Repeat that, please."

Portia gulped, then repeated, "I just saw their entire army, in the grove at the Bloody."

"What are they doing there?"

"What do you mean?" she asked.

"Do they have sacks over their shoulders to cut bark? Or are they in full battle rattle?"

Portia paused, then replied, "Both."

Suddenly, today's mission was no longer about trees. Rafe took the intelligence to Shapcott, who seemed pleased. "Good," Shapcott said. "We can end them after all."

"General," Rafe began, "I suggest we divide our forces into two regiments, sending them not across the meadow but into the trees on the northern and southern ends of the Crown line, to hit the enemy on its exposed flanks." The result, they both knew, would be war inside dense forest canopy. Designed madness. But it would also mean completely surprising the enemy from two directions.

Shapcott approved the plan. The Rogue army divided itself. The general, aided by Maddox, would lead one regiment. Rafe, aided by Beckett, would lead the other.

Word had spread among the soldiers now—they wouldn't be stripping any bark today; they'd be killing Crowns. Rafe ducked into the quarantine tent, which had emptied considerably. Willa was still here, cheerful and excited to see him.

"Machine man!" she yelled happily. Rafe hugged her farewell with a promise to see her soon. She didn't ask where he was going.

At roughly that same moment, Crown soldiers swarmed the grove of sycamores, beginning to cut and collect bark. The mood was celebratory. And wagers abounded—men and women racing one another to fill their sacks the fastest.

But Jule's instincts were pinging. The enemy was coming. She knew it. As her troops happily filled their sacks, she approached Evander, who had smeared mud on his face, as many did before battle. In his case, of course, it was to hide the blotches of yellow beneath his eyes. "You all right?" she asked.

"Fine," he replied.

"Breathing well?"

"Healthy and fit," he lied, ignoring a raging fever that was already impairing his balance and judgment.

She studied him, then moved on to find Chasen, asking the general to order trenches dug on the northern and southern flanks of their lines in the forest.

"What for?" Chasen asked.

"I believe we're going to encounter Rogue companies today, possibly the entire Rogue force. They want the same thing we do. I think they'll split their forces and hit us in defilade from both sides."

"Why?" Chasen asked.

"Because it's what *I* would do. We need trenches, Uncle. It will slow their attack." Chasen ordered it done, and hundreds of Crown soldiers were pulled from bark duty to begin digging on both extreme flanks of the Crown army, soil flying into piles.

Jule organized a small reconnaissance unit to scout the environs south of the Crown line, an endless grove of sycamore trunks and leafy branches. With a rifle slung across her chest and a knife on each hip, she was looking for one Rogue in particular: *Rafe*.

The other night he'd said something about preferring his own death to seeing anything happen to her. Had that been his way of warning her that an attack was coming? She began the scout, looking for him . . .

But the first person she encountered, one hundred yards from the

Crowns' southern flank, was a child: Hollis, dead, where Portia had clubbed him from behind.

No, today would not be about denuding trees.

Jule sighed and lifted the kid's body. The weight of him, the blankness in his face... She carried the tiny corpse to the edge of the wood, where trees met the meadow. There, she saw Liam slumped against a tree, dazed, a canteen in his lap. Another child. Another horror. Another sign that the Bloody was soon to live up to its name. There was no time to attend to the boy. So she poked him and said, "Kid! Run!"

Liam didn't stir. It was all a fog. She'd just have to trust his fate—and all their fates—to Fate itself. She placed Hollis's body on the ground and rejoined her recon unit.

The sun had now hidden itself behind thick clouds, and the air felt still and heavy. Deep in the trees, Rafe and 2,800 soldiers were approaching the Crown army from the south, hidden by the density of the foliage. He had split them into fifty-six companies of fifty and told them to expect a trench at the southern flank of the Crown line. They followed him now as he moved between trees with pace and purpose, heading north. Jule and her unit were directly ahead, moving south, but Rafe did not yet know it. Forest green was all around him. Inescapable. And the sound of crunching leaves beneath his feet felt like a lethal bell around his neck.

To his right was Beckett's company. Rafe monitored their pace carefully, determined to be the first Rogue to reach the Crown line.

Half a mile to the north, and heading south, the Rogue regiment led by Shapcott and Maddox moved just as swiftly. Up ahead, a rabbit saw them, turned in terror, and fled. Maddox hollered, "Run, Old Hare! If I were an old hare, I'd run too!"

He had stitched his name into his shirt just hours before.

Breena was a part of this regiment. She marched with a pistol in each hand and tried not to worry about her brother. He'd be fine. He was always fine. And this army was about to take the Crowns completely by surprise.

Jule continued scouting. She was glad to be on point, in front of her unit, so no other Crown could encounter Rafe before she did. Her eyes darted, scouring the trees for any sign of him. Then she turned to find that Pritchett and Boggs were right behind her. "On your tail, Captain," Boggs said.

"Find someone else to follow," she answered, irritated.

The soldier on Rafe's right hip was named Kimpton. She was deep in the Churn; Rafe could see it all over her. So he decided to tell her a joke. Some soldiers needed a different kind of leading.

But then he stopped. Entirely. And he balled his fist while raising his right arm rigidly to bring this regiment of 2,800 Rogues to a halt. Rafe stood, frozen, breathless, pale, as if he'd seen a monster.

Fifty yards away, also frozen in shock, was Jule, out in front of *her* recon unit, staring at him and half the Rogue army—*thousands*—armed for attack.

Rafe felt his blood congeal. The forest itself stopped breathing. His eyes said: *I'm sorry. I love you. Please run!*

Jule said calmly, "Back to the lines." Her unit turned and sprinted in retreat, shrieking to their compatriots on bark-stripping duty, "INCOMING!!! INCOMING!!!"

Now 2,800 Rogue soldiers looked to Rafe, the tip of the spear, awaiting an order that should have been instantaneous.

Yet he hesitated, unable to speak, watching as she ran away, allowing her precious seconds to get to her southern line.

Finally, Kimpton asked, "Captain?" And Maud shouted, "RAFE?"

Rafe shook himself. Then he nodded to Kimpton, who bellowed, "CHARRRRRGE!"

As one, Rafe's mighty regiment *roared* and began its pursuit, Rafe in the lead. The blood was coming.

There was a sickness in his belly—a first for him in battle—but he ignored it as he hurtled forward, his troops weaving through tree trunks and low-hanging branches that amplified their collective howl.

The sound reached the Crown trench diggers at the southern end of their line.

These soldiers looked up to see Jule and her unit sprinting toward them, death itself close behind. They yanked their knives out of sycamore bark and rushed to back up the trenches.

Shapcott's regiment, approaching from the north, heard the roars too. Sensing the moment, Shapcott screamed, "CHARRRRGE!" and he and *his* troops began a dead sprint as well. Maddox, his speed honed by all those footraces, led the way. The forest echoed, an amphitheater of battle.

Chasen ordered his trench diggers on the north flank to double their efforts.

And still Jule ran, leading her unit toward the southern trench, which was four feet wide and nearly as deep. A hundred Crown soldiers peered out of it, each a sniper with rifle poised. Jule had trained them all.

The feral echo of the Rogues bounced off the trees. At a full sprint, Jule ordered her unit to leapfrog the southern trench and find cover. She launched herself over the trench and came down on the other side. Several of her troops, less athletic than she was, fell short of the mark and wound up landing in the trench itself, a few of them atop fellow Crowns. One sniper was kicked in the head so hard he fell unconscious. Another soldier landed badly and shattered an ankle. Jule dragged him to safety behind a tree and put a pistol in his hand, ordering archers to back up the snipers in the trench.

And still the Rogue roar echoed. The voices grew louder, from both ends of the forest now, bearing down, disembodied.

Rafe had never led a charge like this. On any other day, in any other battle, he'd be searching for targets, weaknesses to exploit, dangers. Now he was looking only for Jule.

The battle meant little. Surviving meant something. *She* meant the world.

He dashed in and out of trees and branches and leaves, everything bouncing up and down. Finally, he saw the southern Crown trench fifty yards ahead, a hundred Crown snipers waiting there, with more Crown troops rushing up behind it in support.

Then he saw her again. And she saw him.

And neither could say the word *Fire!*

It didn't matter. On Chasen's flank, Crowns in the north trench opened fire on Maddox and his troops. The Rogues returned fire. Deafening volleys echoed. Arrows too.

In the southern trench, Crown soldiers opened fire as well, sluggers whizzing past Rafe into priceless tree trunks as he bellowed, "FIRE!!!" His charging regiment obeyed.

The Battle of the Bloody—an accidental fight—had begun.

Instantly, bodies succumbed—chests, bellies, arms, faces. Rogues in full sprint suddenly crashed to the forest floor. Crowns prone in the trench took bullets to the forehead. Snipers killed and died. Great groans arose. But Jule, unhit, kept firing. The Rogue charge continued.

On both sides of Rafe, luckless Rogues fell while other Rogues fired. A few did both. One Rogue flopped onto his back, gut shot, unconsciously firing into the treetops while screaming in pain. Smoke, mists of blood, and discharged glycol powder filled the air as the Rogues kept coming, and firing, and falling, and dying.

"FIRE!" Jule kept shouting. "FIRE!"

More sluggers, more arrows, more death. The dual Rogue assault had completely bracketed the Crown army, but the Rogue regiments were paying a horrible price for it. In that first unhinged assault, 1,200 human beings lost their lives, most of them Rogues. Yet the tide was inexhaustible.

On the northern flank, Maddox and his company reached the Crown trench and simply dove in with boot heels and blades, starting dozens of clumsy hand-to-hand fights at once. Knives, pipes, clubs, fists, rifle butts. Maddox was gutting a Crown with a long-knife when, suddenly, a female Crown soldier, shorter than Maddox by nearly a foot, swung a club at Maddox's legs, shattering his right kneecap. A blinding flash of pain. Breena leapt forward with a knife to the Crown's back, and tried to drag Maddox out of this murderous dugout. But the fighting was on top of them now, leaving no time or room. Maddox yelled, "Go! Go!" and she reluctantly continued to knife her way through the trench, fighting as if she had eight arms . . . until a Crown rifle-butted her to the back of the head and she dropped, unconscious.

The southern trench was just ten yards in front of Rafe now. He ran faster, sluggers slicing the air on both sides of him. Then he and his entire company plunged into this pit of fury feetfirst, knives out, swinging clubs and pipes, firing pistols. No one ran or deserted; they'd been born into this fight. But it was a violence none had seen before. Jule and her unit were behind a few of those noble sycamores, pouring gunfire into the trench.

In less than a minute, all the Crowns defending this trench were either dead or injured. Paris lay unconscious among them, bleeding badly from a wound to his mouth. Rafe climbed over him, out of the dugout and into the heart of the Crown army. Kimpton and the rest of Rafe's regiment followed, trampling bodies as they went. Jule's troops fell back.

The northern Crown trench succumbed as well, Shapcott's Rogue regiment now wading into the main Crown line in such close quarters that before long no soil was visible at their feet, only bodies. A ghastly flooring. Battle had never felt less glorious.

Evander was airless throughout, the Yellowing making every breath hurt. But he did not falter. This was *the* battle; he knew it. Collapse would be unforgivable.

Jule had a knife in each hand. She punched with them, machine-like, recoiling. Throughout, somehow, she kept one eye on Rafe, even as he dispatched scores of her comrades. No one was firing sidearms or rifles now; the density of bodies was too great and the time for loading and aiming too little.

In the northern trench, Maddox tried to crawl to safety—but his right leg wouldn't move at all. A few feet away, four dead bodies lay stacked, like steps, a pathway out of the trench. Maddox crawled toward it, desperate to escape. But a Rogue and a Crown, having just stabbed each other to death, now fell into the trench in a horrid embrace, their combined weight crashing down upon Maddox's useless leg, hyperextending it. The pain shot into his brain with such violence that he blacked out before he could scream. He would sprint no more. Ever.

On the southern flank, all around Rafe and Jule, soldiers would fight, fall, rise, fight more, and fall again. This was not the Churn. This was The End. *No one* in this wood was uninjured. It seemed as though God was above the treetops pulling souls in one direction and the devil was below, pulling them in another. Agony was in the air.

Maud moved like a tornado despite knife wounds to her right thigh and left forearm. She'd also lost the pinkie on her left hand. None of it stopped her, or even slowed her.

Jule was fighting with eight arms too. Then, a horror. She saw a fellow Crown—a sixteen-year-old girl—jam a knife into Rafe's back, just below the shoulder blade on his left side. Rafe pitched forward as the child moved in to kill him. Jule's heart stopped. Then...

Beckett lurched forward, killing Rafe's attacker, and Rafe moved on. Jule's relief shocked her.

Across the forest, Breena got to her feet, concussed by the blow to her head and still reeling from anoxia. She stumbled forth like a ghost in a theater, sounds bouncing and bending oddly, light flashing and then disappearing. None of it felt real.

In the midst of the mayhem, Pritchett and Boggs devised a new kind of combat—crawling along the soil, stabbing short knives into the feet of every Rogue soldier they encountered. Each time, the wounded Rogue would buckle, and then be killed from above by any Crown fortunate enough to be nearby. Then Pritchett and Boggs would move on, knives ready.

Soon they came upon little Liam, still unconscious against that same tree at the edge of the meadow, amid this blizzard of sound and rage. Pritchett decided to execute the boy. Liam was, after all, a Rogue, and this was war. Pritchett raised a blade to the child's throat.

It never got there.

Instead, one of Jule's knives punctured the back of Pritchett's neck just above the shoulder line. He slumped forward onto Liam's lap.

Boggs was stunned; Jule had just killed a fellow Crown. She eyed Boggs and breathed, "Go," until he crawled away. Then she turned . . . too late.

Maud, seizing the moment, moved in and swung a club with all her might into Jule's lower back. Breath rocketed out of Jule's lungs. Her hands went numb. Her eyes glazed and she staggered forward, unable to inhale. An instinct kicked in. *Turn, Jule. Rise. Flee. You can breathe later.* Her eyes opened enough to see Maud swing that club again. Jule sprang to her feet and fled. Somehow.

Maud followed, yelling at her fellow Rogues, "Get her! She's an officer!"

Three other Rogues pursued. In seconds, a breathless Jule was cornered by her captors up against a tree. Rafe saw it all, terrified.

General Chasen saw it too. He rushed forward, a desperate attempt at rescue. But Maud's knife was on its way to Jule's throat. Jule braced for death.

Then the work of a scrawny smithy saved her.

Tied to the back of Rafe's belt, *hidden there since morning*, was a Canner. He'd built this one himself, and had been saving it for just such an emergency. He grabbed it now, pulled the string on it, and tossed it high into a treetop directly above Chasen. The grenade bounced off a branch.

And exploded.

An air-thumping sound, a concussive blast of light, with shrapnel erupting in all directions. A tree trunk sheltered Chasen, but the Crown soldier a foot from him suddenly lost half a face.

And all the Crowns simply STOPPED. Just like that.

Death had never come in a package like this before. It was loud, violent, foreign, *unnatural*. And it froze them all. In the stunned silence that followed, Rafe had become the newly risen Destroyer of Worlds. Awe on every face. Even Jule's.

But not Maud. Her instincts were now telling her that Rafe had tossed that grenade to save the woman Maud had been about to kill. *Could that be possible?* Maud moved in to stab her.

So Rafe produced a second Canner, showing it to Chasen as if to say, *Want another?*

Chasen—stunned, overwhelmed—now hollered, "RETREEEEAT!" until his voice gave out.

And within seconds, the surviving Crowns were racing out of this forest and into the meadow—hundreds of terrified, dispirited, whipped soldiers, suddenly abandoning the fight and surrendering the sycamores to their enemy. Some Crowns helped wounded comrades; most just fled, trampling the tall grass in ignominious defeat. The Rogues, just as bloodied, watched in happy shock as this horrible fight simply *ended*, in an instant. A huge cheer of triumph, exhaustion, and contempt rose from their ranks. They had won. Maud lowered her knife.

Jule stepped away from that tree and entered the human tide, looking for her brother. She found him—on his hands and knees, gasping for air, delirious, mumbling nonsensically. She slung his arm over her shoulder. "Up, Evander. I've got you," she said, and reluctantly joined the retreat.

The last face Jule saw before darting into the lea was that of Rafe. They both knew he had very likely just revealed their secret.

But that was tomorrow's battle; this one was over. She emerged from the shadows of the forest into the gray light of the meadow, bearing her brother. More Rogue cheers and catcalls followed her across the tall bent grass. Rafe remained silent, holding back grateful tears. Jule had survived. He would see her again.

Maud turned to approach him. He simply walked away, beginning to search the ground for the wounded among his regiment while ordering Kimpton to fetch the Rogues' medical units. She obeyed. Around them, Rogue soldiers hugged. Some cried. Many collapsed to the forest floor.

It would take days for a full accounting to be completed, and *weeks* before the last of the wounded from Blood Park would either recover or die, allowing an actual casualty figure to be reached. But everyone knew that the losses had been appalling, unprecedented. Each army had begun the day with well over five thousand healthy soldiers.

The Crown army that retreated had eight hundred and fifty left.

The army mocking them numbered just nine hundred.

The Bloody had taken the rest.

Shapcott, who had suffered a shattered wrist, now wondered what to do with the multitude of corpses. There were too many to compost; no one had that many wood chips. And they couldn't be put in the Thames; the thought was too grotesque to contemplate. Perhaps the *Habs* could haul all this flesh somewhere. They were good at big projects.

When asked by a soldier, "What do we do with the injured Crowns?" Shapcott snapped, "Leave them where they are. Their mates can come for them. But if any have bark in their satchels, take it."

Ignoring this, Rafe assigned search units to find and aid the living, from *both* sides, on the forest floor.

The dying, he decided, would stop here.

In the Crown camp, Nelly awakened with her head on Jameson's chest—noticing that as she'd slept, this remarkable man had indeed built the tower of wooden tiles nearly to the ceiling. "Oh, Jameson," she breathed.

He shrugged humbly, then added, "Tell me what's outside the window."

She hurried toward it and saw a ghastly parade: the remains of the Crown army, crawling back to Eltham. Wounded carried wounded. No one was unscathed. And their numbers told her that thousands had been left behind, dead. She scanned every face, looking for Jule, as they trudged by.

"Tell me," Jameson said calmly.

"There are hundreds that should be thousands. And they are *all* wounded."

"Do you see Jule?"

"No." Nelly sagged hard, bracing herself on the table. The tower of wooden tiles collapsed horribly.

"I'm so sorry!" she exclaimed.

Jameson found his way to her and put his arms around her. She was shaking and her breathing was shallow. The Yellowing made crying feel like drowning.

"Shh," he said.

Then Nelly's front door opened. They both turned.

And there stood Jule. Nelly's knees weakened.

"Jule!" she cried, hurrying across the room to meet Jule in a fierce embrace. Jule began to cry now too, deeply touched that Jameson had waited here.

"Thank you," she breathed.

"Your brother?" Nelly asked.

Jule answered, "I just put him in the Q tent. He's very sick. We need Byron's medicine."

Jameson nodded, then asked, "What were your losses?"

Jule simply could not make the actual figure pass her lips.

Rafe spent the next blur of hours beneath that same canopy of trees, separating the living from the dead, getting the wounded to medics or stretcher bearers.

He neither rested nor ate, and stopped only for as long as it took to have the knife wound on his back stitched by a fellow soldier. Then he resumed crisscrossing the forest floor, the stench of the bloody battle living in his clothes.

Soldiers from both sides were dying, some bleeding out despite medical attention, suffering, calling for water or their mother. Rafe continued to provide water, gauze, and hardtack to dozens of Crowns. That was for Jule.

Late in the afternoon, once the last of the Rogue wounded had been tended to, Rogue soldiers were ordered to complete the massive task of carving and collecting bark from the sycamores. That's when Rafe spotted Paris lying unconscious atop the southern trench, near death. Two Rogue soldiers stood over him, laughing, about to cut the rest of Paris's fingers off. "Better than cutting any more of that stupid bark," one joked.

Incensed, Rafe moved in, grabbing them both and pushing them up against one of the sycamores. "Your knives," he ordered.

Shocked, they handed him their knives. He kept his hands on their throats: "We fight and we kill. But we don't *maim* the defenseless. Understand?"

They nodded silently, as scared now as they'd been during the dying. He hissed, "Get back to your company—and tell your fellow soldiers that any Rogue who harms the wounded will answer to me. Go."

As they hurried away, Rafe knelt down and bandaged his rival. Paris's eyes flickered open hazily, but he was too drained to speak, offering instead a simple nod of thanks. Rafe gave Paris some water, then had two rovers cart him back to the Rogue camp as a prisoner of war. "Take him to Bergen's," Rafe ordered. That was for Jule too.

Maud passed by. When she saw Rafe aiding and comforting the enemy, she asked, "You going gold on us, Rafe?" But even she was too devastated to engage just now. The losses to this army had left her nearly senseless.

That night, General Shapcott lost consciousness and was evacuated back to his headquarters in Paternoster Square, effectively leaving Rafe in command. The work continued and the sun set—darkness bringing no end to the suffering, and no sign of Maddox, who was now listed among the missing.

Throughout, the stripping of the bark continued, and little Liam remained by the tree where Portia had left him. Now and then he would awaken and try to move, but it was impossible. And despite all the activity around him—the stretcher bearers, soldiers, and medics—no one seemed to notice this one child against this one tree. Each time Liam roused, he'd soon fall back to sleep . . . hungry, thirsty, and alone. Dying.

As the sun rose on that second day, a new army—one *without* weapons—appeared in that pristine meadow. It was the Habs, led by Byron, crossing all that tall, lazy grass to the edge of the wood, stunned by the human catastrophe hiding there. Byron could barely breathe. His remedy to ease suffering had now resulted in the bloodiest battle in this rivalry's history. Thousands massacred. He found Rafe and asked, "How can we help?"

Rafe looked at all the Crown bodies still languishing in the dirt, and replied, "You can get the Crown wounded back to their camp. We can't."

Maud overheard this and barked, "Shapcott wants them left as they are."

"Shapcott's not here."

"It was an *order*."

"*And I'm countermanding it.* You want to kill them all? Go stab them where they lie. Otherwise, get out of the way."

Maud stormed away. She'd seen enough now. Rafe was no longer to be trusted. He told Byron to put the Crowns on stretchers, and the Habs began the great task of moving all this human cargo to Eltham Lake.

With the evacuation in full swing, Rogue children began creeping toward the wood, their curiosity impossible to restrain. What they saw left them slack-jawed. Carnage. Forever after, this would be "The Day of the Trees."

Portia was among the children, looking for Liam. To her great horror, she found him where she'd left him—unconscious now, barely breathing. His skin looked gray. Insects crawled across his neck. She awakened him and ran to fetch water.

Heading back, she spotted Rafe and brought him to Liam's side. Rafe was mortified by the boy's condition—barely alive against that tree, his trousers soiled, his breaths faint. He slung the kid over a shoulder, thanked God that the Bloody had not claimed Jule among its dead, and began the hike back to Paternoster, ending his thirty-two hours of sleepless hell here.

Above, in a nest of twigs, a house sparrow looked down upon it all. The din had abated. There were no bullets or screams in the air, so he took wing to see what had happened to his park. From on high, he saw the expanse of the tragedy, and the attempts of a few to bury the many.

It was good to be alive. He filled the sky with song.

SIXTEEN

Byron headed for the Crown camp, his legs and arms aching. Night was coming, and he had carried or carted dozens of wounded today while supervising the transport of hundreds of others, his fellow Habs shuttling the near-dead in a steady stream between the Bloody and Eltham Lake. The number of casualties was staggering. Unfathomable. His last delivery was Boggs, who had fled the battle zone after the explosion of the Canner, badly turning an ankle and then lying in the tall grass of the meadow, awaiting help.

Jule was sleeplessly supervising the care of the wounded here, among them her brother. Evander was mumbling incoherently now, his fever burning without relent. Desperate, Jule spotted Byron and called out: "We need your medicine, Byron! Do you have a price?"

Byron sighed. "I'll bring some. No price."

She nodded a thank-you. Then, "Have you been to Paternoster?"

"No," he replied. "Just the Bloody and here."

"How did the Rogues fare?"

An odd question. He weighed it. "Their losses were heavy."

Jule knew she shouldn't ask, but: "That captain of theirs who was at the palace, the music night. What was his name?"

"Rafe."

"Rafe. Yes. He fought well. How is *he*? Do you know?"

"Injured, but not badly. Said he wouldn't leave the forest until the injured on *both* sides had been evacuated."

A joyous smile threatened to fan across her face. She held it back and muttered, "Good. Can we get you something to eat?"

Byron declined, and headed for the waving fields and meager cabin that were his home.

Darkness had fallen by the time he got there. Everyone in the camp was outside tonight: milling, talking, exhausted. They'd all spent the day as he had, shuttling wounded. The look on every face was shock. And the Habs, tired as they were, couldn't sleep. Minister Dawson shuffled from conversation to conversation. Every cabin was empty and dark.

Except one. Inside Mean's cabin, a candle burned. Byron could see its faint light sneaking under the cabin door. An instinct told him to investigate.

He opened the door, and Mean snapped, *"You don't knock?"*

Byron was glad he hadn't. Before him was a shock:

Maddox, motionless on the floor, his wounded leg exposed. Beneath the skin around his knee was a purple splotch of blood so dark it was nearly black. And his mouth was gagged.

Byron asked, appalled, "What're you doing, Mean?"

"Doctoring!" The peddler grinned. "Saving this man's life!"

"Does his House know he's here?"

"They will, when I ransom him."

"Mean—"

"He's a captain!" Mean exclaimed. "Listed as missing. Know what his safe return would be worth to his House?"

Maddox groaned, his face sweat soaked from pain and shame. Byron felt shame too. He crossed the room calmly...

...then slugged Mean across the temple, dazing the peddler badly. A second punch knocked Mean out cold.

Byron stepped outside and got three friends to help, then offered a bottle of Mean's gin to Maddox, who inhaled it gratefully as the Habs lifted him and moved him into an idle cart. Agony. Byron thanked his mates and began the trek toward the water, which would lead to Paternoster Square. He'd sleep tomorrow.

The Rogue camp was now largely an open-air hospital. Children looked on in silent awe.

The surgeons did all they could, but again, they were implementing twenty-second-century insights with eighteenth-century tools. Henbane and ether weren't enough to put patients out properly, and the suffering was horrendous. More soldiers kept dying, and all Rafe could do was visit them and try to grasp all that had been lost. Many of the wounded were now convalescing in the quarantine tent, which had suddenly become empty, thanks to Byron's discovery.

In a corner of the square, several hundred Crown prisoners of war from the Bloody now huddled behind wooden fencing. Rafe passed them as he headed for the stockade.

It had once been a five-star restaurant called Bergen's, located on the ground floor of the Goldman Sachs building. But it had been stripped bare in the twenty-second century, everything metallic in the kitchen forged for ammunition. Appliances, shelving, countertops, vents, utensils, pans, all gone. Now military prisoners sat in formerly fancy booths, secured there by rope.

That's where Rafe had sent Paris, a kindness bestowed by one captain to another. Rafe entered now and found him.

"I appreciate the courtesy," Paris said, his mouth still swollen, his wrists and feet bound.

"How are they treating you?"

Paris shrugged, then asked, "How much of my army is left?"

"I don't know numbers," Rafe replied.

"Can you find out?"

"Just row over and ask?"

Paris shrugged and let it go. "Our stockade's not as fine as this. Used to be a pig barn."

Rafe breathed out a smile. "Try and get some sleep." Then, respectfully: "I'll get you those numbers if I can."

He emerged minutes later and walked the square. The Crown prisoners were oddly quiet. Numbed, he passed them by. Then a voice rang out from the main gate. "Captain! It's Maddox!"

What? Rafe spun, racing through the open gate to the water's edge.

And there was Byron, nearly unconscious from fatigue, having rowed Maddox here. Rafe hurried to Byron's pirogue. Maddox's eyelids lifted foggily.

"He's had some gin," Byron reported.

"Good," Rafe replied, ordering a few of the guards to get a cart. They hurried away.

Byron nodded to Maddox's leg: "Knee's been shattered."

"We'll see to him. Thank you, Byron." Unable to stop himself, Rafe asked, "How are the Crowns faring?"

"Worse than you," Byron answered. "You won."

"The captain of theirs, the one that played the music—"

Byron was ahead of Rafe now. "Jule."

"Right. That was her name. How is *she*?"

"Well enough to ask about *you*."

A look passed between them—an understanding. Byron's smile said, *It's safe with me.* Rafe paused, humbled and grateful.

The guards returned with a cart. Rafe looked to Byron and asked, "Any gin left?" Byron shook his head.

Breena appeared now, astonished by Byron's kindness.

"I'm glad you survived," he breathed.

"Come in," she said. "We'll feed you."

"That's not necessary."

"It is," she said. "And you can stay here until morning. You look exhausted."

That drew some looks, but Breena went on, "Nothing out there but Bloats and bodies." She extended a hand to him. It remained there, suspended. All eyes upon it.

Byron took it. Rafe smiled, pleased, and Breena led Byron into the camp. Slaughter, oddly, had brought a new decency to this House.

But not to Maud. From the company of fifty that she had led into the Bloody, just nine Rogues had left the forest under their own power. Seven others had been carried out; the other thirty-four had died. And *Rafe*, she now believed, had betrayed them all, ending a battle to save the life of a Crown. She could report that to Shapcott, but doing so without first confronting Rafe directly felt unsoldierly. So she armed herself and appeared at his quarters around one a.m.

Rafe wasn't there.

Rage consumed her. Humiliation too. Suddenly, she *knew*. Everything. And for the first time ever, she didn't want to kill an enemy. She wanted to murder a fellow Rogue.

In the Crown camp, scores of newly orphaned children drifted across the grounds like weightless leaves. Others sat, glassy-eyed, at the base of that mountain of mobile phones. Play seemed impossible today. Their parents, lost in the Bloody, would never come home.

Jule walked through the camp, trying to help. Her heart was in Buckingham Palace—where the music was, where *Rafe* was—but her *duty* was here. Danton approached her, his arm still in a sling, to inform her that General Chasen wanted all his captains to report for a briefing in the bunker. "On the double, please." She followed the boy wearily.

In the bunker, grim work lay ahead; what was left of the Crown Army had to be newly divided into squads, platoons, companies. And

Chasen wanted to know why the hell the Crowns didn't have a grenade like the one the Rogues had just used. No one had an answer. Danton poured water for them.

In a corner she saw Evander. He was barely strong enough to stand, his face fully jaundiced now, his breathing labored. Pride alone kept him upright.

Jule turned, infuriated, as Chasen again gave orders to attack Paternoster. "They think we're whipped," he said. "That makes them vulnerable."

Evander nodded, then collapsed.

Jule felt herself sinking again . . .

Jameson knew the river. No sighted person knew it any better. Today, as London mourned, he followed the sounds, smells, bends, and undulations of the mighty Thames to his home on Prince Consort Road, a building that had once been the Royal College of Music. The water was only two feet deep here. He docked his pirogue.

Six bright young faces awaited him, his own army of sorts. His favorite among them was Carmen, who'd just turned seventeen. She was seven months pregnant. "What do we know?" she asked.

Jameson sighed. "Massive losses."

"My God," she said.

Jameson added, "We may yet see an end to all this."

Jule and two others carried Evander back to the Q tent and laid him on a cot.

He was awake, and feverish. "You promised me you'd rest," she said.

Evander waited until the other two Crowns left, then mumbled back, "Boggs says you stabbed Pritchett."

She recovered fast. "I did. He was about to kill a wounded child."

"A Rogue?"

"A CHILD."

Evander studied her. "What's happened to you?"

Jule's face was stone. "If you try to get up again, I'll have them restrain you."

Suddenly, she was unknowable to him. It felt intolerable.

She left the tent and passed the forge, where Big Lil sat motionless. The two women eyed each other.

"I'm glad you survived," Lil said.

Jule just kept walking—to the gate, where she grabbed a pirogue and rowed for Buckingham Palace in the dark. That fast, she felt a bit lighter, as if the stones in her pockets were magically vanishing.

Of course, maybe he wouldn't be there. It was likely that throwing that bomb, and saving her, had unmasked him—which meant right now he could be facing a court-martial. *For her.* But she kept rowing. Rafe was *life*. She had to get to him.

He was, at that moment, lying on his back atop the aging wooden floor in the palace study where the music had first stunned him. Jule was the world now—the touch, sight, sound, smell, and taste of her.

Jule was beauty. And beauty would save him. He rolled onto his side and prayed she was on her way there. Two moths danced into his line of sight, hearing a music all their own.

Eltham was two miles behind her now, and the sky was quiet; the only sounds in the world were her oars hitting the oily water and her own breathing as she silently hoped—prayed—that Rafe would somehow get to the palace and wait for her.

Yes, he would. He was so capable, so determined. She kept commanding her arms to row.

Then she heard the rumbling.

It was a sound she'd never heard before, entirely foreign to her, coming from upriver, in the darkness. She was rowing *toward* it, her back to it. A deep guttural growling noise; yet it didn't sound animal at all, or alive or organic. But it was real . . . and it was growing louder in that darkness, as if closing in on her fast. She looked over her shoulder but saw nothing. *Keep rowing, keep rowing . . .*

The noise grew louder, more muscular, more foreign. She looked over her shoulder again—

And her eyes went wide with utter shock. Astonishment.

Approaching on her starboard side . . . was a boat ten times larger than her own. And *no one was rowing it.*

Yet it was moving. Rapidly. Somehow cutting through the water. Propelling itself by means of a *motor* mounted on its stern—a functioning, mechanized piece of machinery, with a gas-fed engine churning water in its wake. A *patrol boat*, centuries old. A ghost.

Impossible. But *here*. Moving. A motorboat. A gunship.

Its hull was metal, painted a dull gray. On its bow was the insignia of a flag (Russian, she would later learn). Standing on its port side, staring at her now, were two Russian soldiers, each carrying rifles. They seemed unsurprised by the sight of her. Almost bored. On a railing was a round metal circle of harsh white light, impossibly bright, like the sun. One of the soldiers swiveled it around and focused it on Jule, the beam instantly stabbing her eyes. She shut them tight and covered her face with her hands, but too late. All she could see now was a giant blue *dot*. She was alone, adrift, and now blinded by the first electric light she'd ever seen in her life. It was terrifying.

The soldiers turned it away, and she forced her eyes to squint open, just a bit. But the hot blue dot remained, seared into her retinas. She heard the sailors' voices now, speaking in a tongue she didn't understand.

People. From somewhere *else*. Soldiers. *Here*. In a machine. And she couldn't see them—or anything. A helpless feeling. Perhaps they were as tired as she was. She'd never know. But one of them hit a throttle and the big gray gunship roared loudly, its bow rising while its stern pushed deeper in the water as it accelerated up the river, sending out waves that jostled Jule's narrow wooden pirogue like a toy.

Then it was gone, its exhaust sticking to the air. The waves beneath her fanned out, then became less frothy until everything was flat, like always.

The world was the world again. The water was the water. The present was the present. The monster was a memory. Yet the hot blue dot still blinded her. So she sat, unable to breathe, her wits scrambled, her pirogue gliding aimlessly, the banks a mystery to her.

This had not been a faceless MiG flying so high overhead that Jule could somehow pretend it'd been a mirage. This had been *real, present, physical.* It had power; it had an engine. It made noise and pumped exhaust. It carried soldiers and those soldiers carried weapons. Worse, they'd been utterly unsurprised to find her, as if they'd *expected* to. Did that mean they'd been in London awhile? *Watching them?* It had owned this river, *her* river. Close enough to *move* her in the water, to rock her. It rocked her still.

She sat a few moments longer, in the blackout, her pirogue idly drifting, then bumping into a half-submerged post. She blinked her eyes open and gasped with relief that the blue dot was fading. The night's contours began to appear. A hazy orb in the distance slowly gelled into the moon. Minutes after that, she could see her oars, and her hands, and her arms and feet. She'd never appreciated vision more than she did in this moment.

When it had returned, she began to row again, disturbing the kelp on the water's surface. Soon, she arrived at the palace and saw Rafe's pirogue tethered to a broken window frame.

Rafe. *Love.* More than ever, Jule needed to see him now. She docked and secured her craft, climbing into the building.

The hallways felt longer tonight, darker too. And the air felt heavy. She wanted to call out his name, but that would be suicide. What if someone else were here instead? She got to their study . . .

And there he was. Bringer of death, bringer of life.

"They're here, Rafe. They're on the river. I saw them."

Somehow, Rafe knew who she meant. He held on tight.

SEVENTEEN

Jule described the patrol boat for him, over and over—its dimensions, its power, the guns, the motor . . . None of it felt real. But it was. And so was this: *They are HERE. Not overhead.* Here. *And they know we're here too.*

"It felt like a scout," she said. "A pre-invasion scout."

"Peterborough, Jule," Rafe said. "Let's get away."

"Rafe, there's no leaving all this. How can I leave my House? How can *you?*"

"Our Houses are dead. If we don't leave, *we'll* die too. So will Breena. And Nelly. And probably half the Habs."

"Our place is here."

"Our place is with each other. Don't you know that?"

No, she didn't. And no amount of optimism could get her there. Rafe tried, "I nearly lost you in the Bloody. I can't risk that again. I need you with me, where I can *see* you."

She kissed him. The thought of losing him was unfathomable. When their lips parted, she offered, "Thanks. For not letting your friends kill me."

"We had a date," he joked.

She smiled without meaning to. "You're mad."

He returned, "Never felt saner in my whole life. Let's put on some music." He rose and pulled the Victrola from its usual cabinet, cranking it. Frank Sinatra sang about being young at heart . . .

Rafe let the sounds linger for a moment, then: "Byron knows about us."

Jule went silent and stiff. Exposure meant death.

"It'll be safe with him," Rafe added.

She hoped so. Rafe rose and offered her his hand, to dance. She studied it.

"We fight a lot," she said.

"No, we don't," he returned. "*You* fight a lot. I just happen to be here."

She rose, and they swayed softly to the music. Not really dancing, just rocking, eyes locked. He kissed her hand. "How do you feel about mutiny?" he asked.

"You're doing it again," she said. "I'm *not* going anywhere . . ."

"No, no. Not sailing away. You take command over your House, I take command over mine. And the war ends."

Oh. That actually sounded possible.

"Chasen's lost his mind," she said.

"Then you owe it to your House to replace him. And I owe it to mine." Jule shook her head. Rafe went on, "You want to save people. *This* is how. We end the fight. We *lead*." She was actually imagining it. So he added, "Jule the Peacemaker!"

She eyed him. "You do like to say huge things."

He smiled. "Would your brother help?"

"Might be a lot for him, ending three hundred years of fighting *and* hearing his sister is sleeping with a Rogue in a single afternoon."

Rafe loved that. "Okay. We'll save the world first. *Then* we'll invite him to the wedding."

She shook her head. "WHO ARE YOU?" No reply. She tried again. "Didn't anybody train you to hate your enemies?"

"I've hated my whole life. This feels better. You *love* me, Jule."

That knocked her back. "I do?"

"Yeah," he replied. "You do. Doesn't matter that you can't say it."

She laughed. They both knew he was right.

But just then, suddenly, Rafe stopped swaying, his body rigid.

"Something's wrong," he said.

"What?"

"Do you smell that? Smoke?"

Jule pointed to her nose, reminding him.

"Something's burning," he said. He left the room. She followed into that long corridor, where they both stared in shock—

It was engulfed in flames. An inferno.

The walls, the ceiling, all on fire—a muscular heat, knocking Rafe and Jule back. She looked to her left, into another room, where an even *worse* shock greeted her.

There stood Evander, holding a torch to a back wall, setting it ablaze too. He looked crazed—sleepless and manic—the flames making his skin look even yellower than it had before. His mind had snapped.

Jule could barely speak. "Vander!"

Evander didn't reply. He seemed unreachable. Rafe said quietly, "Captain."

Evander moved to another wall and touched the torch to it as well. The old wood ignited quickly. "Never again, Jule," Evander said. His eyes were murderous.

Jule shook her head. The flames growled as they ate the room.

"Captain," Rafe tried again.

Evander just breathed. He seemed possessed.

But the dying had to stop. Rafe removed the long-knife on his hip and handed it to Jule. The flames were getting louder, hungrier. Rafe started toward Evander, who stood, torch in hand. "Captain," Rafe began, crossing the room. "You and I aren't enemies anymore."

No reply came from Evander. The flames kept growing.

"Our Houses are dead, Evander. You know that. The whole thing has to end."

Again, no reply. He wasn't Evander anymore. The illness had wrecked him.

"Vander, you're sick," Jule tried. "You need rest."

Rafe kept drifting closer. When they were close enough to touch, he paused. The heat from Evander's torch was fierce. Rafe extended a hand to his rival captain.

"Please," said Rafe. "For Jule."

That fast, Evander slammed the torch down on Rafe's arm, setting Rafe's shirtsleeve on fire.

Jule hurried forward as Rafe patted out the flames. "I'm not going to fight you," he said.

Evander swung the torch at Rafe's head. Rafe ducked it, his arm screaming.

"Vander, stop!" Jule implored.

"*You don't get to talk!*" Evander shouted, swinging it at both of them now. The whole room was ablaze around them, and they could hear the hallway collapsing. Windows were the only way out . . . into the water. Evander swung the torch again.

"Don't do this, Evander," Rafe tried.

"Vander, please—" Jule echoed.

"*Don't!*" Evander yelled, crying now. Flames were everywhere. Rafe danced away from the torch as best he could.

"Please, Evander," Rafe said. "There's a whole other war coming. We're going to be *brothers* in that one—"

That was too much. Evander extended the torch like a lance and charged Rafe with a guttural roar. The flames were terrifying. Rafe sidestepped the charge and threw a right hand into Evander's jaw, catching it flush. One punch, and the Crown captain was unconscious. He spun and fell backward into the flaming wall. The torch spilled its fire onto his front while the wall behind him ignited his back.

And that fast, he was engulfed.

Flames ate his clothing, his hair. He awakened and shrieked in pain, arms flailing. Rafe and Jule started toward him. "VANDER!"

But he staggered forward, across the room, and fell, his head slamming into the casing of a window.

A liquid *snap* of the neck and he was dead. Burning, and dead.

Rafe tried to get closer to the body, but the flames were too big, and there was nothing in this room that could tamp them down. Jule couldn't move at all. Her brother lay ten feet away, incinerating. The sounds were ungodly.

Rafe reached for her, spoke her name. "Jule . . ." She pushed his arm away.

The walls around them were beginning to bend; soon they'd collapse entirely.

The heat was unbearable. And the look on Jule's face was empty, glassy, almost catatonic.

Rafe tried again. "Jule, we have to go."

She didn't respond, as if she hadn't heard him. "Jule!" Rafe shouted.

She turned, a hollow look in her eyes, and floated past him, sleepwalking into the study. Something told him not to follow; so he stood, motionless, his head swimming. The smell of the burning corpse was intolerable. And the floor was beginning to catch fire as well. When Jule returned, the Victrola was in her arms. And that same empty look filled her eyes.

"I'm sorry," Rafe said. "You know I didn't mean to—" She drifted by him again, like a phantom. "Jule . . . wait." The vacancy in her eyes . . . She climbed out the window, mumbling, "The records will melt." Then she was gone.

Rafe dashed through flames to get to the study, where he grabbed as many records as he could hold. The palace was defenseless now. Hungry flames everywhere. He got to the nearest window, climbed out, and slipped into the cold water below, holding the records above his head. Jule was doing the same with the Victrola, despite its weight. She was fierce, even in grief.

"Jule!" he called out. "I'm sorry! I love you!"

Again, no reply. Jule was somewhere else. She boarded her pirogue and cast off its line. Her brother was dead. Her lover had killed him. Pain filled every breath.

Her body rowed on its own. Arms, legs, back—they knew what to do. Soon all these flames would tear the palace down and consume everything inside. But then they would hit the river . . . and die.

No, she thought, *you can't burn the water.*

Rafe stood in the shoulder-deep blackness, watching her push the river away. His face felt hot. His heart hurt. He took the hymnal from his coat and held it up to keep it dry. He could follow her to Eltham, he knew that. But it would be folly. She wouldn't listen. And he'd be shot on sight.

So they rowed in opposite directions, leaving behind a palace whose top two floors were consumed by a raging and giant midnight sun, all that brilliant white and yellow reflecting on the slick black mirror of the greedy river.

Jule's pirogue looked tiny. And Rafe felt weak and small—defeated—as he rowed their records to safety. Some Rogue, no doubt, would ask him what those strange discs were, and where he'd gotten them. He couldn't imagine a sufficient reply. But leaving them to burn would be unthinkable.

They were music. They were Jule . . .

The building was screaming now, centuries-old wood and metal howling in a final surrender to the inevitable. Once-noble walls breaking and bending, defenseless. Smoke curling up toward the moon. Monarchs had walked these floors. Their ghosts were no doubt burning now too. And no one—not Rogue nor Crown nor Hab—would ever know that this palace, now suffering a violent death, had given *life* to two people. No one would know that love itself had been born there, had danced there, had hidden there.

And now had burned there. Rafe grieved it like a relative.

Jule's pirogue was halfway to Eltham before the fugue began to slowly release its grip on her. Her senses crept back, and she awakened a bit, surprised to find herself rowing. She turned and looked back to see the glow of the firelight above the palace. In the morning, nothing would be left of it. She knew—to her core—that she would never see Rafe again. The water would win. The water *always* won. That made her feel ill.

My brother is dead. My lover killed him. Russians have found this river. With every stroke, every breath, the horrid realities bit into her like a Bloat. Catatonia had been easier. She began to anticipate the questions that would await her once she got to camp. *Where was Evander? Had she seen him?* Perhaps he'd told others where he was going, and why. If so, she'd be court-martialed, perhaps even shot.

Then Crown soldiers would take this Victrola and, unable to guess what it was, they'd tear it apart and repurpose its pieces. Wood, rubber, metal. She wouldn't let that happen. The box was music. The box was Rafe. She sniffed back a tear and rowed for home.

Sleep eluded Byron now; there was just too much grief. And he knew Buckingham was on fire. *Everyone* knew. As he turned onto his side, he heard a sound at his door. Someone was there.

Byron rose, crossed to it, opened it.

And there stood *Jameson*. Waiting. Blind. But here.

Byron shook his head in wonder. Jameson said quietly, "It's time, Byron."

"For what?"

"Change. Before it *all* goes up in flames."

Byron invited him in and shut the door. Jameson continued, "The Houses have had their time; all they've done is kill one another. It's *your* time now—time to lead your people."

"Into war?"

"Into *peace*. Don't you want *more* than this for them?"

"Of course."

"Then *take* it. The water is receding; the world has found us. You can *save* them."

"How?"

Jameson grinned, hope fanning across his face.

EIGHTEEN

The river felt like mud against his oars.

Rafe had always loved the feeling of moving the water, pushing it aside so he could get somewhere. Not tonight. Tonight the river was pushing back; the sky was unnaturally bright, and the air tasted wrong.

Jule was lost to him. That was all. Nothing mattered but her forgiveness. He stared at all those orphaned records at his feet. Without a Victrola, they meant only longing. And their home, their temple, was gone now. He shook his head. Then—

"HALT!"

There were two pirogues off his starboard side, a pair of Rogue soldiers in each. Rafe stopped rowing. He knew these soldiers; he'd trained them. Two male, two female. Finch, Anders, Blakeley, and Shamir. Their pirogues now abutted his. Random patrol? He doubted it. More likely, they were looking for *him*.

"Captain," Blakeley announced, "General Shapcott would like to see you."

Rafe had always liked Blakeley. He knew her to be honest. "Good," he said. "I'd like to see him too. I'll follow you."

"No, sir," she said. "Need you to board one of ours."

"Oh," Rafe said. "How many were sent out to find me?"

"Just need you to board one of ours," she repeated, a grim expression on her face. No one in this army would ever take pleasure in treating Rafe like a fugitive. Or a traitor.

Rafe reached for the records at his feet—but as soon as his hands disappeared from the eyelines of the soldiers, all four of them reached for knives.

Rafe froze. Eyed them. "It's as bad as all that?" he asked. None replied. He grabbed the records. "These are music." The soldiers stared, confused. "Very precious," he added.

"We'll safeguard them for you. Finch, you can row the captain's pirogue back to camp."

"Yes, ma'am," Finch responded.

Behind Rafe, the flames of Buckingham Palace roared noisily into the sky, and the air was ash. Blakeley nodded toward the conflagration and asked, "Know how that happened, sir?"

"A Russian patrol boat with a flamethrower."

Blakeley asked, "Been drinking tonight, Captain?"

"Just take me to Shapcott." Rafe extended a hand, inviting Finch onto the pirogue. Finch took it.

The rest was a blur.

Rafe yanked Finch hard toward the water, and Finch fell in. That fast, Rafe dove into the cold river and went deep, instantly hidden by the oily black surface. He swam as hard as he could, blind in the darkness, kicking and pulling and pushing the water out of his way. Behind him was the frantic rowing of two pirogues, and the muted voices of the soldiers. Adrenaline rocketed through him. But it was hard not to think of the records he'd left behind.

He swam until he hit a wooden wall and surfaced inside what had once been a hardware shop. Behind him, three soldiers were in their pirogues, zeroing in. Blakeley, Anders, and Shamir. Finch was far behind.

Rafe dove down again, swimming for the hardware shop's back exit, its door long since torn off. He swam through the opening, surfaced, and climbed to the shop's roof. The Hab fields were to the west. Elevation lay there—a chance to run.

So he hurried along this rooftop, leaping to the roof of the neighboring shop, silhouetted by the brilliant light of the Buckingham fire, each footstep soaked and heavy.

His pursuers climbed to the hardware shop rooftop, just as he had. "Captain!" Blakeley hollered. "Halt!"

A six-foot gap lay between the rooftop he was on and that of the next shop, which had a fire-escape ladder mounted on its side. Rafe made the leap and got his hands on the ladder, slamming into it. Then he climbed.

They followed. One by one. He had trained them well. "Captain! Halt!"

They wouldn't shoot. Rafe felt sure of it. He dove from this rooftop into the water again, surfacing again, climbing again, scampering across more rooftops.

"Captain! Halt!"

Into the water again. It was shallower here, knee-deep. Legs heavy, muscles screaming, lungs empty—this was the Churn. He'd never felt it before. Maybe it came with wanting to live. To his right, a Bloat began to surface, coming at him. Rafe got to the nearest structure, the facade of what had once been a massage parlor, and up he climbed. The Bloat paused, as if to watch him go.

The soldiers did not relent—Finch still far behind, but gaining. Blakeley scaled the massage parlor. Anders and Shamir too. All of them reached its roof, following Rafe as he made his next connective leap.

But as *Finch* reached for that same facade, the Bloat got him.

One bite. Finch howled, tried to keep climbing. But the poison was too much. He slid back into the water.

Rafe knew that two rooftops away was land—actual pavement, above the waterline—an escape that might mean seeing Jule again. So he jumped, landing hard, running around a corner . . .

. . . and into capture.

Two more Rogue soldiers were here, approaching this same corner from the other direction. Rafe stopped, breathless. Soaked. He had trained these two also; the names were Rodman and Verrone. "Captain," Verrone breathed. His knife was out. "Your weapon, please."

Rafe surrendered. "I don't have one."

Blakeley, Anders, and Shamir caught up now, rounding the corner and bringing the total of captors to five, knives out, patience expended.

Rafe eyed Blakeley. "Is Finch all right?"

"Bloat got him," she replied flatly.

That hit hard. Rafe breathed, "I'm sorry."

She reined in a reaction. "Let's get you back to camp now."

Rafe nodded. Then everything changed.

First came a loud THUMP. Blakeley suddenly pitched forward, face-first onto the concrete. She'd been hit by an oar . . . swung by Jule in the ashy darkness.

Rafe hadn't seen her coming. No one had. Now Jule held the oar with both hands in front of her chest, punching with it, its blunt ends striking Anders across the jaw, then Shamir.

Rafe lunged forward to help, but Verrone tackled him, slamming him to the ground. Everything got woozy, shadowy. Shapes moved in and out of light. Sounds wobbled. And the cobwebs thickened. His body wouldn't move. He heard more of those hollow thumps. Hard wood striking wrists and chests and jaws and temples, all of it inhumanly fast. Groans, cries, falls. Somehow, Jule was disabling these soldiers with that oar. And then it was done. His head was still swimming.

Her hand came toward him. He grabbed it. She pulled him up like deadweight and he got to his feet unsteadily. On the pavement were five soldiers, alive but incapacitated. "You should go," Jule breathed.

"With you?" he asked shakily.

"Just go."

"Jule, I'm sorry."

"Go!"

"Please hear me. I'm so sorry."

She studied him. Then: "You're the worst idea I ever had." Sadness behind that. Pain and regret. It broke his heart.

"I love you," he tried again.

"Go."

She turned and left him there, heading around a corner. As he followed, she got to her pirogue and pushed off. He started to wade toward her. "I'm sorry," he repeated.

"Will that bring my brother back?"

He had no reply. She and the Victrola rowed away.

An hour later, he dragged himself across the Hab fields where Byron had long toiled, and reached the row of cabins as the camp slept. He dropped to the ground and pulled himself on his elbows into the crawl space beneath Byron's cabin. Nothing but mud and worms and fetid air down here. But it was shelter. The sun would not be up for another two hours.

Stillness, at last. Quiet. He lay on his back and stared at the bottoms of the floorboards just inches from his face. His head ached. His body was shivering inside wet clothing. His socks were soaked. Behind his eyelids there was nothing but Jule: *Hating him. The worst idea she'd ever had.* And the records—what would become of them?

The coming day promised little. For the first time he could remember, he wept.

NINETEEN

Jule returned via pirogue to a Crown camp that was abuzz, even in this predawn hour. Citizens and soldiers stood, entranced by the bright night sky, gossiping, guessing. A light wind had blown ashes toward Eltham. Jule couldn't smell them, but she could taste them on her tongue as she debarked, Victrola in her arms.

Chasen was the first to approach her, asking if she'd seen Evander. She swallowed hard, said she hadn't. Then asked why.

"He went out, didn't give a reason." That drove the guilt deeper into her chest. The last thing her brother had done as an officer in this army had been to lie, to protect *her*. "Let's assemble a search party," she said. "I'll lead it."

"Need you *here*, Jule," Chasen replied. "With the wounded."

"General, he's my brother. With your leave, I'll lead."

"As you wish."

She asked, "No more talk of attacking, then?"

Chasen sighed. "Just find him."

Two hours of sleep weren't much. As Rafe awoke, his head throbbed and his throat tasted like spoiled meat. His damp clothes stuck to his skin and rubbed it raw. And he couldn't tell if the insects crawling across his torso were imaginary or real. He was sure that he would never again feel clean.

Directly above him were the sounds of stirring. Byron's footsteps. Rafe tapped on the underside of the floorboards, repeatedly. Byron's footsteps stopped. Rafe continued to tap.

A moment later, Rafe heard the door open, and he saw Byron's feet appear, just beyond the crawl space. Then the Hab dropped down to investigate, his eyes quickly going wide. From Byron's perspective, Rafe appeared to have this cabin sitting on his chest. "What're you doing here?" Byron asked.

"I'm a fugitive," Rafe said. "Can you get me into the Crown camp?"

Byron sighed. The idea sounded like suicide. Even kneeling down to talk to him like this was a risk.

"Please," Rafe added. "I have to get to her."

Byron paused for what felt like forever. Then: "Jameson came to see me. He has plans. You should know that."

"I hope they're good ones."

Byron exhaled hard. "Don't move. We'll go when the sun's down. I'll try to get you some food."

"I don't need food."

"Just don't move." Then Byron vanished.

At that same moment, Jule rowed sleeplessly atop the swollen Thames, flanked on all sides by her fellow Crowns, searching for a brother she already knew was dead. Chasen and the captains had been pointing all morning to the palace, a soldierly sense that Evander's disappearance had to be connected in some way to the fire. So this flotilla was heading there, Jule in the lead despite deep exhaustion.

Her last three days had been Rafe, risk, battle, death, blood, casualties, defeat, a patrol boat, her brother's immolation, and a series of giant lies about it. No sleep. No time to breathe. And now she might be called upon to identify a body; she prayed it had floated away. Each time she closed her eyes all she saw was her brother in flames, his neck snapping, his life ending.

Because of me . . .

As the pirogues cleared a grove of aquatic trees, the now-skeletal palace appeared, rising lifelessly out of the briny river. The soldiers gasped at the sight of torched columns framed by blue sky—empty space where walls and rooms and a rooftop had been for ages. History, gone.

Jule mourned it. And so much else.

All around her, soldiers now tied their pirogues to the remaining ribs of the palace, which were charred black down to the waterline. She rowed forth and stared into the water, able for the first time ever to see into first-floor rooms that no longer had a ceiling above them. So she could suddenly view them as they'd been preserved, oddly pristine, for centuries. It was like looking into a dollhouse without a roof. The past. One of the spaces now visible beneath the surface was a grand ballroom, under five feet of water. Kings and queens once danced there, unconcerned by the vast calamity that was coming their way.

"Captain?" someone called to her. Jule turned. It was a young private who explained, "They have something."

Jule rowed toward a pillar rising out of the water. A charred body had lodged itself against it—water lapping at the human form, its clothes and face burned beyond recognition.

Evander. Her brother. Brave captain. Loyal Crown. His body now carbonized. Jule recoiled. Beside her, Boggs said flatly, "It's him. Sorry."

"How do you know?" Jule replied, although she knew.

Boggs leaned down and lifted the corpse's blackened left hand out of the water. There was a wedding band on its ring finger. The only jewelry in all of London. Boggs held it up. "See?"

All eyes on Jule now; she turned her face away, as if to hide her grief—which was very real. "The general will want to know of this immediately," she mumbled. "I'll tell him." With that, she grabbed the ring and rowed for Eltham. The men and women watching her all agreed: No braver soldier had ever served this House.

The trip back was long and lonely. She was tired and thinking too much: *Rafe didn't kill my brother. I did.*

There was no one aboard to disagree with her.

Upon arriving at the Crown camp, she briefed Chasen, then walked to Big Lil's forge, where she slapped the wedding ring down and said, as if ordering a sweet, "One slugger, please."

Big Lil quickly complied, and the family heirloom became ammunition. That seemed fitting now.

Rafe spent a lifetime beneath Byron's cabin, watching a Hab workday from the stale darkness, flat on his back. This was harvest season, and Habs large and small poured hours into threshing, cutting, gathering, carrying, struggling, as Rogue guards periodically strolled past, looking for signs of lapsed productivity.

Rafe saw it all while drifting in and out of sleep—feeling hunger, thirst, exhaustion, despair, and deep shame as he watched the toil of the Habs. Theirs was constant effort. But unity too. They all seemed to be helping one another, like limbs of a single organism. Rafe wondered why he hadn't stopped to watch them before.

The sun finally dipped, and the Habs came in from the fields bearing sacks of grain. Rafe's muscles had all cramped into one unyielding block. His back and legs had stiffened; every inch of him hurt. Byron knelt down again at the crawl space, extending a skin filled with water. Rafe downed it greedily.

"You've been bountied by both Houses," Byron reported. "The guards here were told to look for you."

"I understand," Rafe said. "If you don't want to help me—"

"Of course I don't *want* to help you," Byron interrupted. "But let's go. Take that armband off."

Rafe removed it, then rolled out from beneath the cabin, his body utterly wrecked. "I don't think I can walk," he said.

"That won't matter."

Rafe didn't understand at first. But soon he was beneath a tarp inside Byron's cart as the Hab pushed it toward the edge of the Hab camp. Two Rogue guards stopped him, questioning him out of habit. "Where to?" one asked.

"Eltham," Byron replied. "Found three more of their dead at the Bloody." He pulled back the tarp, revealing three bloody bodies: two dead Crowns in rigor mortis and a deathly still Rafe, face down, crammed between them.

The guards nodded with distaste. One said half mockingly, "Aren't you too famous to be pushing corpses?"

Byron shrugged that off. "Gotta respect the dead." He put the tarp back in place and pushed along. In the cart, Rafe kept still. The stench around him was horrendous.

Yet there he lay as Byron pushed the cart to the water, then onto a wide wooden raft, and rowed upstream to Eltham—the two corpses pressing against Rafe, their weight shifting each time a ripple on the water made the raft lift or settle, their rot dancing in and out of his lungs each time he drew a breath.

At the main Crown gate, Byron climbed off the raft and pushed the cart toward two bored Crown guards. They'd seen waves of bodies since the Bloody, many of them delivered by Byron, who was indeed now a celebrity. One guard asked, "More?"

"More," Byron replied.

"Thank you, Byron."

Byron shrugged. They waved him through.

The sun was down now, and most Crowns had retreated to their quarters. Some ate quietly. Byron rolled the cart past them to a shadowy spot behind Big Lil's forge. There, Rafe's ride mercifully came to an end. He rolled off the cart, his joints stiff. The stench of death deep in his chest.

"Her place is there," Byron said, pointing at Jule's dormitory building. "Second floor, facing the lake."

"Thank you."

"If they see you—any of them—they'll kill you."

"I know."

"Might kill her too."

Rafe grabbed a few items Byron had stashed beneath the bodies—trousers and a shirt, the daily uniform of the Habs. Rafe desperately needed a wash after that ride. "Thank you, Byron."

"Good luck." Byron nodded.

At the lake, Rafe shed his clothes and waded in, soaking his head beneath the surface as he scrubbed three days of dying and disaster off his skin. Then he emerged, and threw on the peasant garb Byron had provided, plus boots. Still unseen, he headed for her dormitory. There, he noted the strangler fig tree that grew beside the building, its leafy branches extending over the roof. He climbed it stealthily, crawled along its branches, and dropped quietly to the dormitory's flat rooftop. A skylight appeared, a few feet away. It had a latch.

He crept toward the skylight and opened it carefully. Then he lay flat on his belly—and painstakingly peeked inside.

Nothing moved in there. No signs of life at all except for the flame of a single candle. Where was she?

Behind him.

"Up, Hab," came her voice as the edge of her long-knife pressed against the back of his neck. Somehow she'd heard him from below and climbed up to this roof without a sound. A warrior.

"Jule, it's me," he said, his body perfectly still. "Me."

He half turned his head, catching just enough moonlight for her to see his profile. Her knees threatened to buckle. It was forever until she spoke.

"You'll get us both killed."

"*Not seeing you* was killing me," he replied, reaching for her hand. "I'm so sorry, Jule—"

"Don't," she replied, shaking her head. "Don't ever talk again. I don't want to hear your voice anymore."

"Jule, I—"

She cut him off. "I hate you even more than I hate all of them. *They* never tricked me into believing anything."

She was crying now. It gutted him.

"It wasn't a trick," he said. "I promise." He got to his feet, close to her. She didn't recoil. He put a hand to her face, wiping her tears away. She still bore that knife.

"I'm sorry," he repeated.

"I hate you," she repeated.

Her tears kept coming. Again, "I hate you." But the knife fell from her grasp. He kissed her, his hands on her face. Those arms, the ones she'd once longed to touch, they were around her now, pulling her close. He was death, he was life, he was everything. Mostly, he was hers, all hers. And that's what she wanted.

The night was cool and the moon was high. Rafe and Jule pulled each other down to the rooftop in an urgent tangle, breathless and sacred. A couple.

Later, they lay in her quarters by the light of that single candle. Behind her was the Victrola, which made Rafe think again of the records he'd left behind. He hoped they'd been saved.

"Thank you for rescuing me from my soldiers," he said.

"That? I just made a wrong turn and happened to see you."

"Don't ever lose that." He grinned. "That edge of yours. It'll keep us young."

"Yeah," she mumbled. "Young."

Her brother was dead. Her world was on fire. Yet Rafe was here and she was open to him. That confounded her.

"I've been bountied," Rafe said.

"Then you should go. It's almost light."

The urge to run away with her felt powerful. But he knew he couldn't. The dying had to stop. "I'll be all right. I can get my House to listen." She handed him a gold armband. He went on, "I'm going to make them understand. You have to do that too. You have to lead your House."

"I don't *want* to lead my House," she said.

"No," he laughed. "You just want to lead *me!*"

She laughed too, her eyes wet. "Yes. That would be nice."

He eyed her adoringly. "We're going to end this war," he said. "You and me."

It seemed impossible. She sighed. "You have to go, love."

She'd never used that word before. It filled him. They held each other and tried to say goodbye. But prying themselves apart felt impossible, and another hour passed before they actually let go. They really had bet everything on each other. He couldn't leave her.

But he had to. A last embrace, then he climbed out that same skylight, onto her roof, and along the branches of that same strangler fig tree, then down to the ground, landing lightly, right in front of . . .

Nelly, who opened her window and asked, "Rafe?" He nodded. She went on, "You'd better run. Don't want you getting caught."

"Thank you." He swallowed hard, then turned and ran. Someday, maybe, they'd meet again.

He skirted around the lake, into a grove thick with more strangler figs, until he found the perimeter wall at the back of the camp, unguarded. He climbed it and disappeared into the night, shedding the gold armband . . .

At that same moment, *another* Rogue soldier arrived at the main Crown gate, beneath a white flag.

Maud. It was somewhere near five a.m.

The guards here aimed weapons at her; she didn't flinch. Instead she said, "Bring me to General Chasen."

"Like hell we will."

"Bring me to General Chasen. I have information he needs."

"Who the hell're you to be giving orders?"

"I'm a captain in the army that just routed you at the Bloody. Bring me to General Chasen."

"Rogue bitch."

"I'll wait."

Chasen soon came to her, arriving at the gate alone and greeting her under watchful eyes. "I'd appreciate it if you'd state your business quickly, Captain," he said.

Maud complied: "A trusted member of your inner circle has betrayed you, General."

Chasen reacted, then glanced back at his sentries. Yes, they'd heard it too. "Walk with me," he said to Maud.

She obliged, and they strolled outside the oaken wall. "Please say more," the general requested.

She began, "You have a captain who has coupled with a Rogue."

The idea sickened him. "Why are you telling me this?"

She hesitated. "Because the Rogue was meant to have been coupled with *me*."

Chasen's breaths began to grow shorter. "Who?" he asked.

"Don't you know?" Maud replied. "The one you adopted when her parents died. The one you raised as your own and groomed to be your successor. Jule."

Chasen's knees weakened, and his stomach turned. "This is a lie."

"No," Maud returned. "And it's how Evander died."

That was damning. Chasen whispered, "Say more."

Minutes later, Jule was in her bed when she heard her door open. A grin fanned her face. He was back.

No. He wasn't. Instead, four Crown soldiers barged in, sent here to place her under arrest. The soldiers pinned her, restrained her, and carried her from her quarters like a criminal.

Downstairs, Nelly heard a commotion outside her door. She peeked out and saw a horror: Jule, struggling and kicking, being carried away by four Crown soldiers.

Nelly tried to intercede, but they pushed her over like a standing broom, and she fell to the floor. War was hell.

They carried Jule outside the building and into the night.

As dawn broke, having run, swum, and hidden, Rafe appeared on Prince Consort Road and moved furtively toward Jameson's building, climbing to the top floor, room 301. Again, there was no lock on the door, no handle... but he knocked as a gesture of respect. Footsteps shuffled within. Then the door opened. And there was Jameson.

"I need your help," Rafe said.

"I know. Come in."

TWENTY

Rafe and Jameson discussed it all: Jule, the Russians, Byron and the Habs, the falling of the water. Then Rafe slept for ten hours and woke up at midday. Jameson was gone.

Rafe stood and looked around, impressed by the order in here—everything in its place. There were even a few books. A Bible, *Paradise Lost*, others. The door opened, and Jameson entered alongside Carmen and a young woman named Daisy, who bore supplies and bread. Again, they were neither Rogue nor Crown nor Hab. Rafe found it dazzling, but reassuring too.

"The House of Jameson," he breathed. Carmen's belly had grown. Her movements were slower.

Jameson replied, "I've been considering your predicament, Rafe. And I've decided: All this death has to end now. And you have to end it."

"I know."

"You have to return to your House and tell Shapcott about the patrol boat, as if you'd seen it yourself."

"I don't know how to get him to listen."

"If you walk in there as a *prisoner*, he won't," Jameson said. "You have to march up to the gates on your own, a free man, as if you've come back to *save* them."

"Can you safeguard me there?"

"No. You're a fugitive. If Rogue soldiers spotted us on the water they'd arrest us both. And I don't fancy being a prisoner."

That sounded true. Awful, but true. Jameson added, "But I think I can help you get there on your own."

"They're looking for me everywhere," Rafe said.

"Not everywhere," Jameson replied. "Come with me."

Carmen and Daisy moved to a table. On it was a contraption Rafe had seen in pictures but never in person. It was centuries old, yet seemed remarkably well-preserved: a stainless steel cylindrical tank connected to rubber tubing, and a mouthpiece. It also had a glass face mask attached. "For the water," Jameson reported.

For the water. To allow a person to *breathe* under the water. People had done this centuries ago, routinely.

Carmen said, "Self-contained underwater breathing apparatus."

Awed, Rafe ran his fingers over the tank. "Where did you . . . ? How did you . . . ?"

Jameson smiled humbly, nodding to the women. "They're *my* rovers, found this years ago. Just never had anyone desperate enough to *need* it before now. I believe this part goes in your mouth." He handed Rafe the breather. Rafe inserted it into his mouth and inhaled. Incredibly, there was air in there. "It works," he reported.

The women eyed him, almost insulted. "Then it will get you home," Jameson said.

"How?" Rafe asked.

"You can take the Tube."

Rafe, with the tank on his back, emerged from Jameson's building, noting that the water here was two feet deep. "Used to be two and a half," the blind man said. Again, Carmen and Daisy flanked him. On a nearby corner was the South Kensington Station entrance to what had indeed once been called the Tube, the city's massive subway system. Rafe waded toward it, scanning for hostiles.

At the station's entrance, a once-useful escalator now plunged into black water. At its bottom, Rafe knew, would be a subway tunnel, connected to all of London's other subway tunnels like a vast lake of sprawling fingers. It was hard to imagine sinking into that darkness, Bloats on all sides, and a cylinder of air on his back. *Suicide.* The water could claim him and no one would ever even know it. He edged toward the escalator and looked down. "No light down there," Rafe mumbled.

"No." Jameson grinned. "You'll be blind. At the bottom of the escalator will be a platform. Turn right, into the tunnel. It's a two-mile swim to your stop. You've got plenty of air."

Rafe felt for the metal steps of the escalator beneath his feet, and tried not to look terrified.

"Talk some sense into them," Jameson added. "Else we'll all be dead."

"I will," Rafe mumbled. "I'm sorry it's come to this." Then he looked to the women. "Thank you."

Carmen replied, "Your House is a buncha maggots. Shame they didn't *all* die at the Bloody."

Jameson chided her gently. "Now, now, Carmen. We'll all be fellow Londoners soon enough." Carmen rolled her eyes.

Rafe extended a hand to Jameson. Somehow, Jameson sensed it, and they shook. Then they both heard the familiar rowing sound of a pirogue outside: two more Rogue soldiers patrolling, looking for him.

"Go," Jameson repeated. "And take this." He handed Rafe a knife, which Rafe tucked into the back of his trousers. Then Rafe inserted the mouthpiece and breathed loudly. Carmen reached forward to tighten the fit of his goggles. He smiled gratefully and turned, those metal steps beneath him. For centuries, Londoners had descended this same escalator to a network of destinations, safe and secure. Now Rafe stared into its blackness.

His legs locked, just for a moment. The water. The debt. In that split second, he was a trembling child with urine-soaked trousers in the hold of a Belgian sailboat. A six-year-old making a deal with the river to spare his parents. The water had honored that contract. He tried to steel himself.

A memory of Jule helped. Picturing her on the other side of this underground lake. Her face, her eyes, her hands . . . That gave him strength.

"Go," Jameson repeated.

Carmen tapped her belly and added, "And end this bloody war, yeah?"

Rafe was able to say "Yes," but nothing more. Then he descended into the wash. Hips, chest, head—a last look back at Jameson. There was a half wave from Carmen, a gesture of hope. He appreciated it.

Then he was gone. Under. Liquid filling his ears. But he was breathing—the tank was working—and he was about to touch things no Londoner had seen in three hundred years. He pitched forward and began to swim down—deeper . . .

At the bottom of the escalator, as promised, a platform sprawled. Rafe swam through turnstiles in utter blackness. Things bumped up against him as he pushed and pulled at the water—refuse that had lived here since the Great Soak: plastic bottles, the lids of coffee cups, a tiny box he recognized from photos as a mini-refrigerator. Someone had once *lived* down here.

Again he thought of the millions of Londoners who had stood on this platform every day, for decades, fretting about meetings they'd be late to, checking their phones for news of the stock market's latest hiccup, or a child's report card, or a birthday they'd forgotten, or a sports score, or a politician's gaffe, or a video of a clever housecat, or groceries that needed to be bought, or a technology that thought it was a person. Or an unread article about the calving of a distant iceberg.

Then the water. Then the wars.

Marine life swam toward him now, fish. Some of them had adapted to the lightless water and had developed an electric glow, illuminating pockets of space for him. He followed one to the edge of this platform, where he found an empty track. "Turn right," Jameson had said. Rafe followed it into a tunnel. Water, water, *everywhere*, waiting, as it had for decades, to consume him.

Severndroog Castle, built in the 1700s, was a single stone tower, four stories in height, triangular in shape, sitting at the edge of the Crown camp like an abandoned toy. It had little turrets atop it, as if it had once hoped to become a castle when it grew up but never quite got there.

Tonight, it had become a jail with a single prisoner, Jule, confined to a room on the third floor. No iron bars, of course, but her hands had been shackled with a leather strap. The room had a small window. She felt utterly alone.

But she wasn't. A soldier stood guard outside the cell door. Another soldier sat *inside* the room as well—her jailer, ever watchful and vigilant: Boggs. His ankle was still painful, but he couldn't contain his grin. "What're the chances, eh? Me being your jailer! Justice does work in odd ways."

Jule was silent. Her face a mask.

On the other side of Eltham, Nelly entered the now-empty unit Jule had lived in since her teens. Soon, it would be assigned to someone else; Nelly knew that. Jule wasn't coming back. So the old woman toured the place, remembering moments she'd spent here, and Jule's remarkable kindness. Here was the knife Jule had used so often to cut bark from beech trees, which had given Nelly strength.

She grasped the knife by the handle. It was hers now . . .

In the subway tunnel, Rafe continued to swim, sustained by the air in the tank, his path partially lit by the electric fish that swam alongside him. He couldn't see much of his surroundings, just the faintest outlines of shapes: stanchions, walls.

Just two miles. It's only the next stop.

He pushed on, his legs and arms strong, swimming through a museum. History all around him. Then—

THUMP. He swam headfirst into something solid and substantial. A large flat surface in the middle of the tunnel. Glass.

It was the back of a train that had been sitting here for centuries underwater. He pulled himself alongside it, fifteen cars filled with water, to the lead car, where conductors had once sat. On the other side of the front window he saw gauges and knobs and levers, the tools of a brilliant technology. Mass transit. Genius, really. He thanked God for the air in his lungs and continued his swim, leaving the dead train behind him until . . . IMPACT.

Something from the darkness suddenly plowed into him, brutally driving him backward into that front window. His head hit the glass with concussive force, knocking the mouthpiece from his lips. Dazed, Rafe reached for it blindly. A glowing fish scurried by, giving Rafe a brief glimpse at the lethal beast that had just driven into him so viciously.

It was a Bloat. Inches from his face now.

Rafe reached for the knife Jameson had given him—but it was

gone, knocked loose by the collision. And now the Bloat attacked, mouth agape. A single bite would mean death. The Bloat's jaws snapped at him while its tail coiled around in an attempt to hold Rafe still. Rafe tried to grab the beast's head, but the Bloat shook Rafe's hands away.

Desperate for air, Rafe ducked down and put the breather back into his mouth, unaware that the device had filled with subway water, which he now sucked into his lungs, sending him into a spasm of choking. As Rafe gagged, the Bloat attacked again, knocking Rafe back. He squirmed away to the tracks at his feet—and shoved the breather back into his mouth, this time blowing hard into it before trying to draw a breath. It worked. Air filled his lungs.

The Bloat came back. Rafe punched its nose, the predator recoiling for a moment. Rafe searched for the fallen knife, but the glowing fish had all scattered, and he could see nothing. One of his hands poked at the tracks while the other tried to keep the beast at bay, his fingers brushing against detritus from centuries past—old cans, a hypodermic needle...

The beast surged again, into his ribs, trying to bite him. Rafe kicked at it, screaming in the darkness, the toe of his boot poking one of the Bloat's eyes until the predator backed away for a moment. Rafe sucked in another breath. Then it came at him again.

They were wrestling now, Rafe trying to stay clear of the teeth, the venom, the Bloat trying to wrap around him and squeeze him to death.

Rafe pushed it away, reached down blindly to the tracks again. Desperately, grasping . . .

There it was. The knife. He felt it. Grabbed it. The Bloat barreled in and got its mouth around Rafe's breather—

—just as Rafe plunged the blade into the Bloat's body . . .

The Bloat gasped, its eyes rolling over, its head spasming right and left with the breather still in its jaws, yanking the device out of Rafe's lips.

Then the Bloat sank, still thrashing—biting through the rubber tubing that had been keeping Rafe alive down here.

The beast hit bottom. Dead.

Rafe froze for a moment, Bloat blood warming the water around him. The breather was now destroyed. Bubbles raced out of its shredded rubber. He put the tubing into his mouth and tried to breathe again.

No good. His lips wouldn't seal around the tubing. The tank was now useless. And water, as always, was everywhere. *Drowning* was everywhere, the river claiming him at long last. He kicked madly, swimming *up*. To his right was an alcove, a recess in the tunnel. He swam for it. Maybe there'd be an air pocket there; his lungs were beginning to collapse.

He got to the alcove and looked up, desperate, his hands feeling along the alcove ceiling. Then he felt a familiar sensation against his fingertips. A circle of glass, sealed airtight against tile, housing a light bulb that must have provided light in this alcove when subways still made sense. There might be air in there. And it was above the waterline in this tunnel. *Dry.* He yanked the air tank off his back and thrust it toward the circle of glass, his lungs shrieking for air.

The tank slipped from his grasp but didn't sink. He grabbed it again, praying to God. All this water—it had been trying to claim him all his life, as it claimed everything else. He could not let it win. Not now. Not after loving Jule. He thrust the tank at the glass again, hard as he could.

Success. The glass cracked. He thrust the tank again, breaking more of the glass, pulling away the shards with his fingers. Then he pressed his mouth into the light housing and inhaled.

Air. *Centuries*-old air, hiding in this tiny space as it surrounded a light bulb. Rafe sucked it in greedily, his hands up against the alcove ceiling to hold him in place, remaining there, breath after breath. . . . until the air was gone, and the housing had filled with his own exhalation. He needed a way out of this tunnel. *What way was this?* Rafe didn't know. He knew only that Jule was aboveground.

And Jule was all that mattered.

So he pushed away from the alcove and swam desperately, leaving the tank behind him. The glowing electric fish joined him again, lighting his way. If there was another Bloat in his path, maybe this time he'd see it coming. Maybe.

He felt his lungs emptying again, beginning to burn. *Keep kicking, keep moving the water. It's the next stop. It's reachable. Just GET TO*

HER . . . But soon his lungs emptied, and dizziness struck. He pulled at the water frantically until his hand brushed up against something in the semidarkness. It was plastic, cylindrical: an empty one-liter soda bottle, centuries old.

It might contain air. Maybe. He grabbed it, felt for its mouth, which was sealed tightly by a cap. Yes, there might be air in there . . . Please, God . . . He held the bottle upside down and unscrewed the cap. To his immense relief, no water rushed into the bottle. *There was air inside.* He pressed his lips to the opening, sealed them tight around it . . . and inhaled.

It worked. More of that glorious, ancient, three-hundred-year-old air filled his chest.

He resealed the bottle and began swimming again, keeping it on hand while pulling at the water, hoping to see light somewhere up ahead, some sign that the next platform was nearby.

Nothing. Darkness.

It's just the next stop. It's reachable. SHE IS REACHABLE.

Rafe went as long as he could until the dizziness returned, then stopped for another breath from the bottle. He sucked it in. But this time the bottle began to collapse in his hands, as if being crushed by the water.

It was empty and couldn't help him any longer. Damn it. He pushed it away and kicked madly. *God, do not let me drown today. Not now. Get me to Jule, just once more. PLEASE . . .*

Every muscle in his body was working to propel him, head

throbbing with anoxia. Then, in the hazy light of the glowing fish, he saw promise, just ahead: A platform. Turnstiles. *The Holborn Tube Station.* THE STOP.

He swam for it in a fury and reached the platform, pulling desperately past the turnstiles, past the windowed station where people had once bought their passes and asked directions . . . into a corridor with tile walls. Nothing in his lungs but acid now. *God, do not let me drown today.* Up ahead was another endlessly steep escalator. He pulled and kicked, reaching the bottom of the escalator—and looked up, praying to see daylight above.

Just more darkness—with no alcoves or light housings or soda bottles. There was nothing to do but swim, straight up. So he began, his lungs empty and aching. Every part of him was working now, trying to move the water from his path. *Don't think about drowning. Just think about Jule. BEAT THE RIVER.*

Then he began to see the faintest glimmer of light. *Daylight.* His imagination? No. It was real. Definable. *I am not going to drown. I am not going to pay this debt today.*

But his chest was compressing. He could feel it. So he swam harder, pulling and kicking—despite the wobbly vision. The light above got brighter, closer. That was *Jule* up there. She was the light. Just get to her . . .

The surface was twenty feet away, he guessed. But he was slowing. His body was failing, his consciousness fading. Everything burned. Then his limbs stopped cooperating entirely. His arms and feet stopped moving. He could feel himself sinking down again—falling in the water, dropping like a weight . . . the light suddenly *farther* from his grasp. Worse, his mouth—desperate to breathe—opened involuntarily. And filthy water rushed in, seeking his life. He gagged, choked, screamed. No one heard. Somehow, his brain kept trying—

No. Not here. Not with Jule so close . . . He somehow got his arms to move, and pulled harder.

Kick. Pull. Live.

His legs and feet came back to life, even as his body convulsed, coughing all that water into *other* water. *Just get to her again . . .* Twenty feet away. *Please, God . . .* Fifteen feet now . . . The light getting brighter . . .

Ten feet. *Jule's face . . . Her touch . . .*

Five feet. A body length. *I cannot die now, this close . . .*

Jule, Jule, Jule . . . She was reaching out to him, urging him on . . . One more desperate pull, one more agonized kick . . .

And his head breached the surface, crown first, forehead, eyes, cheeks, ears, nose . . . mouth.

An instant primal inhale, sucking in an agonized breath.

Then a second breath, and a third, his body still shocked. By the fourth breath, his brain was beginning to lose some of that fog. Beneath his feet were the steps of the escalator. His clothes were heavy and cold, his boots filled with ugly water.

He started to cry without meaning to. Hysterical. Childlike. He had survived. He was *breathing*.

Only now did he remember that Paternoster was just across the street from this station. There would likely be Rogue guards all over the intersection outside, looking for him.

They could wait. For a moment, breathing was all. Above him was the glorious sun.

It had Jule's face.

TWENTY-ONE

The grain didn't care.

Byron was a hero now, a leader—the only Hab on this whole benighted island who *wasn't* anonymous. But the grain didn't care. It needed to be threshed and bundled and carried and weighed; and there was too much of it in the fields for the Habs to manage without him. So he pressed sycamore paste and then went into the waving wheat to lend his boundless energy to the taming of all those tall stalks.

At the end of another endless day, their hauls having been weighed, Byron and his fellow Habs dragged themselves back to their cabins, where he was met by children asking if they could come over later. Yes, he would find the energy somehow. He would entertain and teach. And then he would sleep, and the next day he'd do it all again. Endurance was his gift.

But just as he reached his shack, he paused. Jameson had returned.

Moments later, they walked the silent fields. "It really is time now, Byron. The Houses are done. Someone is going to have to show the Habs a new way."

Byron sighed heavily. "And if I don't?"

"Can you speak Russian?"

As night fell in her makeshift cell, Jule sat pensively. Boggs was on a stool across from her, eating a chicken leg. Finally, she spoke. "I'm sorry, Boggs. For what I said about your detaining Breena. You were only doing your job."

"That's the fact," Boggs replied.

"Anyway, sorry."

"Are you sorry about killing my friend?"

She eyed him somberly, then she lied. "Yes." Boggs weighed that for a moment. Jule went on, "I wasn't thinking right—I'd gotten hit in the head and had lost so many of my troops. I just couldn't watch a child die."

Boggs sighed. "He was a good soldier, Pritchett. A loyal Crown. He admired you."

"I know. I lost my way."

Boggs studied her. Then: "You hungry?"

She smiled. "Very!"

He handed her another chicken leg.

For over a day now, Rogue soldiers had blanketed every soggy street within a five-mile radius of Paternoster, looking for Rafe. They'd been in every structure, every alley, above and beneath the surface of the water. A thorough search.

So there was utter shock on the faces of the sentries at the main Paternoster gate when Rafe emerged from that Tube station, crossed the intersection, and awaited entry. Dozens of soldiers now stared at him, wondering how the hell he had eluded their citywide dragnet. And why had he come back?

"I demand to see General Shapcott," he announced.

A guard answered, "He demands to see you too."

"Open the bloody gate." He would *not* enter this camp a prisoner. And he didn't.

As he crossed the square, every citizen watched him with mild awe. He'd been a hero to them all, and none believed he was capable of treason, despite the coterie of guards accompanying him. His chest out, he nodded to all as he passed, even the Crown prisoners behind a fence.

He entered the Stock Exchange and marched to the trading floor with utter defiance. There sat Shapcott, flanked by his remaining captains: Beckett, Maud, and Maddox, who lay on a cot, recovering from his shattered knee. And Breena, who stared at her shoe tops. The air hung heavy with dismay. All of them were shocked—but entirely unsurprised—to learn that Rafe had evaded capture and entered this camp of his own volition. "Sit down, Rafe," Shapcott intoned.

Rafe didn't. He simply *would not* behave as a prisoner. "I need first to brief all of you on something I saw."

"You can speak when spoken to," Shapcott said. "Not until."

"Sir, you need to know about it."

"Captain," Shapcott said, "there's no need to make this harder on yourself."

"You idiot," Rafe interrupted. *"We're being invaded."*

Everything in this room—even the walls—seemed to gasp. Rafe

went on, uttering a lie that was partially true: "I saw a patrol boat on the water. Made of steel, propelled by an engine. Russian insignia on its bow, two Russian soldiers aboard, both armed. They saw me, then went up the river."

Silence fell hard. Rafe added, "They're *here*, General. Not overhead. *Here*. And they will be back, to occupy us. Only question is when."

"He's lying," Maud growled.

"Wish I were. Boat was about forty feet long and half as wide. Big motor."

"He's *lying*," Maud repeated. "To distract us."

Rafe shot back, "I'm trying to *save* you."

"That what you were doing at the Bloody? *Saving us?*"

That fast, Maud had reclaimed the room. Rafe eyed her. "All I did at the Bloody was kill dozens of Crowns, Maud."

"Rescued one too."

Silence. They all studied his reaction. Even Breena. "Rafe," Shapcott said. "How do you answer this?"

"General, it was my estimation that our field losses had become unsustainable and that our only chance of emerging from the forest with our army intact was to drive the enemy from the fight. So I employed the weapon."

Maud became his prosecutor now. "Captain," she began formally, "you threw that Canner because a particular Crown was in jeopardy. Her name is Jule."

"I threw that Canner because General Chasen was in range. The demonstration was for him."

"She was about to be killed. *I* was about to kill her."

"*Chasen* was the point," Rafe answered. "And by the way, it worked. They surrendered and fled. We won the day without losing any more of our troops."

Maud did not relent. "By using a weapon you yourself had told our general and our troops not to use."

"That is a fact," Rafe answered. "General, am I being court-martialed?"

Shapcott answered flatly, "You're being debriefed, Captain. And it's your duty to answer the questions."

Rafe looked to Maud: "Yes, I used a weapon I'd advised the general to exclude from our prior battle plan."

"To save her life."

"To save my company and what was left of our army. You should know that better than anyone, Captain. You led fifty troops into that forest and only nine walked out."

Maud drifted toward the desk that had always been Rafe's. From it, she grabbed one of the tiny twig boats he'd made and crushed it in her hands, continuing, "Then you attended wounded Crown troops in direct defiance of an order. And arranged with a Hab for their safe transport back to Crown camp."

She crushed another twig boat. Rafe said: "That I did."

"Why so concerned all the sudden with the welfare of our enemy?" She crushed a third twig boat, then a fourth.

Rafe tried, "It is my estimation that before long the Crowns will be our *allies* in a much larger struggle against a far more dangerous enemy."

That was blasphemy, and shock painted every face. But not Maud's. "I see," she said. "How many nights did you leave this camp for the express purpose of seeing her?"

Rafe spat back, "This is a waste of our time."

Shapcott jumped in, "Answer the question, Rafe."

"I will not!" Rafe barked. "A hostile force has now encroached on us by air *and* water. They—"

"Just answer the question, Rafe," Shapcott interrupted.

"THE QUESTION IS THE PROBLEM, GENERAL! Crowns aren't our enemy anymore. Crowns don't *matter* anymore!"

Maud now destroyed the last of his twig boats. "I never did understand your fixation with these," she said.

"You wouldn't," Rafe sighed.

"Enough!" yelled Shapcott. "Captain, you'll answer these charges in a formal court-martial." Then he ordered two guards, "Detain him and take him to the stockade!"

No one spoke. Maddox stroked his beard and stared at the floor. Beckett and Breena were too stunned to move. Rafe replied calmly, "General, my oath is to the people of this great House. And I now believe that your leadership is going to get them all killed or captured by an enemy you are unwilling to acknowledge. Therefore, my duty demands that I replace you. Please stand down, sir."

There it was, officially. No one in there could breathe—except Shapcott, who said flatly, "Arrest him." The two guards now approached Rafe, bearing rope shackles.

And in that moment, Rafe saw an inevitable future—capture, confinement, trial, conviction, execution . . . and the news reaching the Crown camp, where someone would have to inform Jule, "Your lover is dead." Fierce as she was, it would cripple her.

No.

When the guards moved in, Rafe exploded in a blur, one shoulder into each, spinning them backward as he burst past them, across the trading floor, toppling two oil lamps. Then through the lobby and into the brilliant light of day. Behind him, Breena silently begged Rafe to run faster.

The Rogue camp was tranquil: children sitting in class, patients healing in the med tent, food being distributed to waiting families— daily disasters held shakily at bay. Rafe raced through it all, voices behind him rising, guards calling to other guards, "STOP HIM!" And the camp took note: A Rogue hero was being pursued like a fugitive.

Children bolted from class. Adults stopped their chores. Rafe ran between tents and carts—darting, leaping, as more and more guards began to follow. Soon, the entire camp was watching. Many cheered him along the way, Willa's voice among the chorus. His only thought was to get to the Cadbury Wall. Slaloming through bodies and other obstacles, he dashed around a corner and into the alley that led to the wall, only to find it guarded.

By *Maud*. Waiting. Knives in each hand. Scowl on her face. Twenty yards away, standing still.

Rafe kept moving at full speed. Without slowing, he called out, "Maud, don't do this!"

Maud hollered, "Sod off, traitor!"

Ten yards separated them now. His speed increasing. Five yards. Bearing down on her. She balled her fists, the blades sticking out. He stuck his head down.

She bowed her neck, refusing to clear a path. Then—

Impact. Rafe barreled into her, his shoulder to her chest, driving the air from her lungs. She flew backward, one knife knocked from her hand while the other grazed Rafe's cheek. He stumbled too, and they both fell to the ground, each shocked by the violence of the moment, eye to eye, breathless, his weight atop her.

"I'm sorry," he whispered. She spat in his face.

Behind them, guards raced into this alley. Beckett too. Rafe rose to his feet and scaled the Cadbury Wall. Then he heard Maud's voice: "Where're you going?"—each syllable labored.

Straddling the wall, he replied: "Don't you know?"

"Yeah," Maud said bitterly. "But you won't find her there."

Rafe doubted that. "No?"

"No," Maud growled. "She's dead."

Time stopped.

Rafe froze, his blood no longer moving. *Dead?*

Overhead, the sky was empty. Not a sparrow or goldfinch or starling to be seen. No creatures moved on the ground—no martens or feral cats. Life had blinked.

Somehow he just knew, intuitively, that Maud was telling the truth. Jule was dead. He tried to speak but couldn't.

He could feel, vaguely, that the soldiers were still coming. He didn't see them, really, or hear them; those senses had shut down. And he couldn't swallow.

Maud went on, "I went to Eltham last night under a white flag and told Chasen about the two of you. They killed her right in front of me. High treason. Six troops, thirty stabs before she finally stopped breathing. But she never made a sound. A soldier to the last."

It made a horrible kind of sense. Of course Jule was dead. Of course Maud had killed her. No, *Rafe* had killed her, the moment he had set all this in motion—knowingly, willfully, recklessly, selfishly. His head was on fire.

Beckett and the others arrived at the wall now. Maud added, "Chasen told me to show you this . . ." She pulled something from her coat and held it aloft.

The arm of the Victrola. Amputated. Useless. Once, its needle had produced sounds that changed his life. No more. Like Jule, it was dead now.

A tear began to form in Rafe's eye. He felt himself getting dizzy; air swam around him. Beckett looked up at him. "You ready to come down, old friend?"

Rafe breathed out a sigh and asked, "How soon can we attack?"

Maud swallowed a grin.

Jule's mind raced, inventing strategies to manipulate Boggs—to disarm him, trick him, conquer him. It all made sleep impossible.

Past midnight, she heard her cell door opening. She closed her eyes, knowing he'd be happier to find her asleep. So she was lying on her back, breathing deeply, as Boggs entered and drifted toward her without a sound. Was he here to touch her? He might be. She prepared herself for that.

Instead he knelt beside her and whispered in her ear: "Are you awake?"

She opened her eyes but didn't turn her head. "I am now," she said kiddingly, as if they were friends.

"Your lover is dead," he reported flatly.

TWENTY-TWO

That fast she was a child again, the stones pulling her down as the lake rose above her chin. Breathing became impossible.

Her body shut down so instantly, she forgot how to blink. A gasp wanted to fly from her mouth, but she clenched her jaws tight to hold it in and remained perfectly still, even though her bones had just gone liquid and her brain felt like it had unmoored from her skull and was now sliding down her back.

Boggs went on, "The woman he jilted for you—Maud is her name. She denounced him to Shapcott, and Rafe was executed on the spot. No trial. I'm very sorry."

Boggs stood and left the cell, proud of the lie he'd invented, thrilled to see it wound her. The door shut.

Only then did Jule allow herself that convulsive gasp. It rose through her belly like a geyser, pushing its way past her ribs and lungs, making her throat bulge unnaturally, then exploding into her mouth.

The sound it made was alien to her—hardly human, a feral shriek. This wasn't grief. It was agony. The molecules around her felt evil. Unclean. Rafe was dead. Rafe was dead. Rafe was dead. Her shoulders shook so hard that her teeth chattered. She shut her eyes tight, but tears came anyway. Her body curled up like a comma, pain in every empty space. Torment. She had killed him—knowingly, willingly. And her punishment would be eternal suffering. She knew it.

Suddenly, her breathing stopped. The room felt airless. She bolted up and ran to the tiny window. It wouldn't open. She punched the window hard, shattering it. Her knuckles screamed and bled—but the pain felt satisfying somehow. She pressed her face into the night air and sucked in as much of it as she could.

But air was not enough. Her eyes went glassy, her knees went soft. And she sagged to the cold floor, unconscious.

In Paternoster Square, soldiers and citizens had amassed now. A "purification ceremony," ordered by Shapcott, was set to take place. Rafe was surrounded by Rogues as he sat at a table in the center of the square. On it, three candles burned.

Shapcott announced, "Tonight, we take the Mark, all of us. A soldier we thought we knew is now dead. We must mourn him and his treachery."

That was to be Rafe's punishment. No lashing, no torture. Rather, he'd be forced to sit here and endure the pain of others in his name. Nothing else would penetrate. The night air passed right through him. Overhead, bats circled, their screeches filling the sky. Shapcott stepped to the table now, nodding to Maddox and Maud to join him before those three candles. They eyed him soberly. Maddox had to be carried to the spot. Then Shapcott nodded flatly. "Commence."

And each put a palm into a dancing flame.

BURN THE WATER

Thus it began. Their hands held steady, the flames doing the work of purification—discomfort becoming agony almost instantly, tissue becoming smoke.

And Rafe forced to watch.

Three sets of eyes locked with his. Three fellow warriors, burning their flesh willfully, to purify *him*. He could smell it. He could *hear* it—fire eating bare skin greedily. And he could see it in their faces. Anguish.

Yet these three did not flinch, their jaws set tight, their eyes never wavering, their expressions saying, *YOU did this. YOU caused this. YOU burned me, not this flame.*

He knew they were right. His crimes had put them there.

After thirty seconds, sweat began to pour down Rafe's face. He felt his legs going liquid and his hands beginning to spasm. He tried to rise from his seat.

"DO NOT!" Shapcott barked.

Rafe sat down again, sending up a silent prayer, begging God to make it all stop. Maddox's arm began to tremble. He let a howl escape his lungs. Would he be the first to waver?

Yes. He yanked his hand from the flame, plunging it into a nearby bucket of water. Rafe gulped with relief.

Shapcott pulled his hand out as well. Into the bucket it went. Rafe shut his eyes tight with thanks.

But Maud's hand remained in place. Her arm was shaking. Her body began to shudder. Yet her hand stayed in the flame. Behind her, Breena began to weep. Several citizens did. Children began to cry.

She didn't move. Shapcott, his hand screaming inside that bucket, breathed, "That's enough, Maud. You may remove your hand now."

Yet Maud would not relent—it was as though she wanted to burn a hole right through her palm and *make* Rafe bear witness to it. So she kept it there, smiling because she knew that her pain was doubling, no, tripling, in him.

"Maud, please," Rafe begged.

Maud didn't move.

"Maud, enough," Breena called.

Maud didn't move.

"Maud!" Shapcott yelled. "The point is made now. You're of no use to us in battle if you injure yourself."

Maud didn't move.

The stench now drilled into Rafe's nostrils in a way that felt permanent, a smell he would never shed. And still she did not relent.

"Maud!" Rafe pleaded. "STOP. Please!"

Maud didn't move. Tears began to stream down her cheeks. The flame was hitting bone now. And Rogues in this camp were beginning to swoon. Two passed out. Yet her arm was locked.

"General," Rafe hollered, "STOP HER!"

Mercifully, Shapcott pulled her hand from the flame.

"No!" she yelled.

"It's an order!" He stuck her hand into that same bucket. Her knees buckled.

Silence blanketed the camp. She sagged to the ground, gasping, shaking. "Never to forget!" she growled.

Shapcott and Maddox repeated together, "Never to forget."

Then, hissing between her teeth, "And never to forgive." Shapcott and Maddox repeated, "Never to forgive."

Rafe was a puddle. They all were. But the purification had not ended. The *entire Rogue Army* was expected to follow, hundreds of troops, waiting in three lines. The next group of three stepped forward. And Rafe gasped. They were *children*. Liam and Portia . . . and Willa. Each extended a hand.

Too much. Far too much . . . Rafe erupted, bolting out of the chair, lurching to the table and swiping his fist through the three candles, knocking them to the ground, startling Willa badly. Then Rafe turned to Shapcott, pleading, "General. Hang me. Shoot me. But not this. I beg you. Not children."

"Who, then?" the general asked.

"ME. ME. BURN *ME*. Please. No one else."

The whole world awaited Shapcott's reply. It came: "Do you acknowledge your crimes against your fellow Rogues?"

"I do."

"You pledge undying loyalty to this House, and to your commanding officer, upon penalty of death?"

"I do."

"You will lead this army into battle, under my direction?"

"I will."

"You're in Bergen's tonight. We attack in the morning."

Rafe nodded, grateful, his knees shaking, and took a first halting step. The crowd parted grudgingly.

He felt close to collapsing. On his second step, he nearly fell. Breena lurched forward and joined him, taking his arm. They began a slow walk. On all sides of him he saw scorn, judgment, sympathy, empathy, fear. But no one uttered a word. He had lied to them all, betrayed them all, endangered them all.

And if it would bring her back, he would do it again. He knew that. But she was gone . . . because he'd endangered her too. He and Breena left the crowd behind, no one else within earshot. Rafe whispered to her, barely audible, "Get to the Habs. Get to Byron."

She was shocked but did her best not to react. "What?"

Rafe replied, "After tomorrow, they'll be the only people alive. Just get to him."

"I can't abandon this House. Look what's happened to *you*."

"Breena, you're not abandoning this House. You're gonna help him build a *new* one, something better." Breena was silent.

Rafe took her hand, desperate: "Do this for me. There's nothing left for you here. We're all going to die tomorrow."

They'd reached Bergen's now. Rafe eyed his sister. "Yes?"

She didn't answer. Two soldiers guarding the door pulled him inside. Last thing he said was, "Breena! Please!"

Inside now, a guard led him to the "cell" beside Paris's. The two captured captains acknowledged each other with a nod.

"What're *you* doing here?" Paris asked.

"Fell in love with a Crown."

"That was a stupid thing to do."

Rafe breathed a smile and extended his wrists to be roped. *This*, he thought, *will be my last night alive. Good.*

"Which one?" Paris asked.

Rafe turned. "What?"

"The Crown you fell in love with. Who is it?"

Rafe paused a moment, weighing his reply. Then, calmly: "Your army suffered 4,287 casualties. Your company sustained forty-seven losses."

Paris swallowed hard. "Thank you."

At the same time, Breena stood in the square, alone. The crowd that had witnessed the purification had dissipated now, and a thousand conversations were happening at once—in tents, on cots, around tables. The whole camp seemed shaken. These were her people; this was her home. Defending it had been her life. Now she knew it would be her death as well.

Hours later, at Severndroog, morning light streamed through the broken window in Jule's cell. She hadn't slept. Every heartbeat was a hammer. The pain was just too great. She'd always worn a certain kind of armor with Rafe—she knew that now. She'd been dismissive of him at times, even withering. That had been a lie. She had loved him but refused to say it. And now she couldn't. She couldn't say *any* of the things she'd meant to. He was gone. And he'd died never knowing. That was torture. She doubted the pain would ever fade, and she didn't want it to. She had betrayed them both.

The door opened. Boggs entered with a sandwich for her. She produced a wounded but brave smile, thinking it would please him. It did. "How are we this morning?" he asked.

She didn't reply. He added, "What happened to the window?"

She held up her right hand, its knuckles bleeding. "Needed some air."

"And now?"

"Just need some breakfast." Boggs handed her the sandwich. She added, "Can you get a message to General Chasen for me?"

"I can try. What is it?"

Jule eyed her meal, then said, "If he still means to mount an attack on the Rogue camp, I'd like to lead it."

Boggs nodded with a smile.

At that same moment, the Crown camp at Eltham was silent, almost numb, still reeling from the string of recent disasters that had left these grounds feeling empty. Thousands were lost. Death had shredded this House, and no one knew what to do.

Except for Nelly. She sat calmly by the lake . . . sharpening Jule's knife.

In the Hab fields, the rows of tall wheat swayed happily in a light predawn breeze. A few mice made their homes here, smart enough to eat the grains that fell from the stalks rather than the stalks themselves, which made killing them unnecessary. They nibbled, and chattered about the day to come.

Byron awakened to find a hand over his mouth and Breena beside his bed. His first thought was to scold himself for sleeping so heavily. Breena whispered, "Good morning. Another battle is coming. My brother says the Habs will be all that's left when it's done. May I move my hand?"

Byron nodded. She uncovered his mouth and went on: "He says *you're* going to have to lead everyone when that happens. There won't be any Houses anymore. Are you prepared for that?"

"Do I have a choice?"

"Do you want a partner?"

The "Yes" escaped his lips without a thought. Their eyes met. He touched her face. One kiss... then he pulled her down to him. Outside, the fields lay still.

Rafe stood on the trading floor with the other captains, gearing up for war. Maud, her left hand tightly bandaged, dressed as well. Silence hung. No one spoke. Maddox could only watch. Rafe said softly, "If Chasen is found, he's mine."

"Understood," Beckett replied.

"Sod that," Maud grumbled. "He's no different than any other bloody Crown. If I find him, I'm killing him. Isn't that what we were taught?"

Rafe nodded, well rebuked. But he added, "Every soldier should be carrying a Canner today."

That drew some attention. Shapcott nodded. "Beckett, see to that."

"Yes, sir."

Rafe continued to apply the tools of war. He had some killing to do today.

And some dying.

TWENTY-THREE

Breena awoke in a panic. Byron was beside her. His cot was beneath her. His cabin was around her. The fields were quiet.

And her brother was about to die.

"I have to go," she said urgently.

Byron stirred, groggy. "What?"

"I have to stop him! I don't know what I was thinking!"

"Breena—"

"He's going to die today!"

She started to rise. Byron stopped her with a gentle hand. "You don't know that."

"He *wants* to!"

"He sent you here so you'd be safe."

"No. If he's going into battle, I should be next to him."

"So you can die too?"

"Then I'll stop him."

"Breena, you can't. They've been doing it for three hundred years. They don't know anything else." That was true. She knew it. He went on, "He wants something else for you. So do I. After all the fighting is done. I want to build that with you."

She sighed. "Maybe I don't belong here."

"But you keep coming *back* here. To the church, to me. There must be a reason. I think you want *more*. Don't you?"

That was true too. She bit down lightly on her lip, thinking. He put a hand to her face. "Help me. I need you."

Jule had spent her life in *motion*. It made things bearable.

But confinement had killed all that. Her world was now this cell, and the numbing hum of seven hundred years of stillness in the air around her. The stone floor was cold, and the walls felt damp. Cobwebs in each corner. Gnats and mosquitoes.

She would awaken each morning alert, ready for a mission—yet her body had nowhere to go. Rafe was in the walls, but she couldn't touch him. It was torment. She lay on her side, the shape of a comma again, as the door behind her opened and General Chasen entered without a word. Jule turned abruptly. "General," she breathed. Chasen nodded to Boggs, who left the room.

"How are you doing?" Chasen asked.

"I'll feel better in battle," she said. "I always do."

Chasen sighed. "Yes. Your request was made known to me."

"And?"

"And I'm afraid I can't grant it." Jule sagged, replaying the words in her head. He went on, "You betrayed us. All of us."

"I'm willing to die for it. But what good would it do anyone for me to die in here?"

"Child, it's the only place your death *can* do us any good." That sobered her. He went on, "You have to suffer. More, you have to be *seen* to suffer, as an example."

"You need me in the field," she said.

"This was my fault," he said. "Something in how I raised you made you hate this House. I'm—"

"It wasn't hate that put me here, Uncle. It was love."

"*DON'T,*" he snapped angrily. "Ever. What you did wasn't love. It was filth. It was hideous. It cost *lives.*"

"Uncle, I—"

"It would be best if you called me 'General.'"

She tried again, calmly. "Our ranks are thin. The Rogues are far better armed than we are. You—"

"Do you know why they always followed you? Your troops?"

She did. But she dodged it. "I trained them."

"They followed you because you inspired them. They looked at you and saw a hero, a leader. Loyal and fierce. But you've broken all that. They won't see you as a hero now, or even as a soldier. They'll see a whore. And no one's going to follow *that* into battle. Why would they?"

That made her head spin. He went on, "So, no. You're never going to lead your company again. And you'll certainly never be a general—although I'd always hoped one day you would."

He rose, heading for the door again. Jule mumbled, "I have more fighting to do, General. More killing. I can help you."

"You want to kill?" he asked.

"Yes."

"And die?"

"Yes."

He eyed her sadly and offered: "Then do *both*. Right here. As soon as I leave. Make your death a lesson your troops can carry into battle, an example of what happens to traitors. It's the only thing you *can* do for them now."

Staggered, she could barely spit out, "Uncle. General—"

"Goodbye, Jule."

He was nearly out the door when Boggs entered. "General," Boggs began. "Scouts are reporting that the Rogues are nearing our position in Eltham Village."

Jule tightened. Chasen too. He asked, "How many of them?"

Boggs replied, "All of them, sir."

Chasen nodded, then asked him, "Soldier, can you shoot? At a distance?"

"Yes, General," Boggs replied.

"Then tie the prisoner to her bed and take up a sniper's post at the window. When they get to the common, wait until you have at least ten abreast. Then open fire."

"Yes, General."

"She does *not* leave here! No matter the result!"

"Yes, General," Boggs returned. And then Chasen was gone.

Boggs did as ordered, securing Jule's wrists to a leg of her cot, which forced her onto the floor. Then he stood in that window with his rifle, scoping the landscape below. "Clever of you to clear the glass out for me," he said.

From here, he had a clear line of sight to the center of the common, where the gallows stood, ringed by two-story buildings. Just to the west of it lay three north-south streets: Eltham High Street, Red Lion Lane, and Constitution Rise. He could do some real killing from here. And Jule could do nothing to stop him.

Home was home. It had to be defended.

At the same time, eight hundred and fifty Rogues emerged from a fleet of pirogues on Crown turf, where the A205 road sloped out of the water. Today, finally, they would kill the last of the Crowns. Here. Forever. They stacked their boats, then followed the road to Eltham Common, which looked exactly as it had on the day General Shapcott's son, Alger, had died here after trying to flee across the square—the gallows, the old abandoned police station. *Here*, Shapcott thought, *my son ran for his life. Then they caved his head in.* It fueled him. Dogs barked. Dread was in the air. By Shapcott's side, at the head of the Rogue army, was Rafe.

This was where Rafe had come to claim Alger's body mere weeks ago, when Jule could have killed Rafe but for some reason did not. The memory made Rafe ache now. Pausing at the entrance to the common, he stared across the grass to Severndroog as it loomed ominously. A soldier's instinct told him that the tower would matter today.

Maud was on their right, fuming as she led her company. Beckett, with Kimpton as his second-in-command, was on their left. They were going to die soon—Rafe had decided that. So too would he, and every Crown. And all this would end, finally. The Habs would inherit London. He prayed they'd rule in peace.

The common itself lay flat and unprotected, surrounded on all sides by those two-story buildings from which arrows and sluggers had been fired at Alger, a perfect killing ground if there were Crowns hiding inside. Rafe could see that. "Not through here," he said. "Through the village."

He ordered his troops away from the common and onto Eltham High Street, one of those three north-south streets in the village, west of the common. Eltham High, like Red Lion Lane and Constitution Rise, had once been a place of commerce and community. But there was no concrete visible underfoot now. Grass had overtaken it centuries ago. Vines climbed the exteriors of the streets' once-charming shops on the ground level and the tiny apartments above. As he led his army onto Eltham High, the street's former shops and their glassless windows sat on his left. He had defilade cover on his right from thick trees whose roots had powered their way through helpless pavements back in the 2100s. His company would stay here and do a sweep. Beckett's Company B had Red Lion Lane. Maud's Company C had Constitution Rise.

From the tower, Boggs could see it all . . .

TWENTY-FOUR

The Battle of Eltham began properly on Constitution Rise as Maud's Company C covered it in measured steps, shop to shop. A stray cat leapt out of one, skittering across the street like the hares had at the Bloody. Animals always seemed to know when to flee.

Just then, BANG—one of Maud's men was shot from a second-story glassless window. He dropped on the spot.

"FIRST PLATOON! CANNERS!" Maud howled.

And the battle was joined. Twenty soldiers in C's first platoon pulled the strings on their Canners now, and began lobbing them at every second-floor apartment visible.

The world soon exploded. BA-BOOM! Huge blasts, some followed by Crown bodies falling from the windows.

On the neighboring street, Red Lion Lane, Beckett heard the explosions and ordered the same thing. Canners flew, then detonated, as helpless Crowns fired their last. Soon that street was a bloody mess as well, shards of wood and plaster everywhere.

On Eltham High Street, Rafe ordered his troops *not* to use their ordnance—and sent them instead into every shop and apartment. Rogues from this company pounded up stairways now, pushing in doors, and hand-to-hand fighting commenced in what had once been living rooms and bedrooms and hallways. Knives, clubs, axe handles, screams . . . Three streets, bleeding at once. Smoke and debris.

In Severndroog tower, Boggs remained perched at the window, watching the madness. So many targets down there. It was hard to choose. Chasen had told him the rules of engagement. He was to wait until he saw ten Rogues abreast.

But a voice arose from behind Boggs. "Shoot the bombs."

He turned. Jule stared up at him from her spot on the floor.

Below them, more gunfire could be heard, the village erupting. She went on, "The devices they're carrying, on their hips. Do you see them?"

"Yes."

"Can you aim at one and hit it?"

"Yes."

Jule thought that might be a lie, but she wanted this to be the last battle the Rogue House would ever fight, wanted them all dead, as they had killed her Rafe. "Then do it."

"You heard the general," Boggs countered. "He said not to fire unless I had ten abreast."

"That means he thinks you're a lousy shot. Are you?"

"No!"

"Then *do it*."

"That an order?" he asked sarcastically.

"Boggs," she sighed. "Your enemy needs some killing now. Are you up to it? If not, step aside and give *me* the rifle. I'll end this war right now."

That landed. Boggs turned his gaze back to the streets below, specifically Red Lion Lane, where Beckett's Company B had now grenaded nearly every structure within reach, pockets of surviving Crowns continuing to return fire. Through his scope, Boggs saw Beckett, in the middle of the street, assessing the battle. A Canner hung untroubled on his hip.

Boggs zeroed in on it from a distance of about a hundred yards, aiming, his finger on the trigger. Squeezing it. Jule was certain he'd miss.

He didn't. The round hit the Canner dead center. BOOOOOM! The explosion liquefied Beckett on impact, momentarily stunning his troops.

That fast, Crown soldiers on this street understood what to do. Every soldier with any sluggers left took aim at the Canners on every Rogue hip. BOOM! BABOOM! Sudden explosions filled the street as Rogues became mist. In an instant, the Canners had become a liability—and every Rogue knew it. Many of them made frantic attempts to get the devices off their hips. Some pulled the string and tossed the Canners blindly. Some tossed them without arming them first. The Canner of one unlucky Rogue was shot half a second before he could toss it. The blast tore his head off. Another Rogue was so desperate that he armed his bomb, tossed it, and watched in horror as it errantly killed three of his fellow Rogues.

One block over, the chaos had spread to Constitution Rise, where Crown soldiers had learned the same lesson. Five explosions—five

Rogues evaporating. Yet Maud's company held together without panic or alarm. On her orders, they hurled fourteen Canners into a cluster of trees, eviscerating branches, leaves, roots... and twenty Crown snipers.

But Eltham High Street was quiet as Rafe and his company went apartment to apartment, killing several Crowns and flushing the rest onto flat ground in full retreat. Fifteen Crowns now fled into the empty skeleton of a former department store called Marks & Spencer. Rafe and his lead platoon gave chase.

The shop was just a shell; it had no shelves or aisles anymore—so it was an empty arena as Rafe pursued those retreating Crowns here. They'd all killed Jule, each of them. He kept telling himself that. She'd been stabbed thirty times—Maud had said so. *These* were the butchers who had spilled her blood. Each would suffer for it.

Flanked by his troops, Rafe waded into the store with long-knives in each hand. With no aisles to hide behind, the Crowns had clustered not far from the door. Rafe charged a pack of four of them, while his troops took on the rest.

The four Crowns could have killed him; he wanted them to. But his rage and skill were too great. Instantly they'd all been slaughtered. The other Crowns in here fared no better. To his right and left they fell, his troops dispatching them.

Moments later, he led his troops out of the department store. Bodies from both Houses littered the streets. *Good*, he thought, *the war is almost over*. Soon there'd be no one left to fight it. Not far from here he saw a pack of wounded Crowns writhing on the street. Ammo was scarce, so he pulled the Canner off his belt, ready to end their suffering.

It was in that moment that Boggs—nesting in that third-floor window in Severndroog—spotted him.

And Boggs's eyes went wide. *Rafe.* Jule's lover. Enemy Number One, with a beautiful Canner in his hand.

"Ya find another one?" Jule asked.

"Oh yes." Boggs smiled. "Standing still, dead to rights."

"Then fire."

"Yes."

On the street below, Rafe moved quickly toward the cluster of Crowns. He liked the idea of killing several at once.

In the tower, Boggs took one last look at the Canner in Rafe's grasp, delighting in the prospect of this kill. He began to squeeze the trigger . . .

And then he died.

It was a *knife*, plunged deep into Boggs's upper back on his left side, puncturing his heart. His last thought was to curse Jule for her treachery. But Jule had never moved. She'd merely *witnessed* his stabbing.

It was Nelly who'd killed him, having entered this unguarded cell, bearing the knife she'd liberated from Jule's apartment. She yanked the blade out of Boggs's back as he slid to the floor. Then she cleaned it on his shirt, and used it to cut the thin leather straps around Jule's wrists.

"Thank you, Nelly."

Nelly replied, "I did this so you could run away. Will you?"

Jule studied her. Lying wasn't an option, but the truth felt impossible, so, again: "Thank you, Nelly." The old woman followed her out of the cell.

Rafe, unaware that his life had just been spared, tossed the Canner into that cluster of Crowns. It detonated. They died.

Nearby, Chasen surveyed the battle before him and knew it was lost. Much of his army had been blown to pieces, or shot, or gutted. Rogues held each of the three streets in this village. The Crowns still alive were hiding or bleeding on the pavement. Chasen didn't yet know the numbers, but he estimated his remaining troop strength to be somewhere under a hundred. A debacle. And he would be blamed for it, forever, his name a shameful wound. So he did something he hoped his troops might somehow forgive one day . . .

He turned and ran. Onto a dirt-and-grass lane that led into anonymous foliage. He'd find somewhere else to live, somewhere upriver, until his name and his infamy could somehow be forgotten.

One block away, Shapcott was evaluating the Rogue losses. Ammunition and ordnance were now low. Casualties had been high, but he estimated his remaining troop strength to be just above five hundred—a triumph when compared to the Crown losses. Just then, he saw Chasen fleeing the battle. That was an even greater victory.

Rafe, however, wanted more than Chasen's dishonor. He wanted Chasen's death. So, as the fighting continued around them on Eltham High Street, Rafe followed Chasen away from the village. Shapcott did as well.

At the same time, Jule emerged from Severndroog tower with Nelly in tow. Before them, the ragged end of this battle unfolded—troops fighting and dying. Acrid smoke from too many Canners. Blood everywhere. At Jule's feet lay the dead body of a fellow Crown soldier, bearing a handgun and rifle.

Nelly touched Jule's arm. "Please, just go home this time?"

"I don't have one anymore," Jule said. There was nothing left to do now but fight and kill and die. She took the guns and the knife.

Nelly begged, "Be careful."

"What for?" Jule asked.

"For me?"

Jule studied her friend for a moment, then whispered, "Find cover, Nelly. I need you to survive this."

As Nelly turned to go, Jule climbed the wall of a nearby shop, reached its roof, and crawled to its edge. The air before her was smoky and dense, but she could see shapes within it, and she knew that anything moving on the street before her—Eltham High Street—had to be a Rogue. She would kill every one of them, until one killed her.

Fifty yards away, behind the village on that dirt-and-grass lane,

Chasen continued his flight of shame, running as fast as he could toward the sanctuary of foliage. Humiliation, pain, regret, defeat, self-loathing... yet the desire to survive outweighed them all. That surprised him; he'd always thought he would die bravely, like a general, like a legend. Instead he'd deserted. And now he'd have to row away from here like a thief—and never return. He turned a corner at full speed, trying his best not to stumble.

Then he came to a sudden stop.

Before him was Danton, his arm still in a sling, tears in his eyes. The deaths he'd just seen had overwhelmed him.

Suddenly, Chasen couldn't get his feet to move. The look from Danton was as painful as a whipping. "General?" Danton asked. "Where're you going?"

Chasen couldn't answer. Instead: "Where're your folks?"

"I don't have any," Danton replied.

Of course not. Chasen turned, mortified, and began to walk back toward the streets he'd just fled, where the fighting was. It was time to surrender. And die.

In the village, on Constitution Rise, a scout unit from Maud's company found two Crowns huddling in a dark basement—ammunition gone, hands raised in surrender. The scouts marched them up the steps to the street and presented them to Maud, who smiled, embracing a teachable moment.

She stabbed them both to death as her company cheered.

"No prisoners today," she said aloud. Her sector now cleared, she began to march her troops toward the Crown camp at Eltham Lake. Civilians would be gathered there. She intended to kill them all too.

One hundred yards away, on that random rooftop, Jule lay flat on her belly, her rifle's barrel extending beyond the roof's edge. Clusters of Rogues splayed before her, unaware that they were now targets. They all had to die. Then she would die too.

On Red Lion Lane, Beckett's troops—now under the command of Kimpton—completed a sweep-and-clear of every shop and apartment, reporting that no Crowns had survived this street's fighting. Kimpton ordered a small force to stay back and guard the street while leading the rest of Company B to merge with Maud and Company C one block to the west.

On the dirt-and-grass lane that had once been his path to desertion and infamy, Chasen now trudged back toward the fighting, until he saw something that stopped him cold again: *Rafe and Shapcott*, heading his way, looking for him.

Upon seeing them, he sagged . . . and raised his hands meekly, his humiliation bottomless. Behind him trailed little Danton. Only now did Chasen notice that the boy had followed him.

"Go home," Chasen ordered.

"I don't—"

"GO!"

Crying, the child turned and ran.

As Shapcott approached, Chasen said, "Congratulations, old friend. The day is yours. The *fight* is yours."

Shapcott nodded, then graciously replied, "Your troops fought bravely today, General. As they always do."

Chasen breathed out a sad, "All but one." Shapcott nodded. Chasen went on, "I don't suppose you'd shoot me?"

"Happy to," Rafe interjected. Chasen had been the monster who had ordered Jule's death, right? That had to be answered.

But Shapcott calmly stated, "Sorry, General, I cannot. Do I need to bind your hands?"

"No. I can make a better show than that."

Shapcott accepted that as well. "Let's go." Now he and Rafe began to guide the defeated Crown back toward the village.

Nearby, prone on that rooftop, Jule identified her first targets. She drew in a deep breath, a serene patience steadying her. Hands calm, eyes lifeless, not a hint of the Churn at all. She exhaled, long and steady, and opened fire with great skill.

POP—POP—POP-POP—POP . . . Through the dense smoke, she hit shapes as they moved, then watched those shapes fall. In that first volley, she killed ten Rogues with ten shots. The rest of the Rogue Army scrambled for cover in confusion. Among them was Kimpton, who stumbled over a body, badly injuring her knee. She dropped to the ground, helpless, the pain excruciating. A stationary target.

But Jule had just exhausted her ammunition. Knives would have to suffice.

Good, she thought. *I'd rather die in hand-to-hand fighting than be shot at a distance. Let them see my face.*

She jumped down to the street, her lungs sucking in the debris of cordite in the air. Sounds were trapped inside the smoke: the groans of the dying, orders barked from soldier to soldier. And there was Kimpton, all alone, hobbling. Easy. Jule moved in on her amid scattered pockets of death in a universe of fog.

At the same time, Rafe and Shapcott led Chasen off the dirt-and-grass lane and back to the village, where Chasen noted a few of his troops fighting to the last. It brought him pride and sadness. "To the gallows now?" he asked.

"Yes," Shapcott answered quietly. "I'm sorry I don't have a blindfold for you. We can fashion one—"

"Wouldn't wear it if you did," Chasen said flatly.

Rafe guided him forward.

Forty feet away, Jule edged toward the hobbled Kimpton, convincing herself that this poor limping nobody had been there at Rafe's death, had cheered it, celebrated it. And this nobody would now pay. Jule moved in, knife ready.

Then some smoke parted. And the whole world simply stopped . . .

She saw him.

Her Rafe. Alongside Chasen.

And Rafe saw her.

He wasn't dead.

She wasn't dead.

The stories had all been lies. The grief had all been for naught.

Now they just stared . . .

For a moment, breathing became impossible. The battle became silent and the air became clear. Even their commanding officers seemed to sense the magnitude of the moment, lowering their eyes solemnly.

Evidence and disbelief collided. He was right there; she could *see* him. The funeral he'd given her a thousand times in his mind was suddenly belied by the fact that she was *here*.

Agony vanished, replaced by wonder. Music. There were still skirmishes around them . . . but these two had *always* made the rest of London disappear. Rafe started toward her. Jule hesitated a moment, her legs briefly unable to move, then she too began to walk, her knife falling from her hand.

When they were just feet apart, Rafe began to shudder; the gift was too much to hold. Her face, her heart, those hands—they'd always seemed too perfect to be real. Now she'd risen from the grave. He opened his arms wide, the battle be damned.

It was then that the shot rang out from behind her.

It struck Rafe on the left side of his chest. He dropped in a heap. Jule turned.

Fifty feet away, Maud lowered a rifle, proud of herself for not having marred his beautiful face.

TWENTY-FIVE

Life froze. Ugliness had won. And Jule now felt unmoored. Her love had died again.

Maud's fellow soldiers didn't know how to react. She'd killed a member of her own House. A hole in his coat marked the spot where the bullet had entered, right over his heart.

The street was suddenly silent. Kimpton screamed. Shapcott could not bring himself to move. Even Chasen was shaken. He took a knee in prayer. Breathless, Jule knelt at Rafe's side.

She was surrounded by enemies, armed Rogues encircling her—and she knew the next slugger would be aimed at her. Or perhaps she'd hang beside Chasen at the gallows on the common. But that hardly mattered; death sounded like a promotion now. She put a hand to his face and waited calmly for capture or gunfire. His eyes were closed.

Then, somehow, they opened.

Jule gasped.

He drew a breath. She was too stunned to react. He reached into his coat. She mumbled, "Don't move, love. Be still," but he didn't stop. And from a pocket inside the coat, Rafe removed that hymnal, the one she'd given him the first night they'd met.

A crushed slugger lay inside, having burrowed into the pages. The music had saved him, once again.

Jule began to weep and wrapped her arms around him. Rafe's fellow Rogue soldiers drew nearer, weapons down, without malice. They no longer saw Jule as an enemy.

But Maud did. She marched forward, furious, her sidearm drawn, and hollered his name. *"RAFE!"*

Rafe looked up. Maud again took aim. Rafe threw Jule aside in an effort to protect her and—

BANG. The report echoed off the empty shop walls.

Maud, struck in the back of the leg, clutched at her new wound as she fell to the ground, having no idea who'd fired the shot that had just hit her.

But Rafe and Jule saw. And their shock was total.

It was *Jameson*, staring at Maud as she writhed, his aim perfect.

His vision was just fine. It had *always* been fine.

Years of deception, plotted in anticipation of this day. He had simply waited, patiently, for the moment when Rogues and Crowns would finally deplete themselves enough to be overrun.

Behind Jameson was an army all his own: his aides, plus a nation of Habs. Thousands. All of them armed. Jameson had rallied Hab Nation, fitted them out, and led them here. He hollered, "THAT IS ENOUGH!"

Two captains flanked him: Byron and Breena. The Rogues were too shocked to respond. *HE CAN SEE?* Jameson ordered Breena, "Get her treated and placed into custody."

Breena nodded. "Yes, sir," she said, and headed toward Maud.

Then, to Byron, Jameson said, "And send a detail to the common to take down the gallows."

"Yes, sir," Byron replied.

Jameson looked to Shapcott now. "General, you can release your prisoner. Today begins a New London. Summary executions won't be a part of it."

Shapcott was speechless—all of them were—each rethinking years they'd shared with Jameson. The patience he'd employed, the sheer will, to fool an entire city for so long... it was dazzling. Shapcott's troops released Chasen as Jameson studied the bloody street—the dead, the injured, the mad. He sighed. "All this over the color of a piece of cloth."

No one replied. They couldn't. He approached Rafe and Jule now.

"Are you injured?" he asked Rafe.

Rafe mumbled, "No." It was all too much to process.

Jameson breathed out a smile. "The rank above captain is a major, is that right?"

Jule nodded. "Yes."

Jameson returned, "Then I'd like you to join my peacetime army at that rank, both of you. We'll need you."

Rafe and Jule were dumbstruck. But everyone here knew their answers would be yes. Jameson had just made their love legal.

Shapcott asked, "Am I to be jailed?"

"Of course not," Jameson said. "But the war is over for you, for both Houses. *War itself* is over now." There wasn't much either general could say.

"All right," Jameson called to his Hab troops, "let's evacuate any wounded we can find, and tend to the bodies of the fallen. May this be the last time we ever need to."

Swarms of Habs, armed for the first time, now filled the street as ordered, wading into all this death. Grim work awaited, but they felt empowered. Jule helped Rafe to his feet. The day didn't yet feel real. Peace didn't yet feel possible. War didn't yet feel antique. But they had each other now, at last. It was good to be alive. And above water. She took his hand. It was shaking.

She put it to her lips and kissed his palm softly. Then, in the awed silence of their fellow soldiers, they made their way through the wreckage of this street where so many had died. Soldiers parted for them and lowered their weapons, a gesture of respect bordering on awe. But nothing was said. They had led without trying to.

Leaving the bloodied street behind, Rafe and Jule crossed the common. A Crown flag still flew proudly atop it. Jule decided that she'd climb up there and pull it down. Tomorrow.

They ambled down the A205 road, following as it sloped gently toward the waterline. Rafe and Jule climbed into a pirogue and rowed north.

Neither spoke. Neither knew what to say.

As they paddled through Woolwich, nothing but rooftops were visible. Crabs crawled, seals squawked. But a light wind had cleared the air around them; the stench was suddenly gone.

Rafe was thankful for that. Jule, of course, didn't notice the difference. "Where should we go?" she finally asked.

It was a fair question. The idea of enemy camps suddenly seemed so odd, archaic. But familiar.

"Jameson wants us to lead the Habs," Rafe suggested. "Maybe we ought to live with them."

"I like that," she said.

"We'll build a house."

"Yes."

They kept rowing, still mostly silent... until Rafe muttered, "He had books."

"Huh?"

"Jameson. He had books, in his quarters. I saw them. But I didn't think to ask why a blind person would have books. He could see, the whole time."

"Yeah," she said. "Even if we couldn't."

Rafe stopped rowing for a moment and took her hand. The pirogue drifted idly. It was all just too much to believe.

"I love you, Major," he breathed.

She laughed. "I love you too, Major."

They kissed deeply, their eyes locked.

The titles fit. It was as if they knew, somehow, that the fighting might not yet be over.

It wasn't.

TWENTY-SIX

*L*ove love love love hope hope hope hope peace peace peace peace. Three months later, New London had become a new world, and every day felt like freedom. Byron and others worked tirelessly to write a constitution for the city, crafting a representative government modeled on democracies of the past. Election Day was two weeks away. Byron himself was on the ballot, for a council position. No one doubted he'd be elected. His leadership, they all knew, would be vital.

The front gates at both Eltham and Paternoster Square were now open and unmanned. That was progress. Neither House had gotten around to taking down its walls, but everyone agreed it would get done. The former quarantine tents in both camps were now schools where children from both Houses mixed.

Habs still toiled in the fields, but they were now the owners of their own harvest. No guards oversaw them, or weighed their yield, or took their crops. An economy was beginning to form, still based on the bartering of goods and services; yet in it were the seeds of a benevolent capitalism.

To help her build a peacetime army, Breena had invited veteran soldiers from both Houses to become her drill sergeants. Only Kimpton, Paris, and Maddox had said yes. The others needed more time and healing.

No more MiGs had thundered overhead; no more Russian patrol boats had troubled the water. All of that felt like an old dream now—to everyone but Rafe and Jule. War was yesterday. Progress was now. Jule and Rafe were the faces of New London.

Jameson was certain its future would be bright. And dry. The water had receded another two inches in those three months.

Honus and Big Lil still operated their forges, but the urgent market for sluggers and Canners had vanished overnight. Necessary now were hammers and nails. The Habs wanted to build things. And Honus had begun a new product line as well: wedding rings.

Children were thriving. Liam and Portia and Danton had become friends; they took on Willa as a mascot. Chasen and Shapcott were now relics. They visited the injured, and no one ever treated them rudely. But their irrelevance was clear, and each kept to himself mostly. It was easier that way.

For the soldiers on both sides—men and women who had survived the Bloody and Eltham Village and countless other slaughters—life now ran at a new and unfamiliar temperature. War had been their careers; suddenly they were without one. Stranger still, they found themselves without an enemy. Former foes were now fellow farmers, sharing fields all across the Dry Ten—the awkwardness made worse because, while both armies had suffered devastating losses, one House had won and the other had lost. The result had been a few deep silences between rows of tall wheat, but no arguments or fights. The folly of all that seemed clear now.

Rafe and Jule were the proof of it, a constant reminder to the rest of the city about the power of possibility. Among the Habs, these two were simply referred to as "the Majors." In Eltham and Paternoster Square, they were lionized, hailed as the lovers who'd saved the world. Some Rogues may have privately held on to their ancient hatred for Jule. And many Crowns surely still privately despised Rafe. But it was now heresy to say so aloud. So they were cheered everywhere they went, their names synonymous with progress and hope. Parents now raised their children to be like the Majors, an idea that months before would have been treason.

The two lovers lived in a cabin built for them by the Habs beside a field of tall wheat. Music played there every night, the arm on the Victrola having been repaired by Portia of all people. The child had a knack for fixing things. One night, as they lay in the stillness, Rafe laid a hand on Jule's belly, grinning—his eyes full of promise.

"One day," he said, "our baby will be floating in there. Safe."

"Yes," she breathed.

"She'll be so lucky to have you for a mother."

Jule beamed. Rafe kissed her, and fell into a peaceful sleep.

Hours later, Jule awakened alone. That was the norm now—Rafe would creep out of the cabin predawn. When asked, he'd say with a grin that there was something he had to do. But he wouldn't say more. She liked the playful intrigue of it.

Among the things New London had yet to establish was a system of courts. Justice, everyone knew, had to be reinvented now, a set of agreed-upon laws. But Byron's constitution was still being written. And of course, no judges had yet been elected.

So Maud remained in Bergen's as a prisoner, where she awaited trial for trying to kill Rafe—although there was not yet a jurist to judge her or a courtroom in which she could be tried. Her days were weeks. Alone. Confined. A subject of scorn. Fairly or not, she had now come to represent a bygone era of hypnotic hostility, the lunatic who'd tried to kill true love itself. No one in Paternoster would say a word on her behalf. To do so would now be tantamount to a vote for hatred and war.

So she was very much alone in this ghost of a space when Rafe came to visit her on a bright Sunday morning, a trip he'd been dreading since her incarceration. He entered cautiously.

Maud's head lifted slowly. She held up her left hand; the wound on her palm from taking the Mark was a permanent scar now, a badge of honor to her.

"Hi, Maud."

She paused, then said, "Off to marry your Crown whore?"

Rafe sighed. "We shouldn't expect a gift, then?"

Maud would never admit it, but she admired that; Rafe went on, "Yes, we marry today."

"I hope it snows."

"It's June."

"Then I hope it floods."

"Water's receding, haven't you heard? All the fights of the past are over now. Everyone seems to see that but you."

"Nah, I'm just the only one willing to say it aloud."

"Is that so?"

"People might dance at your wedding, Rafe, but every Rogue there would rather stab your Crown to death than celebrate with her. And the Crowns feel the same about us. And the Habs hate us *both*!"

"So cynical."

"You liked that about me once."

They eyed each other for a long, pregnant beat. Then he tried, "You can make this easier on yourself, Maud."

"How? By saying I'm sorry? I'm not. Just sorry I missed."

"You want to be convicted?"

"'Course not. But I wouldn't lie just to avoid it."

"I wish you would," Rafe said.

"*You* told a million lies, Rafe. How'd ya feel doing that?"

"Probably like *you* felt when you told me she was dead."

Maud regrouped. "You were a traitor to our House."

"Yet I'm not the one on trial," he replied.

"You should be."

"You shot me, Maud. And even I don't want you to die."

"If what's out there is a false peace between two Houses that still despise each other, then prison is where I'd rather be."

"You're smarter than this."

"Yeah, well, my mistakes are mine to make."

The conversation was done. They both knew it. He sighed. "Good luck, Maud."

"Congrats on the big day!"

An hour later, Rafe and Jule were wedded—not coupled, *wedded*—surrounded by children and neighbors and Habs and retired soldiers. Minister Dawson officiated.

Two lives, dedicated for so long to battle, were now to be dedicated to something higher. The whole city felt it. Vows were exchanged, as were rings—made by Honus and Big Lil.

And Rafe wept. He looked at his bride—even as the minister was quoting Scripture—and whispered, "You saved my life."

Jule wept too. Today was joy. Today was love. Even the river felt like a friend.

After the ceremony, everyone ate and danced. Portia and Liam and Danton—once taught to kill one another—played happily. Jameson made so many toasts he was soon too drunk to stand. Everyone laughed. Willa spun in place. Promise was everywhere. Paris, once "coupled" to Jule, blessed the event and offered his undying loyalty to the couple with great sincerity. It moved them both.

Then, a sorrow. As Jameson rose for one last toast, he drunkenly stumbled and fell face-first to the ground. Many laughed without meaning to, but Rafe and Jule instantly knew he'd been injured.

Indeed, Jameson was unconscious, his nose clearly broken. And the party was over.

The newlyweds waited until he awakened, then left him in the care of Byron and Breena.

As the sun began to rise, Jule and Rafe exchanged gifts. She went first, placing in his palm a tiny boat made of twigs, fastened with sap.

It took his breath away, the kindness of it. She smiled. "May it be the only boat you'll ever need."

A laugh escaped his lips. "Come with me," he said. "I wanna show you something."

He led her by the hand to a decrepit building, once a garage. Rafe swung its tall doors open . . . and Jule's eyes went wide.

Inside was a sailboat. A real one. Twenty-five feet long—with a beam, or width, of ten feet. Her mast rose to thirty feet.

The wood in her hull—at Rafe's insistence—had come from the Cadbury Wall. He had recently ripped planks from it—personally, joyously. Permanently. Her varnish had come from sap pilfered from sycamore trees. Now she sat on old bricks. Rafe had christened her *The Sun*. He looked to Jule, excited. "May she be the only boat *you'll* ever need."

Jule sighed without meaning to, a disappointment to them both. "Rafe . . ."

"No one can stop us anymore," he said. "We can go anywhere we want."

"Rafe—"

"Yes?"

"Why would we leave? Didn't we survive all this so we wouldn't *have* to?"

"We survived all this so we could be *together*, and happy, just us. I built this for *us*."

"I think you built it for *you*, darling. You know I can't just run away."

Rafe exhaled, crestfallen. "We wouldn't be running *from* anything. We'd be seeing what's out there."

"I want to be *here*."

"Why?"

Jule eyed him, a long beat. Then: "Rafe, people need *leaders*. That's us, whether we wanted to be or not."

"Let someone *else* lead. Jameson, Byron, Breena. They're all capable. I just want *you*."

A disagreement. *The* disagreement. On their wedding night. It frustrated them both. "We promised these people something," Jule began. "We asked them to *trust* us, to give up everything. And they did. They turned their backs on three hundred years of war. Now we're just going to leave them?"

"We're not responsible for them!"

"Of course we are!" she batted back.

"Why are you so resistant to this?"

"*Why are you so set on doing it?*"

Rafe started a reply, then swallowed it . . . and walked out.

He asked a few friends to help him get the boat to the water. And their first night of marriage was spent in separate beds—his on *The Sun*, where he lay belowdecks, listening to the water as it lapped on the other side of the hull.

Rafe awakened on the boat, and deboarded to check on Jameson. He entered Jameson's apartment, where Byron sat at a table, patiently crafting that constitution. Jameson's face was beginning to turn purple with bruising. He said he felt fine, just hungover.

But something had changed; Rafe could see it. The fall had shaken Jameson. Suddenly, his confidence—his certainty—seemed gone. Rafe went outside with a baited line, caught a few fish, and insisted that Jameson eat a meal.

That same morning, Jule rowed to Eltham and entered Nelly's unit without a knock, then prepared a light breakfast for them as silence hung. Nelly had been newly coupled once. She didn't feel the need to say much except, "They do have egos, you know."

Jule said nothing, just nodded.

The whole city, it seemed, now knew that Rafe and Jule had slept a mile apart on their first night as a married couple. They'd been the first soldiers in centuries to actually *choose* each other. But now it all just felt empty.

When night fell, Jule checked in on Jameson, who seemed disoriented. Then she returned to the cabin beside the tall wheat, where she found Rafe sitting on the floor, his back propped against the splintery wall.

He'd been crying. That melted her.

"I'm sorry I built you something you didn't like," he said. "I just thought, if you and I were on that boat, I'd always know where you are."

That melted her too. She breathed out a smile. "C'mere, Major," she said, and crooked a finger, leading him to the bed.

Later, languid, she smiled. "Can I offer a compromise?"

"Sure."

"A honeymoon on the boat? A week or two out there . . . then we come back here and make a new world?"

Yes. A big yes. His heart felt full. He put his arms around her. She leaned in. And they stayed there for a moment, as happy as they'd ever been in their war-torn lives. "Thank you, Wife," he said.

"Thank you, Husband."

London, surely, would survive two weeks without them. The land seemed healed. The sky seemed calm. The people seemed hopeful. And Jameson, although not yet ready to leave his apartment, swore that he was fine.

Then a wind began to blow . . .

TWENTY-SEVEN

An impenetrable fog clung to the river as morning broke on what Rafe and Jule had named Sailing Day. The dense whiteness was thick enough to make the opposite bank invisible. Yet great excitement was everywhere. Their voyage to the Continent was about to begin.

Everyone had debated whether the newlyweds should bring weapons aboard, but Rafe and Jule had settled the matter quickly. They were soldiers. They'd bear arms. Now, as they loaded in, a party of well-wishers had gathered. Byron, Breena, Shapcott, Chasen, Maddox, Paris, Kimpton, Nelly, and all the children. The gifts were food. The joy was sincere. Jameson was here too, using a cane to keep himself upright.

His balance was off. They all saw it. But the real damage from his fall had been done to his psyche. This man whose courage had fooled, and then transformed, all of London, no longer seemed like himself. The confidence was gone. Falling had made him feel mortal.

Nevertheless, he had come today to celebrate, to wish the newlyweds well.

"We won't be long," Jule promised the crowd.

Breena asked Rafe, "You really know how to sail this thing?"

"I think so," he said. "And we did bring oars."

Everyone laughed. Rafe took Byron's hand and said, "Keep leading."

"Hurry back," the Hab replied.

Rafe and Jule approached Jameson and embraced him as one. "Thank you," they said.

"I did very little." Jameson grinned. "It was you." His voice sounded thinner now. And his face remained a bruised map.

Rafe looked to his bride and smiled. "Ready?"

"Ready," she returned.

"Let's cast off."

Jule hugged Nelly. "I wish it were clearer," Nelly said. "Ya can't see in front of you."

"It'll be clearer downriver," Jule said confidently. She and Rafe climbed aboard, waving to their friends and former foes. Everyone cheered warmly, especially the children. Beyond lay the future, cloudy or not. Rafe was just about to unmoor the craft from the dock and plunge into the thick gray when—

Uninvited, that *sound* returned . . .

Jule had heard it once before, on this very river. A throaty motor, rumbling powerfully. A *machine*. But this sound was *bigger*. It made her blood congeal. *No. God, no. Not today* . . .

The cheering stopped. The children went silent. Nothing was visible beyond the socked-in cloud that clung to the water and stretched to the sky. Just the sound, the motor, the machine . . . like a villain hiding behind a stage curtain. No one knew what it was. But they could read her reaction. So could Rafe.

The sound grew louder, coming closer, still invisible. Rafe tried to identify it—they all did—but that was impossible. The twenty-fifth century didn't *have* sounds like this. Yet somehow everyone knew—intuitively—it meant doom.

Then the fog parted. Or rather, something cut through it, pushing all that whiteness aside in a muscular way, and every jaw on shore simply dropped.

Terror. That fast.

Before them was a Russian warship. Vastly larger than the cutter Jule had seen on this river before. It was metal, impregnable. It had a motor; it belched smoke.

And it carried death itself in the form of long guns—to launch mortars and grenades.

The warship idled in place, as foreign as the monstrous MiG had been. No sailors on its deck; its bridge was hidden from view behind tiny windows, which added to the scare.

On the riverbank, hands began to shake. Knees too. Parents grabbed their children. Confusion reigned. Old soldiers like Paris and Maddox unconsciously reached for the knives on their hips as if knives might somehow help.

Sailing Day had just ended. From his books, Rafe knew that this was a Buyan-M-class Russian corvette, built in the 2000s for river fighting. His fellow citizens knew only that it was death on the water. A stunned citizenry, staring...

Jameson had suddenly gone pale. His breathing grew shallow. His foot tapped nervously. Jule had never seen that in him before.

But there had never been a monster on the water before. It sat atop the river, framed by dense fog. Rafe took Jule's hand and asked, "Was that the—"

"No. Much bigger."

Rafe digested that. The engine's sound hung like the fog did.

Then, on the bridge of the beast, movement...

A hatch opened. And a woman—presumably the ship's captain or ranking officer—emerged. She bore two bottles of light brown liquid—*whiskey?*—which she extended toward the New Londoners in a universal gesture of offering.

On the bank, people stirred and murmured a bit. Maybe the warship wasn't necessarily death on the water. Maybe...

On the bridge of the corvette, the woman smiled warmly and hollered something in Russian that sounded like *"Droozyah!"* No one knew what it meant. They looked to Jameson—

He was shaking now, unable to reply. Everyone saw it. No one knew what to *do* about it. Without a word, Jule and Rafe climbed off *The Sun* and joined Jameson on the dock, beside Byron and Breena.

The corvette's captain again extended those bottles forward, clearly an invitation to come aboard.

"Jameson?" Jule asked.

Again, nothing. He seemed paralyzed.

"Do we respond?" Rafe asked.

All of New London awaited the answer, needing their leader to *act*.

The long guns on the deck of the beast were enough to wipe out the population of this city. The sound of her engine—*machinery, power*—made the men and women on that riverbank feel naked, puny, helpless.

"Jameson?" Jule asked again.

Again, he was silent, frightened, awed. This was NOT the man Jameson had been before taking that fall. This was a shell.

And still the captain of the warship waited, with gestures of friendship. Then she looked back to the bridge of her vessel, gestured with her hand, and the corvette's engine turned off.

The sound stopped. The smoke stopped. The warship bobbed. And from her bow the corvette's anchor splashed into the water, followed by an unending chain of metal until the anchor hit bottom.

"That was a statement," Jule said.

Indeed. The warship was going nowhere. It wasn't a MiG roaring past, or a patrol boat disappearing into the night. It was here. Fixed. An invasion? No one knew.

"Do we approach?" Rafe asked.

"Let's discuss that," Jule replied.

She reboarded their sailboat. Rafe, Byron, and Breena followed.

Jameson did as well, albeit numbly. Rafe whispered to his bride, "I really did want to sail away with you."

She breathed out a smile. "Someday."

Belowdecks, they talked for an hour, while all of New London waited breathlessly. The warship, like the fog, didn't move.

The options were few. Either they would row out to the warship, as invited, or they would not. Neither sounded good.

"We have to find out why they're here," Rafe said.

Jule said flatly, "They're here to conquer." No doubt in her voice.

Byron replied, "Not everyone is an enemy."

Rafe thought about the strangers who had kidnapped him as a child, and the deaths that had followed. "Not every visitor is a friend," he said.

"Majors," Jameson finally breathed, his voice shaky, "what do you recommend?"

Byron interjected, "Why do *we* get to decide? Nobody elected us." He was a Hab to his core. Jule admired that.

But she replied, "Sometimes you can't stop to take a vote." That swayed him.

Minutes later, on a pirogue, Jameson—who insisted he was fit—Rafe, and Jule rowed toward the Russian corvette. Their entire city watched.

The captain's name was Vazlav. Irina Vazlav. Average height, a plain face, piercing eyes. She had a crew of sixty, lining up now on the deck to greet—and salute—the visitors in the rowboat. Each sailor looked tired and worn. The men were unshaven. Their uniforms were frayed and saggy. The women looked no better. *All* the crew members needed a belt. But they stood with pride as the rowboat moored with their vessel and Rafe lowered his oars.

Then he and Jule helped their shaken leader onto the corvette.

Vazlav welcomed the three New Londoners warmly, her English surprisingly good. "I'm sorry we interrupted your sail." Vazlav smiled. "Where were you headed?"

"Honeymoon," Rafe said.

"Ah!" she shouted joyously. "Congratulations!"

"Thank you."

"Come!"

They boarded warily, returning the salutes of Vazlav's crew—and half waving to their New London neighbors on the shore. Vazlav beamed. "Let me show you our bridge." And in they went, Jameson balancing on that cane.

The bridge was stunning, a time machine showing the past *and* the future all at once. Candle-less light. Power. Electricity. Energy. Rafe and Jule just stared, dazzled by a technology that seemed almost mythic. A dashboard full of instruments unlike anything they'd ever seen before, dials and readouts, all brightly lit, measuring speed, fuel pressure, engine temperature, voltmeter, carbon dioxide, comms, navigation, radar, sonar. Overwhelming.

And *weapons* systems, control boards dedicated to killing. From here, Vazlav could press a button and launch a deadly grenade from the deck with pinpoint accuracy. "I hope never to press such a button again," she sighed. "There's been too much death already. Everywhere."

"We seek only peace," Jule replied.

"That comforts me," Vazlav said. "So much to discuss!"

Rafe continued to study all the technology before him. There were actual *clocks* aboard—digital readouts telling the exact time of day. Not a guess, not an estimation based on sun and shadow. Numbers. 8:14 a.m. Jule and Rafe had never been fixed in time before.

It was all too much to believe, and they stared like children, too fascinated to be frightened. Vazlav seemed to enjoy that.

Jameson, though, remained pale. And every time he swallowed, they heard an audible gulp. Vazlav slid cups of whiskey to them, which Rafe and Jule sipped politely. Jameson, his hands shaking, downed his in a single swig. That fall, and this shock, had unmoored him completely.

"Would you like a tour?" Vazlav asked, touching Jule's hand.

"Yes, please."

Jameson said nothing.

Vazlav led them through the vessel, every inch of it daunting. The muscularity of the engine room left them stunned. Jule noted barrels of fuel stored here, in rows that seemed endless.

The galley boasted kitchen appliances made of *metal*. Coffee makers, stoves, ranges, an oven that used *microwaves*. It all seemed impossible. And Vazlav was now delighting in their awe. They felt like Neanderthals.

The corridors, the breezeways, Vazlav's quarters. Only the sick bay was off-limits. "For your protection," Vazlav said. Rafe and Jule couldn't help but view this craft through soldiers' eyes, each silently searching for vulnerabilities, weaknesses. There weren't any. Vaslav seemed to know it. The end of the tour was the armory, where they saw weapons entirely foreign to them. Automatic rifles in rows, uniform in their lethality. And body armor, rows of that too. No hand-forged slugger was going to pierce those. His eyes darting, Jameson's face was an anxious map. He looked haunted.

They returned to the bridge, where he slugged down another whiskey as Rafe and Jule asked Vazlav endless questions—probing, trying. It was hard to order their curiosity. They wanted to know *everything* . . . starting with why Vazlav was here.

Vazlav smiled. "I am here for the same reason my crew is here, because we can no longer stand to be *there*. In Russia."

Her story—and that of her country—followed.

Russia's devastation from the Great Soak and the wars that followed had led to utter collapse. Hundreds of millions of people dead. Hundreds of years of darkness. Cities standing but barely breathing. An absence of government and order. And from the ashes came the rise of factions, gangs.

"Houses," Jule muttered.

"Yes," Vazlav agreed. "St. Petersburg alone had five ruling Houses, constantly at war, sometimes fighting with sticks and knives, over scraps. It was butchery. Our House was called Vlast. That means *power*."

Jameson still hadn't said a word. Vazlav went on, "Then a rival House, Dynamo, found a giant underground fuel depot that had somehow survived all the wars. It would have allowed them to use *machinery*. Boats. Planes.

"So the other four Houses in St. Petersburg joined forces, and GazWar began. It lasted fifty years, with so many dead. We all did things no human should do."

Rafe and Jule nodded knowingly.

"Dynamo won the war," Vazlav said, "just last year. They seized the fuel and harnessed all that machinery."

She sighed heavily, looking back at her crew. "They intended to make slaves of us and the other Houses too. So I gathered this crew and we stole this boat and as much fuel as we could take, and we fled by night."

The New Londoners said nothing, until Jule asked, "Captain, did Russia have any contact with the outside world?"

"None. Communications never returned. Not even radio."

Rafe nodded. The captain continued, "Dynamo looks for us; they even sent planes! We had to move quickly."

"There was a MiG overhead," Rafe said. "A few months ago."

"And a patrol boat, on this river," Jule added.

Vazlav nodded, unsurprised. "War is all they know. But they haven't found us yet!"

No one replied. She went on, "We thought perhaps you might've rediscovered machinery here too."

"No," Rafe sighed.

Vazlav entreated her guests to have more of the whiskey. Only Jameson accepted.

Hours of conversation followed—about the rivalries that had torn their respective cities apart, and the privation brought forth by all that unwanted water, and parents and friends and loved ones who'd died . . . and unanswerable questions about the rest of the pain-soaked world. What had happened to the US? To China? To Japan? To Australia? Had the African continent survived? No one knew. The world had lost all connections to itself. Vazlav offered, "We came in contact with a sailboat just days ago, in the North Sea, a family fleeing the Continent. They said they were from Alsace, said that used to be Germany and France, one country now. Did you know that?"

None of the New Londoners had.

Vazlav went on, "I am heartened by your love. But your story could never have happened in St. Petersburg! Someone from Dynamo and someone from Vlast? In love? Neither would survive."

"We almost didn't," Jule said. "I died once. Rafe died twice."

Vazlav chuckled, then repeated some version of the story in Russian to a few of her crew. They laughed too.

Throughout, Jule kept waiting for Jameson to behave as a commander might, to inquire of the Russian captain what her intentions were. But Jameson wasn't Jameson anymore. Finally, Jule launched, "Captain, what are your intentions now?"

"My intentions?" Vazlav returned.

"Yes."

"To live here with my crew, among you, in peace. A quiet refuge."

That fast, the world shifted. Jule looked to Rafe. "You mean to *stay* here," Jule restated.

"Yes! I have always wanted to see this city. The land of Shakespeare! He taught me English!"

More silence from Jameson. Rafe asked Vazlav, "Do you have means of camouflaging this vessel?"

"No," Vazlav replied, surprised by the question.

Jule pressed, "Would you be willing to moor it a few miles upriver? The cover is better there, and it would present less of a threat to us."

"A threat in what way? We come here in friendship."

"I doubt the MiG looking for you will take that into consideration," Jule said.

"I'm sorry," Vazlav returned. "But no, we could not do this. Those logistics would not benefit us."

Again, Jule awaited a contribution from Jameson. He simply stared. So Jule spoke. "Captain, if you're discovered by Dynamo and bombed from above while so close to our shore, or attacked by another warship, *our people* will pay for it."

Vazlav nodded, unsurprised, but didn't reply.

Rafe asked, "Would you be willing to *scuttle* your ship? As a gesture of good faith—and a condition of our welcoming you and your crew to our city."

The Russian laughed, incredulous. "I don't understand. You live three hundred years without technology, then someone brings it to you, and your first thought is to sink it?"

Jule replied: "To protect our shores, yes." Her voice was calm and unwavering.

"No. We could not do this."

Finally, Jameson spoke. "Nor should you have to!" Jule and Rafe stared. He went on, "We can be better neighbors than that!"

Hours of silence, and now betrayal. Jule and Rafe looked sickened.

Vazlav smiled. "You know, a friendship with us might be very good for you. My guns can protect you from *your* rivals." Vazlav picked up the whiskey bottle and asked, "More?"

Only Jameson extended his cup.

That digital clock read 2:32 p.m. now. Jule eyed it, dazzled. It was the first measurement of time—six hours in here—in her entire life. She absently wondered what life with a watch must have been like. "Captain," she said, "we and our colleagues need to convene to discuss all this, as I'm sure you can understand. Thank you for your hospitality."

"Thank you for the warm welcome," Vazlav replied. "I know the vessel must have seemed frightening at first!"

There was a feeling of make-believe in the air—pretense and

performance. Every nerve in Jule's body was howling, alerting her that this captain and her ship were not to be trusted.

The trio of New Londoners rose to leave, whereupon every crew member on the bridge—led by Vazlav herself—again stood as one and offered a brisk salute. Rafe and Jule returned it. Jameson, beyond drunk now, staggered a bit. "I am not from the military," he slurred.

Vazlav, still saluting, went right past that. "And if any of the children in your camp want to come aboard, they're welcome! We want to be the best of neighbors!"

Pretense. Again. Jule was sure of it.

They nodded in thanks, then emerged onto the deck of the corvette. The dense fog had vanished into bright sunlight, Jameson silently staring as his majors rowed him to shore.

Jule suddenly saw the next six months of her life unfolding with hideous clarity: Vazlav and her crew, heavily armed, taking control of this new city. A rebellion forming to resist them, Jule and Rafe obliged to lead it. Jameson lost to his new fecklessness. Weapons and battles and death. The cycle repeating, forever. "Jameson," she said. "That was unacceptable, cowering like that."

"You are confusing silence with weakness," Jameson replied unconvincingly.

"I don't think so," Jule said. "Leaders *lead.*"

Jameson replied, "They have arms we can't match."

"Leaders lead," she repeated.

Rafe kept rowing. And when they reached shore he ran as fast as he could to the quarters in which he'd once lived, and tore through his books on warships until he found the one that described the Buyan-M-class Russian corvette. He needed to know it capabilities, its vulnerabilities.

He needed to know if it could be sunk.

TWENTY-EIGHT

Suddenly, all of London was looking to the Thames. Citizens did the day's chores—feeding, cleaning, building, fixing, stitching—but their eyes were trained on the visitors anchored off the riverbank. All that unyielding metal. The faceless bridge. And the long guns, giant reminders that this city could be leveled at any moment. The result was a dull dread. They knew that if attacked they'd be called upon to fight. And they'd comply, and then die—not as members of any House, but as the first, and last, citizens of a doomed New London.

The children were equally fixated on the corvette bobbing innocently on the water. They asked their parents if they could go aboard and see it.

The answer for each was, "Not today."

Rafe watched those children—Willa, all of them—and wondered what kind of London they'd inherit. He asked Jule, "How about the name Hope?"

"For what?" she asked.

"Our baby. When that happens. When it's time. Hope."

Jule nearly melted. Hope was at Rafe's core. It had brought them together, and then brought an entire *war* to an end. She smiled. "I think that's a lovely name."

That night, Rafe taught Jule everything he knew about the

corvette: its history, its design, what it could and couldn't do. They studied the photos of it for hours. The vessel displaced five hundred tons of water; its top speed was twenty-eight knots. It carried four kinds of naval long guns and the grenade launcher. Its systems were pristine. Its onboard fire control was brilliantly designed. In every way, the boat seemed impregnable.

"But it isn't," Rafe said. "There's a way to attack it." And he told her how.

The next morning, on the trading floor, surrounded by Rafe, Byron, and Breena, Jule briefed Jameson on their options.

Jameson was trembling, further devolving right before their eyes.

Breena asked, "What kind of light weapons are aboard?"

Rafe answered, "Automatics. I counted five dozen, but there might be more. Plus the body armor."

Jule added, "She cannot be allowed to remain on our shore."

"So we do what?" Jameson asked. "Ask her to sail away?"

"We keep talking," Jule replied. "Keep learning about her, gleaning information, looking for weaknesses."

"They don't have any!" Jameson said.

"Every vessel has weaknesses," Rafe replied.

"Not if our entire navy is a single sailboat!"

"Jameson," Jule blurted, "all of their fuel is in the engine room. Barrels of it, highly flammable. One Canner, properly placed, could blow up the entire ship."

Jameson replied, "And kill the person placing it."

"That's war."

"That's *madness*."

"I volunteer," Rafe announced.

"Out of the question," Jameson replied.

Jule asked, "What's *your* plan, then?"

"Give her what she wants and invite them to stay."

"*That's* surrender!" Jule argued.

"It's peace in our time," he returned.

Jule was beginning to despise this man.

"We must have something they want," Rafe suggested.

Jameson shot back, "Such as?"

"I don't know. Grain? Medicine? There was something about the way she kept us from the sick bay."

Jule said, "I saw that too. But if they wanted grain or medicine, they would have asked for it. Or just demanded it."

Rafe said, "Maybe we should row back and ask her."

Jameson's eyes became fixed, as if the thought were too awful to contemplate. They all saw it. Jule shrugged, then looked to Rafe. "I want to check on Nelly. Come with me?"

The answer, of course, was yes. As soon as they'd left the trading floor, she said, "He's not worthy of command."

"No," Rafe agreed.

At Eltham, Jule and Rafe joined Nelly outside by a fire. The old woman had been to the still tonight, and was in a mood to talk about the day she'd saved Jule in Severndroog tower—her first kill in decades. Rafe thanked her for it.

But that deadly boat remained on the river, and the air felt thick. The future, which just days ago had looked like a sailing trip, now looked like an enemy invasion.

"What're you going to do?" Nelly asked.

"We don't know yet," Jule replied. "What do people want?"

Nelly scoffed. "They don't know. They want *you* to decide. Leading frightens most people."

Rafe sighed. "Nelly, we don't know either."

"Sure you do." Nelly smiled. *"Attack."*

They thought she was kidding.

The next days were *non*-days. Nothing moved. The corvette sat on the river. Fish swam under it. Birds spied it from above. Wind whistled across its deck. The water jostled it slightly.

And the people of London, having no better alternative, returned to their lives as if the threat now anchored off their shore had always been there. They gossiped, they exaggerated, they opined, and they went on.

But Jule knew an enemy when she saw one. So did Rafe. Each day he took his deepest breath and dove into the river, staying under for as long as he could. It was practice; if an underwater assault were to be launched on that corvette at some point, Rafe wanted to lead it.

On the fourth night of the corvette's presence, Rafe and Jule sat on the deck of *The Sun* and stared out at the gray, faceless boat. Two crafts, sharing a river. One mighty, one slight.

"Attack," she breathed, mimicking Nelly.

"She's right," he replied. "Better than letting *Vazlav* decide when the battle ought to begin."

Jule nodded, then changed the subject. "You built a beautiful boat, Rafe. I'm sorry I didn't say so at first."

He took her hand and smiled.

On the fifth morning since the corvette's arrival, London was stunned yet again. The sun was high overhead, suggesting noon. And life was crawling along at its usual pace, the city's new cloud of dread becoming just familiar enough to be tolerable. People worked, ate, slept, minded their children.

Then the shock. In a quiet midday moment, as Rafe and Jule visited with schoolchildren, the throaty rumble of a *second* Russian boat jarred the city.

New Londoners watched with dread as this patrol boat hurried up the river, turned to starboard, and throttled down beside the corvette, weighing anchor.

This was the craft Jule had seen before. The same two Russian sailors were aboard, looking tired and sunburned but resolute. Mounted 50-caliber guns extended from the boat's bow and stern.

The murmur of commerce stopped. Everyone hurried to the banks and stared out at the new arrival. So did Jule and Rafe. "Was that the same boat you—"

"Yes."

They knew they couldn't show the slightest hint of fear without panicking the citizens, so Jule said calmly, "Back to work, everyone. We'll investigate this and let you know what we find."

No one wanted to move, but Jule and Rafe ushered them along, sending them back to their daily cares.

Jameson then arrived with Byron and Breena, just as the sailors from the patrol boat boarded the corvette and disappeared inside without gunfire or any hostility at all. It felt like allies uniting, which suggested that Vazlav's story had been a lie.

The leaders of New London—Rafe, Jule, Byron, Breena, and Jameson—now gathered on the trading floor of the Stock Exchange at Paternoster. Maddox, Paris, Chasen, and Shapcott appeared as well—an expanded cabinet—to weigh options. None sounded good, and Jameson looked shakier than ever, steadying himself with gin.

"Okay," Jule said. "Now we know she lied to us. The sailors on that patrol boat are *not* her enemy."

Jameson replied, "I know no such thing."

"They boarded her vessel without event."

"Perhaps she surrendered."

"Jameson," Jule shot back, "surrender comes harder to some than others."

He sipped his gin. Jule went on, "The point is, she is no longer commander of a single vessel. She is now commander of a fleet. And we have no reason to believe there won't be other warships joining them soon."

"I agree," Jameson said. "That's why I believe we should be drafting plans to evacuate the city, immediately." His hands shook.

Jule and Rafe tried not to sag.

As hours fell away, the corvette and patrol boat—happy neighbors now—jounced on the Thames. Jameson's cabinet continued to implore him to act. Rafe believed a successful attack was possible. Jameson wouldn't hear of it.

And life went on.

The following morning, Rafe awoke first and watched Jule's belly rise gently with each breath. It shocked him—daily, repeatedly—how tightly his happiness was tied to her. Russian ships of war lolled right off his bow, but Jule was all Rafe could see. She was everything. Even drowning no longer scared him. Her eyes opened slowly.

He touched her belly and grinned. "Any signs of Baby Hope in there?"

Jule smiled. "You'll be the first to know, I promise!"

Rafe pulled her in close. "It's a great thing," he said, "having someone to say I love you to."

"Yes, it is."

He kissed her softly, and she breathed out a laugh. "No one knows! Fierce Rafe, soldier of soldiers, such a romantic."

"Shh," he whispered.

There was bliss on this boat. They'd earned it.

But just then, they heard a familiar sound, the rowing of a dinghy, just outside. They rose from their bed and climbed to the deck.

There, they saw a surprise—Vazlav, rowing a small lifeboat from the corvette, by herself, heading for the riverbank. She spotted Jule and Rafe and waved cheerfully. They half waved back, then hurried below to throw on clothes . . .

"What's it mean that she didn't bring any security with her?" Rafe wondered.

"She knows she doesn't need it," Jule answered.

Rafe considered that, and offered, half-jokingly: "You sure you don't want to just sail away?"

Jule whispered, "I love you"—and grabbed a sidearm and a long-knife. "Semi battle rattle," she said. "You too."

He obeyed. Jule was always right.

But even as he was arming himself, the urge to touch her was irresistible. He pulled her into his arms.

There they stood, kissing, their knives and sidearms banging into one another. And it didn't seem crazy at all.

Moments later, Vazlav's tiny lifeboat sat on the shore, twenty feet away from benches where Vazlav now met with Jameson, Rafe, Jule, Byron, and Breena. Again, all of New London waited and watched.

"Forgive me for not asking before," Vazlav said to Jameson. "I don't know how to address you. Are you President? Prime Minister? Chancellor?"

Jule interjected, "You can address us all. We lead together."

"How very Soviet of you." Vazlav smiled. "My crew is anxious and tired, and they wish to know if we are welcome here."

There it was, officially. A request for a decision. Jameson, as before, was silent. Paralyzed. So Jule began, "Captain, it's difficult for us to negotiate with you. We haven't found you to be an honest broker."

Jameson stiffened but didn't interject.

"How so?" Vazlav asked.

"The patrol boat that you had claimed was looking for you. It's moored to your craft now."

Vazlav smiled. "As you know, yesterday's enemy can be this morning's friend. Nevertheless, we would still like an answer."

"Would our answer actually matter?" Jule asked.

"One would always prefer cooperation," Vazlav returned.

"Captain," Jule said. "This would all be so much easier if you'd just state what you intend to do."

Now Jameson jumped in. "Major—"

Jule turned to him. "She appreciates the candor, I'm sure."

"I do," Vazlav agreed. She exhaled hard, then: "We intend to occupy this sector of your city."

An awful truth, bracingly clear, shaking Jule and Rafe into silence for a moment. Finally, he asked, "'We.' Your country?"

"My crew. We'd like to settle here. It's ideal for us."

Jule stepped in now. "Settle. Occupy. And what do you plan to do with the people who *live* here?"

"They're welcome to stay, of course. We'll need food, and you have fields and hands."

Their heads were swimming. The air felt thin. Jule asked, "As serfs? A conquered people?"

"As comrades."

"And if we refuse?"

"Then force, I'm afraid."

Again, silence. Jule and Rafe began calculating the risks of battle against such a well-armed foe.

But Jameson had other ideas. "You'll get no fight from us. There's been enough loss of life already."

"Good," Vazlav answered.

Again, Jule jumped in: "Would you give us a moment to discuss all this, Captain?"

"Of course," Vazlav said. "I'll await you on my vessel."

No one replied. They couldn't. Vazlav continued, "If one of you might help to push me out?"

And the meeting was over. The smiles were tight and formal.

Jule and Rafe walked Vazlav to her lifeboat in silence. Finally, Jule asked, "The story you told us, about having to flee Dynamo, was any of that true?"

"Every word. Our city is no longer our home. We had to find another."

"But why ours?" Jule asked. "It's not really your love of Shakespeare..."

"Do you know your country's history, Major?"

"Some."

"Every army that ever mattered wanted London. The Romans, the Vikings, the Normans, the Saxons, the French, the Nazis too. It's a perfect port on a perfect river. And when the world is the world again, its economy will run through this city again, as it always did before."

Jule asked, "You plan to reconnect the world?"

"Eventually it will reconnect itself. Human nature."

"Not exactly a 'quiet refuge' for you and your crew," Jule sighed.

"We've been quiet long enough. It's time to conquer now, time to build."

"How very Soviet of you," said Jule.

Vazlav shrugged. "Perhaps you'll stay and be a part of our administration here. You'd be a great asset, I know. You're fine soldiers. Your commander is not."

Jule eyed her, then said, "He's not our commander."

"So abandon him. I'm sure we'd all be speaking the same language before long."

Rafe couldn't contain himself. "Get in your boat, Captain."

Vazlav grinned. "Very well." She climbed in and rowed away.

They watched her go in silence. When she was out of earshot, Rafe asked, "Did I just hang us?"

"*Jameson* did," Jule said. "But, my love, I think we'd better assemble our forces. She's going to attack."

Rafe nodded in agreement. Jule put a hand to his face and held it there for a long while. Deep regret in her eyes. "I can't believe how much time you and I spent fighting each other. We should be on our boat right now, at sea, music playing . . ."

"One of these days." He smiled.

"Yes. When the fighting is done."

"Yes. We'll sail then."

Vazlav continued to row toward the corvette, with all of New London watching. On the shore, Jameson walked away. Byron followed. Watching them, Jule stiffened.

"Be right back," she said.

"You really should be leading us, Jule," he said.

"You'd follow me?" she asked.

"Anywhere."

She hugged him, and held on . . . and felt a small miracle—

Suddenly, briefly, his *scent* registered inside her.

It happened so quickly she almost couldn't feel it. But it did happen. An olfactory pop in her brain—visceral, almost a taste in her mouth. She could *smell* him, musky and real. She held on tighter, breathed it in.

It vanished fast. But it had been *present*. She decided to tell him about it—next time she saw him. The embrace ended. Rafe studied her . . . "Bye, love," Jule said.

"Bye, General," Rafe joked, feeling lucky and blessed. "Give him hell."

She nodded. "For Hope."

Her face—that face. He'd never loved her more.

"For Hope," he breathed, squeezing her hand.

As Jule headed up the bank, eager to scold Jameson, Breena arrived at Rafe's side: "Proper couple, you two are."

Rafe breathed out a grin. "We are."

"Happy for you, brother. You deserve it."

"Do I?" he asked.

He kept his eyes on the water, watching Vazlav row away with calm, muscular strokes. Oddly, the Russian stopped for a moment—her tiny craft beginning to glide peacefully . . .

As it did, she raised her right hand and signaled something to the unseen crew members on the bridge of the corvette, making a circular motion with her index finger. Rafe didn't recognize the gesture.

Then Vazlav resumed her rowing again, Rafe and Breena continuing to watch.

. . . which was when an odd sound squeaked into the air . . .

. . . the long guns on the deck of the corvette began to lower slightly . . . as if being aimed.

And on that lifeboat, Vazlav ducked and covered her head.

And Rafe knew . . . *No. God, no.*

He pushed his sister to the ground and hollered: "JUUUUULE!"

Jule, just now catching up to Jameson, turned. And she too saw the guns adjusting.

Her heart stopped. Her eyes locked in on his as Rafe started toward her—a step, a second step, a lifetime, every feeling all at once—then—

Black fire erupted from those guns, before the sound could register—a deafening BOOM.

And Rafe and Breena were no more. The *shore* was no more.

As Jule watched, the entire riverbank simply vanished into a cloud of launched earth—love itself, exploding into disappearance.

Vazlav resumed rowing again. Then, as she reached her vessel, the guns rose a bit.

They were now aimed at Paternoster Square . . .

PROCESSION

Every day is a gift, but not all gifts bring joy. All music is a wonder, but not all songs inspire.

Every life is a miracle. But some lives are not fully lived.

And all deaths matter, but some deaths matter more.

Westminster Abbey had once housed the dead bodies of kings, queens, authors, poets, and inventors. Rafe was none of those things, and the abbey had been underwater for centuries now. So there would be no splendid procession for him, no robed Reverend Dean to conduct a service, no stone vault chiseled with his name.

There should have been.

He was, by any measure, a hero. A lion. He risked and dared and warred and suffered. He taught and fought and defended and inspired. He healed and hurt and cried and cared and ran and swam and drowned and survived. He listened and lied and tore down and built up again. He ached and trusted and forgave and made peace. He lived and he led—every day.

Most shockingly, Rafe loved. And he suffered for that too—for showing us something true. He was a soldier, a captain, a rescuer, a counselor, a captor, a jailer, a prisoner, a fugitive, a partisan, a savior, a student, and a husband. He was faithful to all that was good in himself.

Not a king. Not a poet. Just a man who adored one woman, despite the unthinkable cost.

No, not all deaths are equal—nor all lives. *This* life made other ones better. This one made halves whole. It ennobled and enthralled and soared . . . and refused to sink.

This one left a mark. I feel it still.

TWENTY-NINE

Chaos, devastation, terror . . . and no time to mourn.

Jule's world had evaporated into sand. She stared in horror for a half second, then opened her mouth to call Rafe's name, but no sound emerged. Her hands—those hands he so adored—began to spasm.

Around her, citizens screamed as they fled. Parents gathered children in their arms. Bells rang in the square. Jule raced for the battered bank, even though she knew there would be nothing left of Rafe to retrieve. Byron did the same for Breena, his heart shattered.

Then the long guns boomed again. Fire and fury. This time the target was the square itself. That fast, the building housing the Stock Exchange floor was belching black smoke and flames from a hole in its face the size of a truck. The inhabitants of the square shrieked, nowhere to hide. The reach of the guns seemed limitless. Hundreds of people in mass panic. Jameson was so confused and frightened, he jumped into the river, covering his head. Paris dove in to retrieve him.

Jule and Byron met at the bank—breathless, stunned. Just then, the corvette's grenade launchers opened up. KA-CHUNK. KA-CHUNK. Fists of death flying right at them. She grabbed Byron's hand and called out, "RUNNNNN!"

And they did.

Behind them, a grenade detonated ten feet off the ground, decimating a tree that had been growing by the river's edge.

Madness surrounded them, a mass exodus. Another grenade traveled farther, exploding atop the medical tent. The loss of life inside was instant and unspeakable.

"INLAND!" Jule screamed. "GET TO ELTHAM!" It was all she knew, the defensive properties of her home. The long guns couldn't reach that far. So she ran blindly, knife and sidearm bouncing on her hips. She wanted to howl and cry—RAFE WAS DEAD, TRULY DEAD NOW—but there were lives to save, one of them her own. She and Byron raced for Paternoster, where they spotted Maddox hobbling on one good leg as he tried to evacuate citizens. They put him in a soldier's carry, rushing him away from this place. "I can walk!" he protested.

"You need to run!" Jule yelled.

A moment later, a shell eviscerated the spot he'd just occupied, leaving nothing behind but a crater of char, smoke, and debris. Another shell blew a section of the Rogue wall to pieces. Right behind it, now shielding themselves from wooden shards, Jule and Byron threw Maddox into a waiting pirogue, debris flying as they pushed the craft into the flooded street. Maddox paddled with all his might until he realized that Jule and Byron had not boarded behind him. "What're you doing?" he yelled.

They had already run back into the square to rescue others.

Moments later, Maddox had company. Jameson, soaking wet,

emerged from the square, hopped into that same pirogue, and paddled for his life.

From her vantage point inside Bergen's, Maud watched the catastrophe calmly. Her hands were bound to the booth around her. The building above her was on fire. And the square, the only home she'd ever known, was a mass of panic and terror. Flight and fright without an ounce of fight. Shapcott, once her general, ran past the restaurant's glassless window. Then a grenade exploded in midair, separating his legs from his torso, a life erased. Maud's death now seemed certain. And almost welcome.

Then Jule appeared in the doorway.

Knife in hand, she approached without a word and began to saw at the leather straps securing Maud to the booth, their eyes locked, as Jule warned: "You should get to Eltham. It's far enough inland. We'll rally there."

"Who's we?" Maud asked.

"Everyone."

Maud eyed the wedding band on Jule's left hand. Infuriating. "Where's Rafe?" she asked.

Jule kept cutting . . . "Rafe is dead. Breena too."

The words knocked Maud back. She didn't speak, couldn't. When the straps were cut, Jule pulled Maud to her feet. "Eltham," Jule repeated. "But if you try to harm anyone, ANYONE, I'll gut you."

"Jule," Maud muttered. "How can I help?"

Minutes later, they were outside together, hurriedly sorting through fallen bodies, looking for survivors. Among them was Liam, his adolescent face and shoulder bloodied, lying beside Portia, who was wounded as well. Jule grabbed the boy and threw him into a fireman's carry. Maud grabbed the girl and did the same. They hauled the children through the wreckage that had once been the main gate, where they found Byron loading two maimed soldiers into a pirogue. "There's no one else," he said. "No other survivors."

"Then let's go." The three rescuers pushed off and began the journey to Eltham. Behind them, Paternoster burned.

For the moment, Eltham was the panicked sanctuary of all London. Roughly five thousand people, all of them in shock, and far too many in mourning, now crowded into what had once been the Crown camp.

Jule's agony was whole. Rafe was gone, and there was no time to mourn him. She entered the bunker and assumed tactical command of what was no longer a peacetime army. Of the five thousand inside the camp, perhaps two thousand were fit to fight. But all they had were sidearms, knives, clubs, and the like.

Playthings.

She sat with Paris (once her intended mate) and Maddox (once her sworn enemy), ordering them to send out recon teams to see if Vazlav's crew had stayed on the water or made landfall, and if so, where they were going.

Step two was an organization of those two thousand soldiers into fighting units. Two battalions—Paris got one, Maddox the other. Companies, platoons, squads. The charts were drawn on a bare wall. At one point, Jule noticed that her hand was shaking, almost too wildly to write. Rafe, poor lovely Rafe. She inhaled deeply and went on, briefing them on the level of weaponry she'd seen on board the corvette. She wanted to cry out . . . But grief and shock were luxuries just now.

So too were old wounds. Maud was assigned to be Maddox's second-in-command. She nodded, grateful for the chance.

Step three was preparing the citizens for the full-scale invasion Jule felt certain would come. She turned to Byron. "Someone needs to be in charge of civilian defense now. That would've been Breena. Can you do it?"

Byron shook himself enough to reply, "I'd rather be in the fight."

"Byron, this *is* the fight."

He accepted the assignment, and asked Kimpton—still badly hobbled by her injury—to help. She agreed. Jule scrawled it all on that wall chart as Jameson drifted in, his face pale, his hands shaky, his clothes still soaked.

"Now we evacuate," he said. "I'll need to see plans for that."

"Jameson," Jule said, swallowing rage, "we're *staying*. We're defending our city. You need to step down! NOW!"

"I answer to the people. They chose me."

"Nobody voted for you!" Byron shouted.

"Nor you," Jameson replied. "I armed them. I led them. They want me here."

"No," Jule said. "They want their homes defended!"

"Some, maybe. But most just want to survive."

"Fine, you take the ones who want to flee. I'll take the ones who want to fight."

"So you'd divide this island into two Houses again? Is that what you want?"

Jule tried to steady herself. "God, what a coward. We're in a *WAR* now."

He replied, "I'm very sorry for your loss." And he drifted away, like a ghost.

Jule wanted to scream. Jameson, who had fooled so many for so long, who had organized and armed all the Habs, was now a shell. Here but gone. It was infuriating.

She went back to work, despite the grief and agony clinging to every cell in her body, despite the tears and the screams she could now only barely contain. New London needed defending.

As night fell, there was only silence from the Russian warship that had so devastated the city. And all throughout Eltham, the shocked survivors of New London now gathered in their homes around candles and took the Mark for the loved ones, colleagues, and heroes lost that day. Old, young, civilians, soldiers, teachers, parents, nurses, the wounded and the well, the shaken and the sleepless. Former Rogues, former Crowns, former Habs . . .

And one former enemy of the state. Maud.

In the bunker, Byron had completed the ritual in the name of Breena, and Chasen had done so for his former rival, Shapcott. Now Jule stood before a lone candle, her hand extended—under the watchful eyes of Byron, Chasen, Maud, Nelly, Maddox, and Paris. A few of the children had asked to attend: Willa, Liam, Portia, Danton. They were here too. Jameson's whereabouts were unknown—but word had reached this bunker that he'd found a nearby gin still.

Jule steeled herself. She had spent the day being a soldier. It was time now, at last, to be a widow. She placed her palm over the welcoming flame, wanting to be branded forever. The others watched, their hearts full. Jule shut her eyes. In this moment, she wanted to see only Rafe. The shape of him, the feel of his arms, everything about his face—eyes, jaw, nose—against the black canvas of her eyelids.

He had loved her utterly. It had swept through her body, filling every vacancy. She had carried it with her on water and land, in deepest sleep, even in battle. He had inspired her to sail. He had struggled for her, fought for her. He had died and been mourned and come back and died again—and throughout, without letup, without his patience ever flagging, he had held her in love. He was her peak; she knew that. How could any love ever feel as new, any risk as great, any touch as electric, any kiss as brave, any secret as powerful, any song as thoroughly *shared*?

Her hand began to scream, and she removed it from the flame, opening her eyes to find these kind faces holding her, all of them in tears. Byron, who'd just suffered the same pain, led her to a waiting bucket of water. They plunged their hands in together and sobbed, their heads touching, shoulders heaving so badly that the water shook.

"He's gone," she cried.

"He's *here*," Byron corrected her, pointing to her heart. "You carry him."

"And *you*?" she asked. "Are you okay?"

Byron shook his head. *Okay* wasn't possible anymore. Jule nodded understandingly.

Next came the closing of all their eyes. Then the simultaneous tapping of whatever they'd brought with them: a stick, the bottom of a shoe, the butt of a pistol—Jule used the handle of her knife, as did Maddox and Paris—the taps becoming a single sound at once. Then all those eyes opening. Reset.

But of course, for Jule, nothing had reset at all. She felt shattered. Rafe was gone. Her legs felt shaky and her voice felt weak. She did not know how to strengthen them.

And it hit. The wave. Weakening her knees and exploding through her eyes. Squeezing them tight didn't help. It couldn't. The pain was just too great.

"I killed him," she said.

"What?!"

"All he wanted to do was leave . . . and I kept making him stay. I did this. I killed him."

"Jule," Byron said, "you brought him to *life*."

She sobbed, her insides hollow—"I wanna drown." Then she ran out of the bunker. Byron followed, alarmed.

He found her beside the lake, standing in ankle-deep water. "Jule?" he asked.

Her will had vanished. "I want to put rocks in my pockets and dive off that beautiful boat he built for me and never come up again."

"You can't," Byron answered. "Someone has to lead us out of this."

"Look at me!" she yelled. "Do you see a leader here?"

"I do."

She sobbed. Byron put his arms around her. And he sobbed too. They stayed there, crying, alone together. He placed his hands on her face. "I'll follow you anywhere."

"After seeing me like this?"

"*Especially* after seeing you like this." That got through . . .

Paris found them there. "The scouts have all reported back now," he said. "No sign that any patrols left that boat."

"Thank you," Jule said. "Triple the watch on the perimeter."

Paris acknowledged the order and left. Jule exhaled hard, gathering herself. Then she said, "We can't just let them sit out there, Byron. They'll destroy us."

Byron nodded. "I don't know how to help. I don't think like a soldier thinks."

That's when Jule remembered: "Rafe did."

Big Lil was on her nine hundred and sixtieth push-up of the day when Jule and Byron entered her forge. The madness of the morning had rattled Lil completely; exercise was her refuge.

Honus, roughly half her size, sat on a table, watching as Lil pumped herself into a frenzy. He and Lil had come to admire each other a great deal since the merging of the two Houses. A deep professional respect, a shared love of their craft.

Jule entered the forge without a hello. "The Canners you made—do you think they could be fashioned to detonate underwater?"

That fast, Lil stopped the push-ups. And Honus's eyes went wide, excited by the sheer difficulty of such a challenge.

Jule went on, "And is there a resin that could make the device stick to the hull of that boat beneath the waterline?"

Honus smiled. Lil did too. They were smiths, but in their hearts they were armorers. And battle was their passion. "Let us think on that a moment, will you?" Honus asked.

Jule nodded. Moments later, she and Byron strolled the back perimeter of the camp, behind the lake, where Rafe had gone after he'd made love with Jule on her rooftop, forever ago. It was all she could do to push the images from her mind.

Byron asked, "Do you mean to sink their boat?"

"I do," she replied.

"With Jameson's consent?"

"Doesn't matter."

She walked a few more steps, forest twigs crackling under her feet, a perimeter fence to her left, night birds overhead, pain filling the empty spaces behind her ribs...

Byron read her face and offered, "You don't ever get used to their being gone, but you get used to the feeling of missing them." Jule appreciated it. He went on, "After a while, it becomes like walking around with one of your lungs missing. There's a constant feeling of absence. But you can still breathe."

"But I miss *love*. I never knew what it was, and now I don't know anything else. I'm sleepwalking. I didn't think I could feel like that."

"It just happened, Jule. It's gonna be raw for a while. But it will get better."

"It was better *before*—not feeling anything."

"No, it wasn't," Byron replied.

The birds cooed. A few small animals chittered. Jule asked, "And you?"

"Me?" He sighed. "This was it for me. I mourned once already, thought I'd never have to again. Twice is too much."

"*Once* is too much!"

He nodded. "My hope is they build those bombs but can't make them stick to the hull, and you need a diver to deliver them underwater and detonate them to save the city. And I'll volunteer and that will be that. I'll die a hero."

She eyed him. "That's not how this is going to go, Byron."

"Would solve a lot of problems."

"These people need you," she said. "*I* need you."

Byron breathed out a soft smile and shook his head.

Then the world stopped. Again.

Fifty yards ahead of them, dropping down from a tree after clearing the perimeter wall, were four Russian sailors on a mission. On their belts were devices that looked like grenades. Each carried a pair of them.

In their hands were submachine guns.

Everyone froze—Jule, Byron, the sailors. The night was suddenly still and airless. Then, quietly, Jule whispered, "Byron. Run."

And they did, sprinting back toward the former Crown camp at full speed. The four Russians gave chase and opened fire, a steady stream of bullets flying past, shredding branches.

Jule and Byron kept running, zigzagging, faster than their pursuers. Soon the buildings of the Crown camp were in sight; Jule could see her own dormitory peeking out from behind the huge strangler fig tree that sat beside it. She hated leading these soldiers toward the camp, but her obligation at this moment was to survive. *Just run, Jule. Leaders can't lead if they're dead.*

More branches exploded around them. As Jule reached her building, she grabbed Byron's arm, pulling him into the lobby. Bullets kicked off its brick exterior now. The four sailors were still sixty yards back.

She pulled Byron up the stairs where she'd first met Breena, then the two of them burst into Jule's second-story apartment and hurried to the window, which looked out onto the lake. The spot afforded her a view of the sailors as they approached. She quietly slid her window open and handed Byron one of the knives on her hip.

"We're going to kill them . . ."

Byron had never done that before. But he took the knife.

The four sailors passed directly under Jule's window now, slowing as they approached the corner of the building, their guns silent but poised. Then they came to a cautious stop.

Jule exhaled. Then—for Rafe, for New London, and for the future only she could build—she pushed herself out the window. Byron followed.

They landed on their pursuers, knocking the four Russians to the ground. The one directly beneath Jule suffered a broken collarbone. Jule heard it snap on impact. She plunged a knife into the back of his neck.

Byron, a stranger to killing, did the same to another. And before the remaining Russians could even raise their weapons, Jule had gutted them both, Byron watching in silent awe.

And the siege was over.

For a long moment, Byron remained in place. His heart was racing and his mouth was dry. Yet he felt free, righteous, almost joyous. And his hands, to his great surprise, were steady. Four soldiers lay dead at his feet.

"You did great," Jule said.

He nodded and began to gather the submachine guns and ammunition they had been carrying.

Then he noticed: Jule's eyes had suddenly gone wide in terror. She was, for a moment, suspended in place.

"What's wrong?" he asked.

"Byron," she whispered, "get away from here."

"What're you talking about?"

"Please, go."

"No. Tell me what's wrong."

She nodded to one of the grenades on the first sailor's hip. There was a *vial* attached to it. It was labeled VX.

"It's nerve gas," she said. VX—which had once decimated the people of this city.

Byron didn't move. He couldn't. This wasn't a mortar fired from the river. This was extinction. Mass murder. "What do we do?"

Jule answered, "We can't leave it here unattended." She knocked on Nelly's window.

It slid open. The old woman regarded the four bodies, and the concern on Jule's face. "Jule?"

"Nelly, go to the bunker. Get Maud, Paris, Chasen, and Maddox, and send them here."

"Jameson too?"

"If he insists. But don't come back with them. Stay as far away as you can. Okay?"

That night, nature retreated. The sky was clear of birds and bats. Insects hid in holes or brush. Small animals remained out of sight. It was midnight, or near it, when an impromptu meeting took place outside Nelly's window between Jule, Maud, Jameson, Byron, Paris, Chasen, and Maddox—in the presence of the four fallen sailors.

"It's time to attack," Jule said.

"Attack?!" Jameson exclaimed. "That's madness." His speech was slurred.

Jule eyed him: "They want to *eliminate* us, Jameson. And we have to respond *now*, before they realize that these men are missing."

"Respond how?" he asked. "With knives and sluggers?" There was a tremor in his voice.

"We have eight grenades now," she explained. "And four submachine guns. And those sailors can only come out of that bridge one at a time."

"You're talking suicide."

"We also have the VX," she said flatly.

The others fell silent. Even Jameson couldn't think of a reply. *A biological weapon?* Finally he breathed, "We cannot do that."

"I don't think we have a choice."

"Of course we have a choice," he said. "We can *retreat*, as originally discussed."

Maud looked murderous. "Retreat?" she asked. "To where?"

"Anywhere upriver. Why die for our right to live here?"

Jule answered, "Because it's *ours*. Because *they* have no right to it."

"It's just land."

"You don't understand."

"No, I don't," he said.

"That's because you've never been a soldier. You've never fought to defend your home before."

"Yes," Jameson scoffed. "Much good it did, the centuries of fighting over black and gold. What did it gain anybody?"

"Jameson, running won't help; they mean to kill us. There *is* no safe distance."

"Major, all we *can* do is run."

Jule wanted to punch him and thought she might, but Byron interceded. "Hate to remind you, both of you, but this choice really isn't *ours* to make."

Jameson turned. "What're you talking about?"

"The *people* should decide. No one elected us."

"They followed *me*," Jameson answered.

Byron stayed calm. "Jameson, you want these citizens to surrender. Jule wants them to attack. Shouldn't we ask them what *they* want?"

"It's past midnight," Jameson answered. "And we have to *choose*. Right now."

Jule said flatly, "Then we should start waking people up."

THIRTY

Jameson could hardly believe his eyes. Before him, five thousand New Londoners, awakened from their sleep, stood attentively, holding candles and torches, parents hushing small children. Minister Dawson had led them in a brief nondenominational prayer, and Byron had apprised them of the threat represented by the dead sailors.

VX. Death. Extinction.

Now it was Jameson's turn to speak. Jule would follow. And the people would vote with their feet. Midnight democracy. Jameson stood before that mountain of mobile phones, their glass faces reflecting the flickering flames.

Jule was in the medical tent—preparing to speak, uneasy. A handful of sleeping patients surrounded her.

Outside, the crowd hushed, and Jameson began: "I've lived in this city for more than a decade now. I know you. I know that no one standing before me now has *ever* run from a fight."

He looked sober and clear, determined—and, for the very first time since his fall at the wedding—unshaken. "But I also know that what means most to you in this world is not your city. It's your *families*."

The crowd was silent. He continued, "Floating on that river right now is an enemy we cannot defeat—not because we aren't brave enough, but simply because we lack the *arms* to fight them. And if we try, we will perish. All of us. Everyone you love." He held up the vial of VX. People recoiled. "These people are murderers."

"I know you want to defend your city. But tonight I would ask you ... *why*? All your lives, this land has been a battleground. You've bled over every square foot of it, centuries of fighting that left the whole city cursed. If *peace* waits for us upriver, if walking away will save us, how can I ask you to die here?"

Many heads nodded. Byron noted it all with great unease.

Jameson went on, "So I am begging you to follow me out of the north gate, to safety. No, we won't have London anymore. But we will have one another. We will survive, and prosper. Home can be anywhere if your family and neighbors are with you. Let's go somewhere new. Somewhere unhaunted. Let's find a *truly* new London. And leave this one and its ghosts to the invaders."

Silence hung like a fog, dotted only by the small hisses of the torch flames, and the occasional squirming of children.

Jameson had sold this crowd. That was clear. He had turned surrender into something noble. Byron knew it. He walked to the medical tent, where he found Jule, in full battle rattle, applying sycamore-bark paste to her cheekbones, as if for camouflage.

"They're ready for you, Jule," Byron said.

Jule nodded tightly, more frightened than she'd ever been before a battle. "I'm not a speaker," she whispered.

"Then just be a leader."

That helped. She attached the eight Russian grenades to her hips and slung the four Russian submachine guns over her shoulders and headed out of the tent, stopping only to grab a single item: the Victrola . . .

Outside, she carried the big wooden box toward the row of tables and kept her mind focused solely on little things: right foot, left foot, right foot, left foot. Breathing. The feel of the wood in her arms.

The people were waiting. Five thousand of them. Right foot, left foot, right foot, left foot. Breathe . . .

Rafe was with her every step of the way.

She reached the table, set the box down, and opened it. Few in the crowd had seen this device before. People craned their necks for a look. Parents held up their children.

Byron decided to stand beside her.

Jule inhaled deeply, her face camouflaged, grenades on her hips, automatic weapons over her shoulders. She searched for familiar faces in the crowd: children, Nelly, even Maud, who nodded in a sisterly way.

Jameson eyed her—the battle rattle, the face paint, the weapons—and he murmured, "You look ridiculous."

Jule didn't reply, just turned the crank on the box.

Now the New Londoners were truly curious. *What was she doing? What was that odd wooden box?*

Only Byron saw what was coming.

Jule set the needle down on the spinning black disc within, and a crackling sound followed.

Jameson scoffed. Others did too. Jule stood firm. Then—

Beethoven erupted. The first four notes of his Fifth Symphony. DUN-DUN-DUN-DUNNNNNNNNNNNNNN.

The sound knocked everyone back. Some fell. Eyes went wide. Every jaw dropped. The children were breathless—Willa, Liam, Portia. So too were the adults. A moment of shock . . . then the NEXT FOUR NOTES knocked them back again.

DUN-DUN-DUN-DUNNNNNNNNNNNNNN.

Music. Recorded music. Emanating somehow from that box.

The people were poleaxed, all of them. It was overwhelming. Sensory bliss. Jule remembered that first night at the palace, the shock on Rafe's face—and she began to cry, the tears rolling over the bark paste on her cheeks. Nelly wept too. Many of them did. Byron watched, breathless.

Still, the stunning sounds—every note a miracle—kept pouring out of that box, stupefying the citizens. The children seemed to be vibrating. A lifetime without real music and then *this*—magic in the air—bouncing, floating, darting, lifting them as one. Vibrations hitting every chest.

Rafe was here, in the air, between every note. Jule could feel him beside her, urging her on. He was on every face. And inside her.

Maud began to cry. So did Byron. And Paris and Maddox. And Kimpton. Even Mean. Their lives had been pain and struggle and loss and not nearly enough beauty. But this was rapture: the smell of the air, the color of the sky, the tingle between their ears, the wonder in their chests. They felt transported and yet wonderfully present. Alive. Grateful. Thrilled. Proud to be human. Proud to be *here*, together—and proud to share her tears. Jule was making them, at last, a single people. A community.

She wasn't just music. She was New London itself.

Yet she still hadn't spoken. Byron was certain she would. There was so much to say.

Instead, her tears still falling, Beethoven still soaring, Jule merely placed a hand on her heart and said three words: "I have Hope."

Then she turned and left the stage and waded into the crowd in full battle rattle, passing stunned citizens and heading for the main gate. The music continued.

If no one came with her now, she would fight the invaders alone. Leaders needed to do that sometimes. Armed to the teeth and utterly unafraid to die, she kept walking and did not look back.

So she didn't see that Byron was now following her.

So was Paris. And Maddox, despite his wrecked knee. Nelly followed too. And Maud.

And then . . . every single New Londoner in the camp.

Five thousand of them, their faces grim, their fear entirely real but their souls soaring. The music pushed them along—Jameson's dismay growing with each new volunteer.

Jule turned now and saw them coming . . . and she nearly collapsed with joy.

They believed in her. They trusted her.

Byron, Paris, Maddox, and Maud were right on her tail. Jule handed each of them a grenade and a machine gun. It was time to win a battle.

Jule had stacked a gigantic cache of weapons at the main gate, watched over by young Portia and Liam. Now these kids handed firearms to every New Londoner passing through the gate. Honus and Lil had fashioned twenty-five new Canners as well, capable of detonating underwater. Those too were distributed.

"Let's move out," Jule hollered. And this citizen army now filed toward a row of waiting pirogues. The strains of Beethoven could still be heard behind them.

They paddled solemnly away from Eltham to meet an enemy they had not antagonized, to face a danger they did not deserve.

But there was a joy to it, a righteousness. Jule was their true north.

And home was home. It had to be defended.

Soon, there was no one left behind at Eltham except the very old or the very young or the badly injured . . . and Jameson, who had proven himself to be blind after all, for he had failed to see Jule's great gift. She could make people believe.

The flotilla rowed on, Jule and Byron in the lead, Maud in the pirogue alongside them, seeking a redemption nothing but this moment could provide. Everywhere Jule looked she saw former enemies, ready now to die for one another. And for Jule. And for Rafe. And for Hope.

These soldiers would soon be hurling grenades at a boat and the barrels of fuel it was carrying. This army—*her* army—was at last going to burn the water.

And the slugger that had been made from Evander's ring, the one Jule's father had worn so proudly, it sat chambered in her sidearm.

She planned for Vazlav to see it soon.

The pirogues reached Paternoster. From here, Jule could see the two Russian warships, lightly guarded, surrounded by the blackness of the water. She stepped out of her pirogue, unseen by the sailors on the corvette.

Maud approached and embraced her. So too did Maddox, Paris, Nelly, Kimpton. Jule looked to Byron. It was time.

For so long, she had struggled. For so long, she had rejected the idea of command, of being a general. But it felt natural now; it felt inevitable . . . because, she now realized, a fight between rival Houses had not been her fate. *This* was the army she'd been born to lead, and *this* was the war she'd been destined to win. She stared at the river, and saw its lessons so clearly. Every moment in her star-crossed life—every battle, every wound, every argument and heartbreak, the deaths of Dorn and her brother and Breena, even the love and loss of her precious Rafe—had led her here, to this moment, to this history. They'd all been angels in a way, guides who'd pushed her, taught her, honed her, inspired her. And Jule knew things now; uncertainty was no longer her lot.

Yes, London had drowned. Yes, Love and Water had clashed, fatally. But peril had NOT yet won. Peace WAS possible.

And she was ready to lead.

She knew where the corvette was vulnerable. Rafe had shown her. Now she and Byron each grabbed a grenade and a canner. And they quietly slipped into the inky water.

Just before she disappeared beneath its surface, Jule saw the first faint hints of dawn. And she grinned.

Here came the sun.

HAIL

She was all England. And the soldiers and citizens she led truly thought she was magic, mythic, graced, so fearless and noble that they found it hard to believe she was actually real.

They didn't understand.

She was indeed uncommonly brave, an idol and a hero, fierce and unyielding. Righteous, tireless, humble, loving, compassionate, and true. She was a warrior who rejected killing. A fighter who learned to prize peace. A teacher, a friend, an idol, a lover, a leader. She bled courage, and courage matters. Courage wins wars. It builds nations and crosses rivers. And she was the only person on Earth those thousands would have followed into that particular battle on that particular morning against that particular enemy. She—her leadership, her loyalty, her goodness, her love—had *earned* her city's devotion. Jule was remarkable.

But not a myth or a queen or a fable.

No, she was very much real, mortal, entirely human, capable of error, susceptible to the deepest of pain. She wore her wounds openly, in an unflinchingly human way. There was something dignified about that, something loving. Not a goddess. Not a warrior princess. Not a legend carved in stone.

She was *better* than all that, because she was one of us, born in the forge of war. And her standard will never be met—certainly not by *me*. Terror always reduces me to salt.

Jule was ultimately a leader, a guide, an inspiration, a model. And, yes, bigger than the water. And what is more . . .

She was my mother.

This history is hers.

All hail Jule.

ACKNOWLEDGMENTS

My career and life have always been blessed by mentors and guides, exemplars—many of whom I never got to meet. Among them are Shakespeare, Fitzgerald, Hemingway, Nabokov, Hugo . . . and Arthur Miller, Tennessee Williams, Eugene O'Neill, Peter Shaffer.

And my screen angels, who set the bar so high for me: Billy Wilder & I. A. L. Diamond, William Goldman, Alvin Sargent, Francis Ford Coppola, Steve Tesich, Robert Bolt, Robert Towne, Paddy Chayefsky, Rod Serling. There are too many to name.

And the public school teachers whose classrooms were my temples of history and literature: Marilyn Kretzer, Fred Mathieson, Sherry-Beth Sternlicht, Professor Charles Berst of UCLA.

This *book* has had angels too—people who read draft after draft for me, who kept encouraging me, and educating me, people who believed. My thanks to Cari-Esta Albert, Jeff Ford, Josh McLaughlin, Peter Gethers, Rick Ray, Brad Weston, and Anthony Mattero.

I want to thank everyone who ever said yes to me—but also everyone who ever told me NO. You made me work harder.

Above all, my editor, Lisa Sandell, who believed on a different level . . . and guided, encouraged, and taught me. Lisa made this effort so much better than it was. My debt to her is bigger than the water.

To *all* the angels who grace and guide me—my deepest thanks.

All hail Jule.

Billy Ray wrote the Oscar-nominated screenplay for *Captain Phillips*, for which he won the Writers Guild of America Award. Ray's films as writer, co-writer, or writer-director include *The Hunger Games*, *Richard Jewell*, *Shattered Glass*, Showtime's *The Comey Rule*, and the forthcoming *The Hunger Games: Sunrise on the Reaping*. Billy lives in Los Angeles. He believes in democracy, justice, his children . . . and the Dodgers. *Burn the Water* is his first novel.

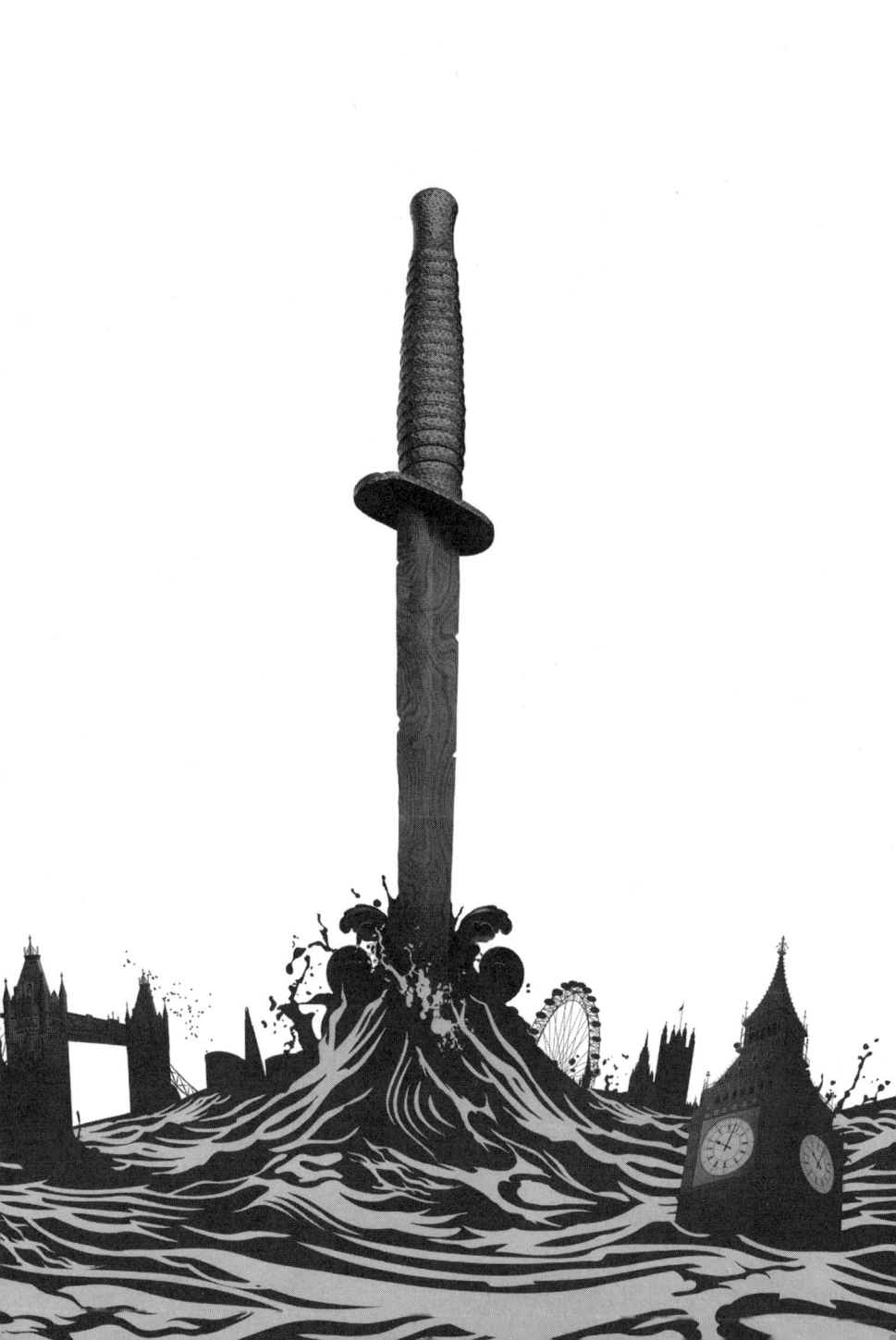